"Why didn't you wait for me?"

The words were out before Rafe could stop them. "I told you I'd be back for you. You couldn't wait six lousy months?" Feeling the anger anew, he rose quickly, knocking their plates aside.

From the moment she'd heard he was on his way, Nora had known they would have this conversation. Why, then, wasn't she better prepared for it? How could she make him see? "I didn't know where you were, if you would return...."

Rafe swung around, reaching for the control he seldom lost. "Why did you marry Ted? Did you love him?"

"It—it seemed like the right thing to do at the time."

"But he didn't make you happy, either, did he, Nora?"

"No, he didn't."

"Maybe it's you, Nora. Maybe no man can make you happy. Have you thought about that?"

She felt the knife twist and fought desperately not to let him see the effect of his words. "Yes."

Rotten. Rafe felt rotten. He hadn't meant to lash out at her with accusations and cruel remarks. Clearly, his pain wasn't as deeply buried as he'd thought....

Dear Reader,

Welcome to the Silhouette **Special Edition** experience! With your search for consistently satisfying reading in mind, every month the authors and editors of Silhouette **Special Edition** aim to offer you a stimulating blend of deep emotions and high romance.

The name Silhouette **Special Edition** and the distinctive arch on the cover represent a commitment—a commitment to bring you six sensitive, substantial novels each month. In the pages of a Silhouette **Special Edition**, compelling true-to-life characters face riveting emotional issues—and come out winners. All the authors in the series strive for depth, vividness and warmth in writing these stories of living and loving in today's world.

The result, we hope, is romance you can believe in. Deeply emotional, richly romantic, infinitely rewarding—that's the Silhouette **Special Edition** experience. Come share it with us—six times a month!

From all the authors and editors of Silhouette **Special Edition**,

Best wishes,

Leslie Kazanjian,
Senior Editor

PAT WARREN
My First Love, My Last

Silhouette Special Edition

Published by Silhouette Books New York

America's Publisher of Contemporary Romance

For Irma Freeman,
our cruising buddy,
for years of laughter and friendship and love

SILHOUETTE BOOKS
300 East 42nd St., New York, N.Y. 10017

ISBN: 0-373-09610-0

First Silhouette Books printing July 1990

Books by Pat Warren

Silhouette Special Edition

With This Ring #375
Final Verdict #410
Look Homeward, Love #442
Summer Shadows #458
The Evolution of Adam #480
Build Me a Dream #514
The Long Road Home #548
The Lyon and the Lamb #582
My First Love, My Last #610

Silhouette Romance

Season of the Heart #553

Silhouette Intimate Moments

Perfect Strangers #288

PAT WARREN,

the mother of four, lives in Arizona with her travel-agent husband and a lazy white cat. She's a former newspaper columnist whose lifetime dream was to be a novelist. A strong romantic streak, a sense of humor and a keen interest in developing relationships led her to try romance novels, with which she feels very much at home.

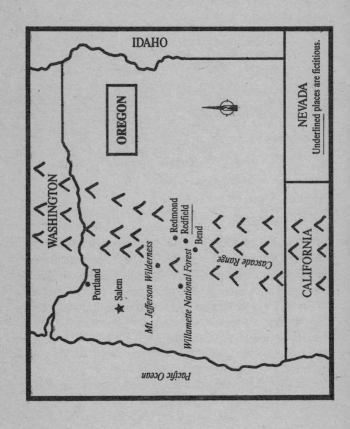

Day One

*K*idnapped. The very word made Nora Maddox cringe. And when she thought of it in connection with her nine-year-old son, Bobby, it struck pure terror in her heart.

Scarcely aware of the damp tissue she held in her clenched fist, Nora walked to the window and pulled back the sheer curtains. Moonlight shone down on the large Douglas fir in the center of her small front yard. Through the open screen door a soft summer breeze drifted in. The wooden porch swing hanging on chains shifted slightly—the swing where she and Bobby often sat rocking in the evening. *Bobby, where are you?*

Choking back the sobs that earlier had drained her so completely, Nora pressed a fist to her lips. She never should have let Bobby go with Ted. But her ex-husband had seemed to finally have his act together since his return to town six months before. He rarely drank anymore and was holding down a steady job.

Again last week, Ted had asked Nora to remarry him. For Bobby's sake, he'd said, his tone pleading. She knew Bobby loved both of them, but she couldn't take Ted back, not even for her son. She didn't love Ted Maddox, had in fact never loved him. She'd never lied to him about her feelings. Yet through the years, her inability to care enough must have eaten at him. Had he taken Bobby to punish her?

Absently Nora scratched at a hive that had popped out on her neck, then moved her hand to rub at another on her shoulder. Since her early teens, whenever she was nervous or worried, she broke out in hives. The tendency doubly irritated her just now. But then, very little would please her tonight. Except the return of her son.

With a sigh, she returned to the couch and curled up in the corner. Bobby smiled at her from the framed photo on the end table. The picture had been taken three months ago in May on his birthday before his top front teeth had come in all the way. Her hand trembling, she picked up the photo, thinking how Bobby disliked this particular snapshot displaying his gap-toothed grin. She smiled at his wavy brown hair that refused to stay in place, so like her own. His face was oval-shaped, also like hers, his mouth full and nicely shaped. But it was his eyes that haunted her, a brown so dark they were nearly black.

Closing her own eyes, she hugged the frame to her. Where in heaven's name was her brother, Jack? He'd promised her faithfully that he'd keep her informed if she'd just sit tight in her house until he organized things. As one of two sheriff's deputies in the small town of Redfield, Oregon, Jack Curtis was widely respected and enormously capable. He'd assured her that he'd use every professional avenue of approach available to him in the huge national police network to get Bobby back for her.

Nora glanced at the clock on the mantel. Jack had left her over six hours earlier. Why wasn't he calling? What was happening? Running a hand through her short hair, Nora wondered how much more of this she could stand. *Ted, Ted, how could you do this to me?*

She'd known Ted Maddox forever, it seemed. They'd grown up together in Redfield, northwest of Bend, one of Oregon's most popular ski towns. They'd attended the same schools and begun dating in junior high. Ted had been fun in those days, though always more intense than she. He'd begged her to marry him right after graduation, but she'd put him off. She'd always wanted to teach and planned to attend Oregon State University to get her degree before even thinking of marriage. They would attend college together then, Ted had declared. Only their plans had changed that fateful summer ten years ago.

Nora set down Bobby's picture and leaned her head back. She never should have let Ted talk her into marrying him. But she'd been barely eighteen and he'd convinced her that he loved her enough for both of them. Her minister father had married them right before Christmas, and everyone had smiled happily. Everyone except Nora.

But she'd vowed she'd be the best wife possible, and she had certainly tried. When Bobby was born the following spring, Ted was delighted. And he'd been a good father always, spending time with him as a baby and later taking him to ball games and fishing and camping.

Yet the marriage had steadily fallen apart. After her second miscarriage five years ago, they'd tried a trial separation. When that hadn't worked out, Nora had filed for divorce. She'd felt that she'd had to because the problems between them were upsetting and confusing Bobby. And always her son and his welfare had top priority.

Hearing a car approach, she sat up expectantly. But it passed on by and she slumped back in disappointment. In her mind she pictured Ted as she'd last seen him, tan and fit, his blond hair bleached even lighter from the sun, his hazel eyes clear once again. He'd recently returned from a fishing trip and had regaled Bobby with the fish stories he loved to tell.

Even though Ted had moved to a neighboring town after the divorce, he'd returned often to see Bobby, to take him hiking and camping. Nora had occasionally gone with them, because Bobby loved to have her along. Ted was an excellent climber and woodsman, a man she trusted implicitly on the many wilderness trails of Oregon. That was why when he'd asked to take Bobby camping, she hadn't hesitated in letting him go.

It wasn't until this afternoon when she'd received the note Ted had obviously mailed yesterday after picking up the boy, that she'd become aware of the danger she'd trustingly sent her son into. "I can't lose you both," Ted had written. "Don't worry. I'll take good care of Bobby." Nora struggled to keep the tears from falling again as she bit down on her lower lip.

Was it her refusal to remarry Ted that had triggered this act of insanity? she wondered. Surely he wouldn't harm Bobby just to get at her. He'd never even been able to spank the boy for an infraction. Despite the problems in their marriage, Ted had always seemed to love Bobby. Yet kidnapping a child, even if that child was his son, was certainly not a rational act. Dear God, what was Ted thinking of?

Nora looked up as the clock chimed nine times. Restlessly she got up and went into the kitchen to put on a pot of coffee. Inactivity and too much time alone were driving her crazy. Jack would probably appreciate fresh coffee when he arrived. She'd just plugged in the pot when she heard another car out front. Hurrying to the door, she watched her brother step out with a mixture of relief and fear.

Jack's footsteps as he climbed the wooden porch steps were heavy and slow. Wearily he ran his long fingers through his dark hair cropped close to his head in an effort to control the curls he disliked. As Nora held the screen door open for him, he gave her a tired smile.

"Is that fresh coffee I smell?" he asked as he walked inside.

"It'll be ready in a minute." Nora clasped her hands together to steady them. "What did you find out?"

Jack sat down on the couch, stretched out his long legs and raised serious blue eyes to her. "It's not wonderful news, Nora. But it's far from hopeless." He patted the seat beside him. "Sit down."

She gave a quick shake of her head. "Tell me."

"We've traced Ted's movements back over the past week. When did you say he came over here asking you to marry him again?"

"One day last week. Tuesday or Wednesday." Nora rubbed her forehead, trying to concentrate. "It was Tuesday. I had two children who had to stay an extra hour at the center that afternoon. Ted was annoyed and impatient while he waited for me to lock up and come into the house."

"Would you say his behavior was unusual? Did he seem upset?"

"Not terribly unusual. He became upset after I refused to discuss marrying him again, but until then, no." She frowned, his delay in telling her what he knew beginning to worry her. "What has that to do with anything?"

Jack sighed heavily. "The next day he quit his job at Benson's Lumber and told his landlady he was moving out of town."

"Dear God, he planned the whole thing." With a shudder, Nora sank into the nearest chair. She closed her eyes, struggling for control.

"I'll get the coffee." Jack rose and went to the kitchen, returning minutes later with two steaming mugs. He placed one on the table next to Nora. "Take a sip. It'll help."

No, it wouldn't, Nora thought, fighting the fear that threatened to take over. Only finding Bobby would help now. She raised anguished eyes to Jack who sat on the edge of the couch taking several long swallows. "What else have you learned?"

"On a hunch, I talked with the manager of the store where Ted usually buys his camping equipment. Ted had been in yesterday morning before he picked up Bobby and bought some heavy-duty stuff." Jack checked his notepad. "A small fold-up tent, a new fishing rod and two winterized thermal sleeping bags."

"Winterized? But it's August. Where is it that cold at this time of year?"

Slowly Jack set down his cup. "Mt. Jefferson Wilderness. We found his car parked near the Whitewater Road entrance."

Eyes wide, Nora just stared at him. Deep in the Cascades, Mt. Jefferson rose to over ten thousand feet. The Wilderness surrounding it was dense and thick and dangerous. Though some of the trails were frequented by advanced hikers, usually even the most experienced campers steered clear of the area Jack mentioned, due to the thick vegetation and steep rock formations.

Because of the density of the trees and greenery, there were sections where even a summer sun had difficulty penetrating. A native of the area, Nora knew that it was a rare night that the temperature didn't fall below freezing in some parts of that untamed region. She reached for her coffee, needing the warmth.

"Where does he usually take Bobby camping?" Jack asked.

"Mostly into Willamette National Forest. There are always lots of campers there and climbers. Sometimes we go around Hosmer Lake. Bobby loves to fish. He . . . he took his pole, the collapsible one you got him for his birthday." Nora stopped as she felt her eyes fill. "But Mt. Jefferson. Oh, Jack . . ." Her voice broke as the tears began to fall again. Bobby was tall for his age, but he was still a little boy. Why had she let him go?

Jack moved to her, covering her clasped hands with one of his own. "It's going to be all right, Nora. We're going to find him."

"How?"

"I've called someone. He's an expert on tracking, the best I know."

"I don't believe Ted would harm Bobby. But it's so thick in there and it can get so cold at night. He's not behaving rationally. What if he doesn't keep a good eye on Bobby? What if Bobby falls or . . . ?"

Jack squeezed her hands. "I've never doubted that Ted loves Bobby. He's just upset that you won't take him back, and in his emotional state, he took Bobby. He wants to hurt you, but he'd never hurt Bobby."

She had to believe that Jack was right. She had to. Nora reached into the pocket of her slacks for a tissue and dabbed at her eyes.

Jack walked across the room and drained his cup. "Several of my men started along the trails to see if they could pick up any signs. But none of them has the experience necessary to track a man far into the wilderness. And then it got dark." Digging his car keys from his pocket, he turned to face Nora. "You get some rest and don't worry. Our expert will be here early tomorrow morning, and we're going in together. We'll have Bobby safely back here in no time."

Nora stood, shoving her hands into her pockets. "I'm going with you."

Halfway to the door, Jack swung back. "The hell, you say. You know what it's like in the Wilderness—dark as pitch, freezing nights, bugs, snakes, bears." He stopped, looking as if he realized he was shoring up the wrong side of the argument.

"Yes, I do know what it's like. I've hiked into Mt. Jefferson with Ted. Not far in, but I've done it. And that's only one reason why I'm going. In case you've forgotten, Bobby's my son."

Jack stretched to his full height, an impressive six feet. "I told you I'd bring him back to you."

Despite his size, he didn't intimidate her. "I appreciate your concern. But I'm going, with or without you."

His frustration mounting, Jack swore under his breath. "Dad's not going to like this."

"Then don't tell him." Nora placed a hand on his arm, feeling the tension. She knew Jack loved Bobby, too. "Please understand. I have to go."

He studied her a long minute, then nodded curtly. "Be ready at eight tomorrow morning."

"Who is this expert tracker who's coming in the morning, the one you have so much faith in?"

Turning, he gazed into her eyes. "Rafe Sloan."

Before she could stop herself, Nora gasped out loud. "No!"

"Nora, he's the best. He's no longer that wild kid you knew ten years ago. Through the years, I've kept track of Rafe. He's a trained field operative, a survivalist. He's affiliated with some department of the government, all pretty hush-hush. He's tough and strong and deeply respected— by his men, by the higher-ups, and by any number of police departments across the country."

Heart pounding, Nora tried to gather her scattered thoughts. "This is hiking country. Surely you could find someone else who could do the job as well."

"Maybe. But with my family, I hate to take chances. With Rafe, it's a sure thing." ·

She narrowed her eyes as she studied her brother. "Funny, I had the impression that you didn't care for Rafe. You were always warning me about him."

"That was then and this is now. I'm not saying I like the guy. What I'm saying is I respect his ability above the others'."

Nora was still unconvinced. To call Rafe Sloan for help, after all these years. "How did you even know where to find him?"

"I have my ways. And I told you, I've followed his career."

"What . . . what did he say?"

"That he'd come. Instantly and without hesitation. He'll be arriving on the seven o'clock plane in the morning."

Rubbing her forehead, Nora shook her head. "I just can't believe there aren't perfectly qualified people right here in Oregon who can—"

"Rafe's had training most guys haven't even read about. And connections. He's already called the FBI."

"The FBI?"

"Yes. Kidnapping's a federal offense, you know. Even if the child happens to be your son. Ted doesn't have custody. But the FBI won't get involved unless Ted takes him over the state line. And he hasn't done that.''

Nora could almost hear the unspoken ''not yet'' that Jack had been thinking. Bobby missing, Ted a hunted man and now Rafe returning. She felt near collapse.

Sensing her turmoil, Jack slipped a steadying arm about her slender shoulders. ''If anyone can get Bobby back, and fast, it's Rafe Sloan. Isn't that what you want, your son's return?''

''You know it is.''

''Then trust him.''

Trust Rafe Sloan? She'd done that once, and it had gotten her only heartache. Still, what choice did she have now?

Jack opened the screen door. ''Listen, you can change your mind about coming with us. I know you and Rafe must have had a falling out when you parted years ago. It probably won't be easy for you to be with him again.''

A falling out. Not exactly. And no, it wouldn't be easy. But necessary. She would do anything, face anyone, for Bobby. She raised her chin. ''I won't change my mind. I'm going.''

Stepping onto the porch, Jack held the door ajar hesitantly. ''I've never asked what happened between you two when Rafe left here that summer.''

Nora let out a deep breath, feeling more tired than she could remember having been in a long while. ''No, you haven't, and I've appreciated that. I don't think this is the right moment to dredge up something that happened years ago.''

''Right. Lock up and get some rest. I'll see you in the morning.''

Nora watched him drive away, closed and locked the door, then turned to lean against the solid wood.

Dear God, Rafe Sloan.

It was ten years since she'd seen him, yet if she closed her eyes, she could picture that rugged, tan face, the coal-black hair, those dark eyes that still haunted her dreams, that hard, lean body that could make her heart race. She remembered every minute they'd spent together that long, hot summer. Remembered and relived all too often, despite her best efforts to forget.

She'd just turned eighteen that June and was planning to go to college in the fall, after spending the summer working at a nearby children's camp. Doc Sloan had been the veterinarian who'd taken care of the horses the children learned to ride on. And he'd introduced her to his adopted son, Rafe, who'd just graduated from college and was home for the summer, helping him out while he waited to hear about a job application.

Ted had already been in the picture, of course. But Ted had been working in California at his uncle's fruit ranch and Rafe had been right there, dark and intense and so alive. Rafe with his quiet eyes watching her, his deep voice teasing her, his strong hands brushing accidentally against hers and sending her pulse into overtime. Her trusting mother and her minister father, to say nothing of her overly protective big brother, would have been shocked to learn how fast and how hard she'd fallen for the handsome loner.

Nora shivered as the memories engulfed her. Pushing away from the door, she turned off the lights and impulsively picked up Bobby's picture to take upstairs. In her room she set his smiling face on the nightstand, then turned to stare into the mirror over her dresser. How would Rafe see her after all these years?

Despite three pregnancies, she was as slender as she'd been then. She even wore her brown hair short and soft about her oval face as she had then. He'd been all over the world, undoubtedly meeting beautiful cosmopolitan women everywhere. She would appear small-town to him, unsophisticated, rural. Perhaps because she was all of those things.

Only her deep blue eyes seemed to hint of a level of maturity that had been missing back when Rafe had known her. And he'd been the first who'd plunged her headlong into growing up. Then Ted had come back into her life and completed the job.

Rafe would have changed, as she had. The work he did, as Jack had described it, sounded hard and unforgiving, undoubtedly leaving marks on him. She'd always known he would be someone others would admire and respect, even before he believed it.

Quickly Nora washed up, undressed and slipped between the sheets of her double bed. Despite the season's heat, she felt chilled, so she curled up, hugging herself. Her thoughts drifted to her son, and she prayed that he was safely snuggled into his sleeping bag and that Ted was watching out for him. That her innocent child should be a pawn in her struggles with Ted made her want to lash out at the injustice of it all.

Jack was probably right. Rafe would find Bobby. She recalled one weekend they'd gone camping together in the foothills of Mt. Washington, another nearby wilderness. She'd lied to her parents in order to be with Rafe, telling them she was going with a group of girls. She'd lied a great deal to her parents that summer. Though her deception had bothered her, she'd set aside her conscience. Being with Rafe was all that had mattered to her.

Doc Sloan had taught him all about camping in the Wilderness of the Cascades, about wild animals and survival, how to build fires without matches, to spear fish with a stick he'd sharpened with the knife he always carried. Rafe was half American, half Mexican, yet during that trip she'd thought he was part Indian, too. He could move soundlessly through the woods, knowing how and where to step, hearing the approach of a stranger long before she could.

Yes, despite the fact that seeing Rafe again would not be easy, she was glad he was on his way. Bobby needed all the help he could get.

She closed her eyes, willing sleep to claim her as she considered how ironic it was that Rafe was the one chosen to help find her son.

As the big jet leveled off at cruising altitude, Rafe Sloan pushed the button that allowed his seat to tilt back and settled himself. He usually flew first-class, not for the status but because at six feet three, with powerful shoulders and muscular legs, he needed the additional roominess.

Glancing out the window, he gazed at the clear night sky. The plane had left D.C. from Washington National Airport shortly after eleven and was scheduled to arrive at seven in the morning at Redmond, Oregon, the closest airport to Redfield. With the three-hour time difference, that afforded him only a couple of hours of rest. Provided he could get to sleep, Rafe thought skeptically.

Oregon. He hadn't been back in nine years, since Doc's funeral. Yet had a day gone by that he hadn't thought of some part of his life in that small town where he'd been born and raised? Certainly not many. Or did his remembrances center around Nora Curtis? No, it was Nora Maddox, Ted's wife. And now, as Jack had informed him only hours ago on the phone, Ted's *ex*-wife.

With a distracted smile, Rafe accepted the flight attendant's offer of coffee, hot and black. He might as well drink coffee since the memories were crowding in on him, making sleep an impossibility. Leaning toward the window, he let his mind drift.

Had his hometown changed much? he wondered. Doubtful, for there seemed a provincial air about Redfield that the residents fought to maintain. Despite the fact that his early years there hadn't been happy, Rafe realized he still had a fondness for Redfield and the way of life it epitomized. And Doc had loved it there.

Doc Sloan, the man who'd saved his life. Leaning back, Rafe felt the jolt of loss anew, thinking of Doc, wishing he were still around. His real father had died in the service when he'd been only an infant, and his Mexican mother, from whom he'd inherited his black hair and eyes, had been run over by a car when Rafe had been ten. A series of foster homes had followed, as well as a few skirmishes with the law and a truant officer, until he'd finally gotten lucky.

Doc had taken him in when the county agencies had finally lost jurisdiction over him at sixteen. And a damn good thing Doc had, or Rafe would surely have wound up behind prison bars. A naturalist who loved the outdoors, Doc had turned the town's bad boy into a strong, proud young man, not only surrounding him with love but teaching him, inspiring him. Nobody had ever bothered before.

Rafe took a long swallow of his coffee, thinking of the soft-spoken man with the bushy white hair who'd never married or had children of his own. Doc had taught him to love animals and independence, how to survive in a tough world, how to cope. And he'd learned his lessons well. Rafe had taken Doc's name to show how much he cared for the grizzled older man. No question about it, Doc had turned him around, had been the strongest influence on his life. Until Nora.

Closing his eyes, Rafe leaned back in his seat. He'd been barely twenty-two that summer, just out of college and hanging around at Doc's insistence, waiting for the phone call that he hoped would change his life. He'd applied for government service. Raphael Robert Sloan intended to make something of himself.

He'd fallen in love with Nora almost the first moment he'd seen her. Doc had asked him to help out with the horses at the summer camp where she was working with the children. At first he'd tried to stay indifferent to her, thinking she'd be like so many townies, looking for a fling with the half-breed, but privately thinking he wasn't good enough. She'd been a minister's daughter from a very conventional family, and she had had a brother who hovered over her.

Rafe and Jack Curtis had attended the same college, but they hadn't exactly traveled in the same circles. Rafe had entered on an athletic scholarship, his height and his love of basketball giving him an edge. Jack hadn't made the team, a fact that hadn't sat too well with him. Later, when he'd learned that Rafe was seeing his sister, Jack had tried to steer her away from him. But Nora had had a mind of her own.

Smiling to himself, Rafe remembered the first time he'd asked Nora out after watching her for days. They'd gone to a local basketball game and afterward he'd asked her how she'd enjoyed the game.

"I hate basketball," she'd answered.

That had surprised him. "You do? Then why'd you agree to go with me?"

She'd smiled that soft, slow way. "I hate basketball," she'd said, "but I love being with you."

From the beginning she'd made no coy attempt to hide her feelings from him. Although she'd been dating Ted Maddox before he'd arrived on the scene, when Ted had called from his summer job in California, Nora had told him that she was seeing someone else. She wasn't like the others he'd known. She was open and friendly and, more importantly, honest and sincere.

And she'd supported Rafe's dream of becoming somebody, of doing something worthwhile, though she'd feared for his safety in the job he described to her. As the summer went on and they grew closer, she'd wanted to take him home to meet her folks, but he'd held off. Past rejections from some of the people in town, because he was a half-breed and because of his early juvenile truancies, still hurt too much. He'd wanted to wait to meet Nora's parents until he could do so with pride and accomplishment, after he was established in government work. Thinking back, perhaps that had been a mistake, Rafe decided.

But he'd been stubborn and single-minded in those days. He'd loved Nora fiercely, but he'd refused to ask her to marry him until he could offer her something solid. When the phone call had come informing him to report to Washington for indoctrination, he'd asked her to wait for him until he got through the probationary period and was certain of his future. Then he would come back for her, he'd vowed. She'd promised she would wait as long as it took, and he'd left with the memory of her kisses to sustain him.

Rafe twisted in his seat, remembering the six months he'd spent training as a field operative, traveling to some of the rough spots of the world, the grueling pace, the loneliness, the thoughts of Nora that had kept him going. He'd just finished his probation in early March when he'd been informed of Doc's fatal heart attack. He'd rushed home to Redfield, and in his grief he'd called Nora's house, needing her comfort and love.

But her brother, Jack, had answered and told Rafe that Nora was happily married to Ted Maddox and had warned him to leave her alone. Stunned, filled with disbelief, he'd asked around, only to learn that she truly had married Ted the Christmas after he'd left. She hadn't even attended Doc's funeral, though he'd thought she was fond of his adopted father. Hurt, bewildered and filled with anger, he'd left his hometown, vowing never to return, vowing to forget Nora.

The flight attendant brought him out of his reverie, offering more coffee. He ordered a scotch on the rocks. He seldom drank, but tonight was an exception. In a few short hours, he'd be landing in the city of his tangled past. And seeing the woman he'd promised himself he'd forget.

Only he hadn't been able to forget Nora, not really. Often he wondered why in all his travels he'd never found a woman who could erase Nora's memory. When he'd received Jack's call yesterday telling of Nora's son being kidnapped by Ted, despite the buried animosity he felt toward her brother and perhaps the entire town, he hadn't hesitated.

Nora needed him. Perhaps their reunion would be difficult, but he wanted to see her. Maybe then he could put her out of his mind once and for all. He'd matured since the last time he'd been home, hopefully enough to handle his feelings. He'd seen a great deal of the world and witnessed more pain and death than he cared to remember. His experiences had changed him, hardened him, perhaps mellowed him.

Besides, there'd been a growing restlessness in him lately, especially since his friend, Skip, had sunk deep into depression. He needed a break from routine. Ten years in the field was a lifetime. A man saw too much, buried too many friends, picked up too many scars. A little time away and he'd be eager to be in the thick of things once more.

Accepting the drink with a brief thanks, Rafe took a swallow, welcoming the rush of heat. Looking through the window, he watched the night give way to the first feathery brushes of dawn.

Nora would have changed, he was certain, as he had. But had she changed inside? Perhaps he hadn't. One phone call and he was racing back. He could label it curiosity, or a desire to help someone in need. But was it? Or was he still searching—for acceptance, for a home to call his own, for love, the love he'd known for much too short a time?

Rafe drained his glass. Nora would be vulnerable, but he mustn't let that soften him. In his lifetime he'd allowed few people to penetrate the wall he'd built around himself, a wall of cool indifference, aloofness, even arrogance. It served as his protection against an unfriendly, sometimes hostile world. First with Doc and then with Nora, he'd dropped his defenses, no longer feeling the need to isolate himself and his feelings. But Nora had hurt him, badly. He couldn't afford to let that happen again.

What had she thought when she'd learned he was on his way? Was she as wary of seeing him again as he was of seeing her? Perhaps she was too filled with concern over her son to give much thought to him. Or was she lying there in her bed thinking of him as he flew to her side, just as he was thinking of her?

A catharsis. That's what this trip was for him, Rafe decided. He'd find Nora's son, return him to her, then be on his way again, hopefully having put to rest his vagrant memories.

He didn't need Nora. He didn't need anyone. If you relied on yourself and your training coupled with good instincts, you were less likely to get hurt. If there was one thing he'd learned in his thirty-two years, it was that. Rafe relaxed his muscles and closed his eyes.

Day Two

The morning sun was climbing in a cloudless blue sky as the plane taxied toward the Redmond terminal. The airport had been expanded since his last visit, Rafe noticed. Everything changed. He unfastened his seat belt and moved into the aisle.

Walking toward the baggage-claim area, he rolled his shoulders, loosening the kinks from the long flight. He'd had only snatches of sleep, but he'd never needed much. Long ago he'd trained himself to waken instantly and be alert. That ability had saved his life more than once.

Scanning the people in the waiting area, he spotted Jack Curtis. A shade under six feet, Jack was carrying a little too much weight packed into his tan deputy's uniform. They were the same age, yet a fondness for the good life was beginning to show on Jack. From behind sunglasses, he watched Rafe approach. Keeping his features even, Rafe stopped alongside him.

Jack held out his hand. "Thank you for coming."

Surprised, Rafe shook hands. The Jack he remembered had never seemed capable of gratitude. Times changed. He would take Nora's brother at face value, but regard him cautiously. "How's Nora holding up?"

"She's upset, of course. But Nora's stronger than most people realize."

He'd always thought so. "She's going to need to be."

The luggage carts arrived, and Rafe walked over to retrieve his leather bag. Hefting it easily, he joined Jack in strolling toward the double doors that led to the parking area. He didn't speak again until Jack started his blue station wagon and headed it toward U.S. 97 and the ten-mile drive to Redfield.

"Did you bring Ted's note?" Rafe asked.

"Yeah." Digging into his shirt pocket, Jack handed him the envelope containing a single folded sheet of paper.

Rafe took his time reading the message. Just a simple statement of the fact that he couldn't lose both of them. Was there an implied threat in that? Then the almost husbandly reassurance that she wasn't to worry, that he'd take good care of Bobby. The handwriting was neat and tidy, almost feminine. Certainly not scrawled as if written in a hurry or in agitation. He'd never met Ted Maddox, but it would appear that Nora's ex-husband was a methodical man who'd planned the abduction, not taken the boy on an impulse.

Turning his attention to the envelope, Rafe studied the postmark. "What time did Ted pick up Bobby?"

"At ten, Tuesday morning, day before yesterday. Nora received the note in yesterday afternoon's mail."

"This is postmarked noon on Tuesday, so he must have mailed it right after picking up the boy." He handed back the note. "Anything new since I talked with you last evening?"

Jack passed a slow-moving van as he shook his head. "I got all the camping gear you asked for, the food and nylon tent. I had to get a few extra supplies." Jack rubbed the back of his neck, clearly uncomfortable.

Rafe shifted on the seat so he could study the man. "Why is that?"

"Nora insists on coming with us."

Stubborn. He remembered how stubborn she'd been. "I'm not surprised."

"Maybe you can talk her out of it. Mt. Jefferson Wilderness is no place for a woman."

It was no place for most men, either. "I can try. Tell me about Ted Maddox. Has he ever done anything like this before?"

"Not that I know of. Nora's always been pretty close-mouthed about her marriage."

Yes, she would be. Even years ago, she'd been a very private person. "What caused their breakup?"

Jack shrugged. "A combination of things, I think. Ted seemed to wander from job to job, never holding one for very long, unable to find something he liked to do. Money was tight, and that's always a strain on a marriage, or so I hear. To make ends meet Nora got a job in a nursery school when Bobby was two, so she could make some money and still keep him with her. Ted hated her working. Said it made him feel like a failure."

"Was he, in your opinion?"

"Nah, just a guy who got married too young. I never did understand why he didn't go on to college, why they were in such a rush." He glanced over at Rafe. "Guess that kind of surprised you, too."

The understatement of the year. "Did you ever ask Nora why?"

Jack hesitated before finally answering. "I interfered in Nora's life once, Rafe, just once. I wish I could undo that. So I don't ask her too many questions. We get along better that way."

A careful answer. "Did Ted finally get used to Nora working?"

"Not really. He wanted more children, even though Nora had had a real difficult time delivering Bobby. We almost lost her. She was hell-bent to make Ted happy, so they tried again. After her second miscarriage, the doctor told her to let her body rest for a while. That's when Ted started drinking."

"A lot?"

"Enough." Jack turned off the highway as he reached the city limits, then angled the station wagon up a hill. "He lost another job and Nora lost her patience. She insisted on a trial separation. Ted moved to Bend and got a job at a ski lodge. He came back regularly to see Bobby, but Nora was always with the boy, making sure Ted wasn't drinking."

"Do you think he ran around on her?"

"Nah. He's been nuts about her since they were teenagers. I think the guy tried to make a go of things, but he just couldn't cope. He came back for a while, but it didn't work out. When Bobby was about four, they talked it over and agreed that Nora would file for divorce. They simply weren't making each other happy."

Rafe crossed his legs. So she hadn't been happy any more than he had. Could he have made her happier, if she'd chosen him? Rafe wondered. Anyone's guess. He turned back to her brother. "Is she working now?"

Jack nodded. "After the divorce I cosigned for her, and she bought this older house on Long Street because it was in a good neighborhood and it had a small building on the back of the lot. She worked like a demon and turned that place into a real nice nursery school for preschoolers. Small Fry Day-care Center, Nora calls it. She's got a full-time assistant and a part-time teenager who helps out, and they have about a dozen kids now. She's doing pretty well.''

"I remember she'd wanted to teach."

"Yeah. She's great with kids. Bobby's her whole world."

"What about Ted? Is he good with Bobby?"

"He's crazy about the boy."

"Then you don't think he'd harm his son?"

Jack let out a deep breath. "Up until yesterday I'd have sworn he wouldn't. Now, I'm not sure. You see a lot of things in my line of work. Yours, too, I imagine. It happens every day—something snaps and people lose control. I've got a gut feeling that Ted took Bobby only to force Nora to come back to him. But I can't be sure."

"Where's Ted been living since their divorce, in Bend?"

"Until about six months ago when he moved back to Redfield. He got a job at a lumber store, moved into an apartment and started coming around to see Bobby and Nora, telling her he was through with booze and settling down. Last week he even asked her to remarry him."

"What was her answer?"

"She refused even to discuss it. Since then we've learned that the next day he quit his job and formulated his plans to kidnap Bobby." Jack pulled the wagon to a stop.

Rafe turned to study the wide two-story gray frame home. At the far end of a cozy front porch, a swing supported by two heavy chains swayed in the early morning breeze. So she'd gotten the swing she'd daydreamed about so often as they'd lain on the summer grass talking about the future. But it would seem she'd not gotten much else she'd envisioned for herself.

"One thing, Rafe," Jack said. "Go easy on any references to possible danger to Bobby, will you? She's probably thought of plenty herself. Nora's wound pretty tight, as you can imagine."

Slowly he swung around. "I think you should know something, Jack. I would never knowingly hurt Nora."

Jack's blue eyes scrutinized him a long moment. Seemingly satisfied, he gave a brief nod and opened the car door.

Rafe stepped out on the other side and took a deep, bracing breath as he gazed at the bay windows that faced the porch. Did he imagine it, or had the curtains shifted slightly just then? With a sureness of purpose he didn't quite feel, he moved toward the porch to face his past.

She'd been up for hours, unable to sleep, showering, pacing. Packing and repacking her backpack, drinking coffee, worrying. Was Bobby warm enough, clean enough, safe enough? Was Ted calm and sane, or had something pushed him over the edge? Something or someone, perhaps her. Her life had changed irrevocably yesterday, as if she'd been on a train that had veered onto a new track, taken a different direction, leaving her lost and questioning. She hated the thoughts that whirled around in her brain, but she couldn't seem to stop them.

Forcing herself to perform little, everyday things, she straightened the house, then made herself a piece of toast. She got half of it down before her stomach rebelled. She resumed pacing, her eyes on the clock. At last she heard Jack's station wagon pull up in front. She moved to the bay windows in the dinette and pulled aside the sheer curtains.

They sat talking while her frustrations mounted. Were they quarreling, these two men who had never really been friends? Not now, she prayed. They needed all their energies to find her son. Finally she saw them emerge, and dropped the curtain before moving to the door.

Nora studied Rafe as he walked up the stairs. He hadn't changed; yet he had. He seemed taller, more solid. He'd been youthfully defiant before, arrogantly sensual, boyishly appealing. He was a man now—harder, stronger, tougher. There was a small scar on his left cheek near his temple. His eyes were worldly-wise and seemed to hide a thousand secrets. And he looked dangerous.

Struggling to keep steady, she swung open the door and he walked in, followed by Jack.

He hadn't known what he'd feel when he saw her again. Anger, resentment. The one he hadn't been prepared for was pain. He hadn't known that just looking again into those deep blue eyes would hurt. As he'd schooled himself to do years ago, Rafe hid his emotions behind a shield of cool arrogance. "Hello, Nora," he said.

Nora stepped back, aware that she owed him for dropping everything and rushing to her side. She hated owing anyone, but this had to be said. "Thank you for coming so quickly."

He brushed aside her thanks and indicated the cup she held in a white-knuckled grip. "Got any more coffee?"

"I'll get it." Jack made his way to the kitchen.

Alone with her, Rafe found he was still unprepared, despite the long hours of conjecturing. He'd forgotten how incredibly beautiful she was. Could that be so, when thoughts of her had rarely left him? Or had he deliberately tried to put her out of his mind so that being without her wouldn't hurt so much? He walked past her, gazing around the comfortable room. It was fragrant and inviting, like the woman whose guarded eyes watched him carefully. "Nice place."

"Thanks." Nervously she sat down in the chair opposite the couch. "How have you been?"

Several sarcastic remarks came to mind. He swallowed them all. "Fine." He let his eyes roam over her and found that time had barely touched her. She looked as young, as innocent as that summer. "You look the same, as lovely as ever." The words were out before he could stop them.

And you look wonderful. Nora gave a quick shake to her head. "I think we've all changed."

Here they were like two strangers, having this stilted conversation. Rafe shoved his hands into his pockets to keep from reaching out and touching her. There was so much to say, so many questions he wanted answered. Instead he nodded toward the fireplace, remembering how she'd fantasized about owning one. "I see you got your fireplace. And your porch swing."

"Yes. Some dreams come true." She felt the quick stab of regret, but kept her gaze steady.

"Not many."

"No, not many." She raised her chin challengingly. "Did yours come true?" How long could they keep this up, this maddening stroll through the mine field of their memories?

Rafe shifted his gaze to look out the front window. He could make out a snow-covered mountain peak miles away. It seemed as distant as the woman seated beside him. "A few. Not nearly enough."

Jack returned, bringing coffee and a welcome interruption. Nora watched him pass out the mugs and seat himself. She wanted to get going, to get her mind focused on finding Bobby and off this unbearable tension. "How soon can we leave?"

Rafe took a hot swallow before answering. "Are you sure you want to go with us? It's going to be rough in there."

Jack evidently wanted to give it one more shot. "We can move faster without you, Nora."

She never took her eyes from Rafe. "I'm sure. And I can keep up."

He'd never been one to try to persuade someone to not do something he was determined to do. Time was of the essence here if they were to pick up Ted's trail before dark, and he wasn't about to waste any more of it arguing. With a nod, Rafe stood. "Where can I change?"

"The bath's upstairs, first door on the right."

She took the time while he was changing to check with Wendy Brown, her assistant at the center. She'd been lucky to get Wendy, a former schoolteacher who loved children. In her fifties, Wendy was dependable, bright and a good friend. She delighted the kids and Nora with her Louisiana accent and her down-home philosophy. Hurrying out the kitchen door, Nora peeked in and saw that the children were happily engaged in a story-telling session with Nancy, the teenage girl who helped out. Catching her eye, Wendy came over and stepped outside.

"All set to go, I see," Wendy commented, her eyes sympathetic as she studied Nora. "Honey, I hope you know my thoughts and prayers will be with you night and day."

"Thanks, Wendy. You know where the numbers to call are, in case you need more supplies, right?"

Wendy patted her shoulder. "Don't you worry about this place. Nancy and I'll be just fine, and so will the children. Everyone showed up this morning except Mark. His mother called to say that he's got a tummy ache. You just go do what you have to do and get our little guy back." She shook her head. "I still can't believe Ted would do such a thing."

"Neither can I." Nora accepted the older woman's hug, and with a wave hurried back to the house. Jack was carrying out the last load of supplies to the station wagon.

Picking up her backpack, she heard footsteps on the stairs and glanced up.

Yes, dangerous looking. He had on a short-sleeved black shirt worn with army fatigues tucked into heavy boots. In one hand he carried a duffel bag. In the other, a rifle. She tried not to gasp out loud, but felt her mouth go dry.

"Is that necessary?" His eyes reminded her of a predator's.

"I hope it won't be." She looked suddenly pale, but he kept his gaze steady. "Jack has one, too. Doesn't Ted carry a gun camping?"

She tried to remember. "I think so, sometimes."

"He should, as a precaution against wild animals."

Though his attempt at reassurance did little to relieve her mind, she nodded and moved outside.

She recognized Ted's car the moment they turned off Whitewater Road and drove into the small clearing. It was parked near the well-traveled, most popular trail leading into the Wilderness. Soberly Nora approached the vehicle, peering through the windows.

"My men have already looked it over," Jack told her. "No clues here." He glanced toward the trail, then back at his sister. "Ted figured we'd eventually track him this far and tried to throw us off. This isn't where he entered."

Nora frowned. "What do you mean?"

"I gave Bobby's shirt—the one you'd given me that he'd worn the day before—to the hunt-and-search team connected with the sheriff's department. Their bloodhounds picked up the scent and led us from the car up over that way, toward that smaller, narrower path." He pointed off to the right about three hundred yards. "The men took the dogs in about a quarter of a mile, but there's so much rich vegetation and small wildlife in there that the dogs got confused and lost the scent. We're sure that's the way they went in, though.''

"I can't believe Ted went to so much trouble to mislead us.''

Rafe walked over, watching her closely. So far she was taking each piece of news in stride. "Probably just buying a little time.'' He turned to stare at the distant path. "He also knew that route was too narrow to take horses in.''

Jack shook his head. "He sure chose the tougher path.''

Ted always had chosen the hardest roads to follow since she'd known him, in hiking and in his life. Nora gazed toward the thicket of towering Douglas firs that lined the narrow, winding path, the huge trees arrow-straight in the pale sunshine. Some of the evergreens were very thick, many at least five hundred years old. These trees would be their constant companions on their hike, she thought, and hoped that they would not be joined by too much wildlife. Maybe it was good that they had two rifles along. Reaching for her backpack, she struggled with the wide straps.

Her expression was an odd mixture of hesitancy and determination, Rafe thought as he adjusted his own gear. He moved closer to her. "Let me help you with that.''

"I can manage,'' Nora said without looking up.

He dropped his outstretched hand. Had he been looking for an excuse to touch her? he asked himself. Probably. Disgusted with himself, Rafe turned back to Jack. "All set?''

Jack checked the safety on his gun. "Yeah. I'm going to take my two-way radio along, though I don't know how long I can hold the frequency in the forest. It's worth a try.''

Rafe headed for the path. "I'll start off and you bring up the rear, okay?'' At Jack's nod, he began walking. Checking his watch, he saw that it was barely ten. Ted Maddox had a day and a half's head start on them. But he probably couldn't make very good time with a small boy along on one of the toughest routes. Still they'd have to set a grueling pace to make up the difference. As he stepped over a jagged rock, he wondered how Nora would hold up.

For the next three hours, Rafe was too busy leading the way to ask himself too many questions. The damp heat was oppressive, the mosquitoes relentless, and the altitude as they climbed robbed them of precious oxygen. He ignored his discomfort and the beauty of the foliage. Instead he watched for signs of recent footsteps in the damp earth that surrounded the deeply embedded rock formations that were liberally sprinkled along the trail. The trail itself was barely visible at times.

He found several sets of footprints, too many to be identifiable. Soon, he knew, the evidence of hikers would thin, as few would have ventured very far into the dense vegetation. The path narrowed to a point where he had to hold tree limbs aside as Nora and Jack followed, then it widened to where they could walk three-abreast for long periods before narrowing again. Fortunately there were no forks in the trail leading off to force choices on them. This area was not so frequently traveled as to necessitate exploration in diverse directions, for which he was grateful.

Stopping at a small clearing he waited for the other two to catch up.

She'd hiked before, but those forays were more like Sunday strolls compared to the pace Rafe set for them, Nora thought as she fought momentary dizziness. The heat and the rarefied air, coupled with the intense march, had her wishing she were in better shape. But she wasn't about to complain to these two men who hadn't wanted her along in the first place. Or to let them see in any way that she had to struggle to keep up.

She came alongside Rafe and looked up at him questioningly.

She was game, he'd give her that, but hadn't he known she would be? When they'd been young and carefree, she'd been willing to try everything he suggested. Rafe hid his admiration behind his hooded gaze. "We'd better stop and have something to eat." If he'd been alone, he'd have kept going and eaten as he climbed. But he knew better than to push his companions too hard the first morning.

Jack arrived, huffing more than the others. Rafe saw him try to hide his relief at the announced break. "I could sure use something cold to drink," he said with a sigh, as he flung himself to the ground.

Easing out of her straps, Nora dropped gratefully to the ground. Her shoulders cried out in protest, as did her wobbly knees. Lord, how was Bobby managing to march along this overgrown path? He had field boots on and heavy jeans, but the gnarled tree roots and sharp rocks were everywhere. What if he...No! She mustn't let fear take over.

"See if this helps," Rafe suggested, holding out a chilled can of orange juice. "Vitamins and a sugar jolt." Her eyes looked haunted, and he could well imagine the path of her thoughts. They were centered on her son.

She gave him a small smile and sipped, then drank thirstily.

Jack dug into his bag and passed out granola bars and fresh fruit. Before he sat down, he tested his radio and gave them a satisfied smile. "I don't know how long it'll last, but I got through. The deputies are taking turns scouring the foothills in case Ted changes his mind and comes out."

Silently Rafe ate his lunch. Four days, tops, and they'd run out of the food they'd carried in. But the streams were full of fish and fresh water to replenish their canteens. If they found Bobby and Ted quickly, it would help. Of course they'd still have to hike back out, either using the same path or the westerly one on the other side. He could manage on little food, as long as there was water. He had done so before, many times. But he wondered about his two companions.

Nora was half reclining on the fern bed, disinterestedly eating an apple. Studying her, Rafe wondered what she was thinking. He saw Jack finish eating, then stretch out and lay a beefy arm over his eyes to rest for a few minutes. Rafe moved closer to Nora and saw her eyes shift to meet his.

For a moment, her look was unguarded and vulnerable. It was all he could do not to reach out and pull her into his arms, to offer her some small measure of comfort. Then he saw the shield go back in place, the wariness return.

"Are you all right?" he asked.

"Yes, fine." She gazed affectionately at her brother. "He didn't get much sleep last night."

Neither had she, Rafe was certain. "You're close, you and Jack?"

"In the past couple of years, yes. He's been very good to me." He'd been too watchful in her youth, too critical later, but now Jack was a friend.

Rafe leaned his arms on his bent knees as he tugged at the stem of a deer fern, absently pulling off the delicate leaves. "How are your folks?"

She sent him a questioning look. He'd never met her parents. "They're well. Why do you ask?"

"Just being polite. I imagine they're upset about Bobby being gone."

Nora wrapped the core of her apple. Polite inquiries were not exactly Rafe's style. He was getting at something. "They don't know he's missing."

He might have guessed. She'd never been one to confide much. There was such a thing as being too independent. "You didn't go to Doc's funeral." He saw the quick flash of regret on her face.

"No. I feel bad about that." She'd been pregnant, feeling awkward and swollen, and hadn't wanted Rafe to see her that way. "I sent flowers."

Rafe threw down the fern and gazed off into the distance. "It's not the same."

Nora sighed. "No, it isn't. I'm sorry. I liked Doc."

"He liked you."

She looked at him then, needing him to understand. "Rafe, these next few days will be difficult enough without us bringing up past hurts. Could we please not do that?"

"Yes, all right." He would give her that, for now. But too many questions churned inside him, questions demanding answers. They'd have to wait. He glanced at Jack. "We need to get going."

Somewhat reluctantly Jack rose, buried the garbage, and then they set off. The afternoon climb was even tougher, Nora thought, with the sun directly overhead. Even though they were in the shade most of the time, the moist heat engulfed them. She felt the dampness roll down between her breasts as she squirmed against the discomfort of the wide straps on her aching shoulders. But the men had even heavier backpacks, so she kept her thoughts to herself.

Rafe kept his eyes on the ground, thick now with the needles from the surrounding trees. Dark green moss covered many of the rocks they passed, the pungent smell of vegetation heavy in the humid air. Tucked under his right arm, he felt the reassurance of his rifle against his side. He hadn't been kidding Nora when he'd told her it was for protection from wildlife that lived in the Wilderness.

Doc had often taken him backpacking into another dense area, the one north of this one, called Mt. Washington Wilderness. They'd run into coyotes, black bears, bats, even wolves. He knew from experience that most wild creatures left humans alone unless the humans were a threat to their young. Or if it had been a long, cold winter and they were very hungry. Still it wasn't something you could rely on. And then there were the two-legged creatures they might run across.

Though it was a mystery to most people how they survived, there were actually a few people who lived in the Wilderness the better part of the year, driven out only by the deepest snow. Grizzly old men who moved about, hermitlike, communing with the animals, shunning people for reasons long-forgotten. Fleetingly Rafe wondered if Ted, in his anxiety to keep his son with him, might have that in mind. Doc had labeled the Wilderness people "the lost and weary," yet he'd had a grudging respect for them. They were doing exactly what they wanted to do and asking nothing from anyone. Doc had valued independence above most other characteristics.

There might also be hunters in the area, poachers really, for hunting here was outlawed. If they felt threatened, caught with their illegal bounty, they might be dangerous. And there would eventually be Ted Maddox to confront.

What was Nora's ex-husband like? Rafe wondered. What had triggered this irrational act? His guess was that when Nora refused to take Ted back, his already confused mind had come up with the kidnapping plan to frighten her. No logical person would believe such a bizarre action would cause Nora to return to him. What bothered Rafe was not knowing what state of mind Ted was in right now, what risk he represented to Bobby. Sometimes people who had nothing to lose, no hope of winning that which they wanted most, became dangerously careless of their own lives as well as the lives of others. He felt certain they'd find Ted, but would they be in time to prevent a tragedy?

At the top of a hill he spotted something. Realizing that Nora and Jack were a ways behind him, Rafe stooped to study the patch of earth that consisted mostly of dried mud. He could clearly make out a series of large footprints made by a textured sole and close to them, a small set. He turned as Nora came alongside him.

"What size boot does Ted wear?" he asked.

"Not real big. Ten or ten and a half, I believe." She angled her head to look at the ground. "Did you find something?"

"Maybe." He shifted so she could see as Jack reached them. "This larger print was made by a boot that's worn at the heel, not ones that are new. The prints aren't as deep as mine, so I'd say the man's smaller than I am and weighs no more than a hundred-fifty or -sixty. The tracks are solid, indicating he was walking along slowly, not rushing."

Jack looked impressed. "That's pretty close. Ted's about five-nine and lean, weighs about one-fifty-five. What about the smaller prints?"

"At first glance, they could be made by a woman. But she'd have to be mighty small. I'd say these were made by someone around seventy pounds. And you see how they're kind of scruffy around the edges? Seems to indicate more how a child walks, sometimes dragging a foot." He pointed to the side. "And over here it appears the wearer jumped up in the air, then landed alongside his own prints." Rafe glanced up at the tree directly overhead. "Maybe to bat at a leaf or grab a small branch."

Nora bit down on her lower lip, fighting the hope that sprang up inside her. "Yes, Bobby does that often when he's hiking, to relieve the boredom. And I remember Ted was wearing his old boots, ones that could be run-down at the heel. Do you think these prints were made by Ted and Bobby?''

Rafe rose. ''I don't want to let false hope carry us away. Let's just say it's a distinct possibility.''

She knew he was right. But it was the first sign, weak though it was, that Ted and Bobby probably had come this way. She needed to cling to it. Nora let out a deep breath as she spotted a couple more similar prints farther along on the path. Without waiting for the men, she began tracking. *Bobby, please be all right.*

Catching up, Rafe touched her arm. Startled, she sprang back from him. ''I'd better go first,'' he said, ''in case we run into something unexpected.''

She let him pass, then followed close behind, her eyes searching for more footprints. They had to be on the right track, they simply had to be. She didn't want to even consider the possibility that they weren't.

It was an hour later that they ran into their first major obstacle. Climbing a somewhat steep grade, Nora had her eyes downcast and bumped right into Rafe, not realizing that he'd stopped. Recovering, she tried to see around him. ''What is it?''

''The bridge has collapsed.'' He leaned to the left, looking down into the gorge at the racing Santiam River coursing along far below.

She gazed at the dangling bridge that had once spanned the river perhaps two hundred yards below. The wooden structure clearly showed the strain of thousands of feet marching across its weathered boards. ''Now what?''

He studied the sloping hillside with a practiced eye, gauging where it would be safest to descend. As Jack came up alongside, Rafe pointed downward. ''See those rocks sticking up in the water? I think the river at that point is shallow enough to walk across to the other side." Carefully he leaned out. "But going down's the problem. It's all lava rock, sharp in spots and probably slippery as hell."

"We could use ropes, go down using the buddy system."

"There's nothing solid enough here to tie the rope to. See how spindly the trees are along the edge?"

Jack looked about. "I don't see any other way then, but to climb down the face of the cliff."

Moving back to the path, Rafe agreed. "Nora, have a look. Do you think you can make it?"

She barely glanced down. "I'll make it."

Why had he bothered to ask? Rafe wondered. Nothing short of a broken neck would stop Nora from reaching her son. "All right. Anyone have anything breakable in your backpack, because if so, we're going to have to leave it here." He shrugged out of his pack and moved toward the edge. "We can climb down better without these. I'm going to roll them down ahead."

He anchored the straps of his backpack, then leaned forward and sent it rolling downward. In moments he saw it land on the river's edge with an echoing thunk. He turned, reaching out to Nora for her pack.

But she hadn't moved, mesmerized by the gaping gorge and the rushing water and sudden new fear. "How did Bobby ever make it down that steep grade?" she whispered, her voice catching on a sob.

Rising, Rafe touched her chin, forcing her to look at him. He couldn't afford to lose time taking her back now if she fell apart. She had to get a hold of herself. "This is the only path through here and we haven't found him, so he's got to be all right. Believe that. We'll find him, Nora. I promise you."

At the edge, Jack rolled his pack down. "You better believe we will. Bobby's a gutsy kid and he loves to climb. And he's wiry and agile, unlike his uncle."

Choking back her fear, Nora struggled out of her backpack and handed it to Rafe. She watched the two men send the two remaining packs to the bottom. The rapids were foamy in places, white and rushing in others. It didn't look all that shallow, either. She hauled in a deep breath. There was no other choice, she reminded herself.

"I'll go first," Rafe told Jack, "and then you start Nora down. I'll wait for her partway and help her get to the bottom."

"Look, I'm not helpless," she said, but with little conviction. She'd camped and hiked many times before. But climbing down lava rock had been one experience she'd missed.

Rafe caught the hesitancy in her voice, but didn't comment. She'd do it by sheer willpower, he was certain. Grabbing a hold of a thick bush, he turned and began to back down the wall. Carefully he found a foothold and placed one boot into it, then the other, his hands gripping tangles of red-twigged manzanita bushes that clung tenaciously to the lava rock. Nearly halfway down, he found a ledge at least a foot deep and two feet wide. Gratefully he wedged his feet into the spot and rested a moment.

Looking upward, he saw Nora poised on the edge. "Okay, ready," he yelled. His words echoed softly in the canyon.

Her descent was more difficult for him to watch than his own had been to endure. If he'd fallen, he knew he had the training to curl himself into a ball and to drop in a manner that would afford him the least harm. If Nora fell, she'd likely take them both down. While sweat poured down his back, he watched her cautiously inch toward him.

She was nearing when her foot slipped and she slid precariously lower. With a yelp, she caught herself on the manzanita vine and found her footing again.

Rafe's heart beat in double-time. "Just take it easy. You're doing fine."

Taking a deep breath, she moved steadily downward. At last her foot touched the crevice only two feet above him.

"I'm going to grab your ankle," he told her, fearing that his unexpected touch might startle her. "Let me guide you down here with me. There's plenty of room on this ledge."

"I'm ready," she answered.

Once he had her on the ledge, his arm automatically circled her, pulling her close to his body for a long moment. He could smell her familiar scent mingled with the unmistakable smell of fear, whether hers or his he wasn't certain. For the first time since his return, she touched him willingly, her small hand sliding around his waist. She clutched his shirt with trembling fingers. "You all right?" he asked.

She nodded, then made as if to look behind her.

"No, don't look. Not until we're all the way down." Slowly he lowered himself, searching with his foot until he found an indentation, a groove, a small shelf. Then he eased Nora down with him, inch by inch, until at last he vaulted clear of the rock wall.

Hearing him land, Nora turned her head, then angled her body and jumped down into the circle of his waiting arms. She closed her eyes as a shudder of relief raced through her. Safe again, fear left her, quickly replaced by a sharp awareness of the man who held her. The nearness of him had her trapped, just as his touch had years ago. She'd suspected as much and had avoided contact until now. Mere seconds in his arms and her treacherous body ached for more. Hearing a noise from above, she moved back from Rafe with a guilty start and gazed upward at Jack.

He'd already started down. The sun was brighter here, and Rafe shielded his eyes as he watched Jack's descent, trying to ignore his pounding heart. Why was he so surprised how quickly Nora could send his senses spinning? She always had.

Jack's added weight and his inactive life-style worked against him as he maneuvered somewhat clumsily downward. "Keep to your left more," Rafe called out. "There are larger footholds on that side."

He was only a dozen feet from the bottom when it happened. Evidently Jack thought his boot was firmly wedged into a crevice, but when he shifted his weight, he slipped. With a faint cry, he came crashing downward as Rafe grabbed Nora out of his path. Jack landed with a heavy thud, his right leg taking the brunt of his weight. He crumpled into a heap and let out a loud groan of pain.

Rafe rushed to him, followed by an anxious Nora. "Lie still, Jack," Rafe instructed. "Let me check you over before you try to move."

But Jack was already trying to sit up, reaching for his right foot. "Damn, I hope I didn't break anything."

"Show me where." Rafe's hands expertly moved along Jack's leg as Nora knelt by him.

"Did you hear a bone snap?" she asked.

"No, but I landed kind of crooked on this foot. Oh, whoa, Rafe. That's the spot, the ankle."

In moments Rafe had Jack's boot off, then his sock. Gingerly he examined the foot and noticed that the ankle was already swelling. "Looks like a bad sprain. Nora, get on his other side and let's see if we can move him close to the riverbank. If we immerse his ankle in cold water, that might do the trick."

Taking most of his weight, Rafe eased Jack to the shoreline, while Nora supported his other side. The big man sat down heavily, sweat on his forehead attesting to his pain.

Just what he needed, Rafe thought as he dangled Jack's leg in the chilled water nearly up to his knee. An injured man along with an emotionally distraught woman. Why in hell hadn't they let him search for the boy alone? Not only would they slow him down, they'd deplete his patience.

Standing, Rafe checked his watch. Already three. Only another two or three hours of daylight remaining in the forest, if they were lucky. Damn!

Nora gathered the backpacks they'd thrown down. Her mind racing through the possibilities, she propped one behind Jack and gave him a cold drink. What in the world would they do if Jack couldn't walk? "Are you in pain?" she asked him.

"It hurts like hell, but the water's numbing it. Got any aspirin?"

She gave him two, watching Rafe out of the corner of her eye. He was walking slowly along the riverbed, lost in thought. Probably trying to calculate the depth of the water and where they could cross. Or would they get the chance? She swung her gaze back to her brother.

Jack was a heavy man. How could they support him between them until his ankle strengthened? She ran a hand through her short hair. Why had this happened now?

Bracing himself on a large rock, Jack struggled to his feet, brushing aside Nora's offer of assistance. Carefully he tested his foot, trying to put his weight on it. Nora watched him grimace in pain.

"You need to rest. It's too soon to walk on it."

Sitting back down, he ran his big hand over the ankle. His skin was red from the cold water and the area was still swollen. He looked up at his sister. "Nora, my two-way radio's in my backpack. Hand it to me, will you?"

She did as he asked, then sat beside him as he fiddled with the dials. It took him a few minutes, but he finally got a response.

"Ken, this is Jack Curtis. You there...? Yeah, we're several miles inside Jefferson...Listen, Ken, we've got a problem. I've sprained my ankle really bad. I don't think anything's broken, but it could be. I need you and a couple of boys to come in and get me....Yeah, I know it's getting late."

Nora moved to his side. "But Jack, I..."

He waved at her, requesting silence. "I've got a rifle and I'll be fine. I'm not sure I can walk well, so you'd better bring a canvas tote...No, not a stretcher. Too difficult on these narrow trails. I'm right at that old bridge, only it's collapsed. So you have to come down the cliff side and pull me up. I'm sitting on the riverbank.... You remember that pulley we rigged up to rescue that kid who'd fallen down the ravine in the Willamette...? Yeah, bring that. There's rope in the back of my wagon. And find Steve. He knows a little about hiking....I've got enough food. Rafe and Nora will build a fire before they go on.... No, just me. Keep in touch by radio, so I know how you're doing.... All right, see you soon."

Slowly Jack turned off the dials and looked up at Rafe, who'd come over while he'd been talking. "You know I can't make it. This is the best way. You'll lose too much time if you wait with me."

Rafe nodded. The more he'd heard, the more his respect for Jack had increased. He'd wanted to suggest that he call his men, but had hesitated. Fortunately Jack had made the decision on his own. "I'll make a fire."

"I hate to leave you alone," Nora said, her expression filled with concern.

"Then stay and go back with me. Not for me, but because Rafe can find them alone faster."

Nora touched his arm, willing him to understand. "I can't, Jack. If Ted is behaving erratically, Bobby will be upset. He doesn't even know Rafe, and I've warned him about trusting strangers. He might be frightened or worse, hurt. I *have* to go. I wish there was another way, but..."

Jack sighed heavily. "I knew I couldn't talk you out of going, but I had to try. Don't worry, I'll be okay." He reached to squeeze her hand. "And I do understand."

Fighting a rush of emotion, Nora leaned over to hug him close. "Thank you." Brushing at a lone tear, she stood. "Now let me wrap your foot and make you as comfortable as possible."

In less than ten minutes, Rafe had a fire blazing and a pile of wood stacked beside Jack to keep it going. "I'll leave the big flashlight and you've got your gun." He stood. "Do you need anything else?"

Jack's blue eyes were dark and serious. "I need you to find Bobby and to take good care of my sister."

Rafe nodded. "I'll have them both back to you as soon as possible." He stretched out his hand. "Take care."

Jack shook hands, then reached to embrace Nora once more. "Be careful."

She blinked back the tears. "I will. You, too." Turning quickly, she followed Rafe downstream.

The shallowest level of the riverbed was about thirty yards from where they'd left Jack. Rafe stopped and stooped down, dipping his hand deep into the water. "It's got a stony bottom, like a floor of pebbles at this point. But they're not sharp." He stood, wiping his hands on his pants. "I think we'd be better off removing our boots and trying it in stocking feet. Hiking in wet boots can be miserable.''

He sounded as if he'd done just that a time or two. She certainly wasn't going to argue. Dropping to the hard ground, she removed her boots, while next to her he did the same.

The first plunge into the cold water was enervating. Fortunately the pebbles weren't too uncomfortable through her thick socks. Nora held her boots in one hand while her other gripped Rafe's as she followed him across the gurgling river. He maneuvered her expertly around the larger rocks, testing each step before he put his weight down. They'd rolled up their pant legs to their knees, and she was grateful to see that the water didn't reach that high.

Rafe made it to the bank and pulled Nora across the last few feet, relieved that they hadn't run into any unexpected dips in the riverbed that might have soaked them. Thick grass grew along the bank, and he sank into it. Digging in their packs, he found the towels and handed her one before stripping off his socks. "That wasn't so bad, was it?"

"Except that I can't feel my feet." Vigorously Nora rubbed her toes, trying to warm them. "I don't think that water ever warms up."

"Probably not." Tugging on dry socks, Rafe glanced across the water and upstream to where Jack sat. Nora's brother was talking on his radio again. Thank goodness he'd been able to reach his men. Rafe didn't want to think about alternatives. Checking the sky, he was pleased that there were few clouds and no rain in the air. "With a little luck, we can cover a couple more miles before we have to stop for the night."

Nora finished lacing her boots. "All right, let's go." She waved to Jack and smiled when he returned the gesture. She prayed his rescuers would hurry.

On this side of the river there was a rough path leading back up to the main trail. Nora found she didn't mind climbing it in the least, for she'd feared they might have to scale the rocky cliff instead. Going down had been bad enough. She wasn't certain she could have managed the climb up.

As they moved along with Rafe leading the way, Nora noticed subtle changes in him now that they were alone. He turned frequently to check on her progress. Without Jack following her, he seemed to be doubly concerned about her welfare. He reached often to assist her around a particularly treacherous rock, a low-hanging tree branch, a prickly bush. Other times his hand touched her shoulder to guide, to reassure, its lingering warmth encouraging. It wasn't that he made her feel that she couldn't manage without assistance, but more as if he cared what happened to her. Nora wished the thought didn't please her so much.

Subconsciously she became aware of something else, of the anticipation of being alone with him. The thought was already making her edgy.

At the top the path was quite narrow, and she had to walk behind him. Though she stayed close, the arrangement didn't seem to suit Rafe. As he helped her around a fallen tree limb, he stopped for a moment, holding her hand loosely, his dark eyes looking down into hers, giving her a choice.

Rafe had always been a man of few words, and asking for anything was not his style. Years ago she'd been able to read him clearly, and that hadn't changed. They were two solitary figures in the wilderness, walking into the unknown. That alone was a powerful bond, but despite the separation of the years there was far more between them, and they both knew it. There was a chemistry between Rafe and her that was as undeniable as it was rare. Tightening her fingers about his, Nora gave his hand a squeeze, letting him know she, too, felt the need for physical contact.

His expression didn't change, but she saw his eyes warm. Turning, he resumed the hike, keeping their hands locked together.

Day Three

Night sounds swirled around her as she rested in her sleeping bag on the hard ground. Nora lay awake long after midnight, listening. The swish of the wind through the evergreens high above their heads. The furtive scurrying of small animals that she fervently prayed would keep on going. The eerie hooting of an occasional owl and the accompanying echo. She took a deep breath of the clean, pure air and tried not to toss and turn, tried not to waken Rafe.

He lay on his back in his bag, close enough to touch. He'd insisted that her bag be positioned between the fire and himself, so she'd be safer. One arm was raised and resting above his head, the other lay atop his rifle at his side. His breathing was shallow and even, as it had been since he'd closed his eyes several hours ago now. She envied his ability to fall asleep instantly.

If only she could, Nora thought. She was certainly tired enough, but sleepy was another matter. Since leaving Jack they'd hiked for what seemed a very long time, but had, in fact, been not quite four hours. By then darkness had been closing in on them rapidly. Seemingly tireless, Rafe had gathered firewood and had a blaze going in no time. Together they'd prepared their dinner—beef stew from an aluminum pouch, oranges and instant coffee to ward off the chill of the night closing in around them.

And they'd eaten mostly in silence, broken only occasionally with pass-the-salt conversation. That's what her father had labeled strained dialogue between two people who weren't communicating, back when he'd done his marriage counseling through the church. She'd seen the questions in Rafe's dark eyes, but he hadn't asked them and she'd been grateful. Small talk was easier, though it was probably only a postponement. Odd that she and Rafe, who'd once had so much to say to each other that they could scarcely wait to be together, now spoke in short polite spurts. Perhaps not so odd considering their circumstances.

Unable to lie still, Nora shifted restively, her eyes on his face. But he didn't move. She'd spent the first hour in her sleeping bag worrying about Bobby's safety, and the past conjecturing about Jack's rescue. Drained from those concerns, she switched her thoughts to the man alongside her, but found the change even more disturbing.

Since they'd set out alone, Rafe had kept her hand nestled inside his, releasing her with obvious reluctance when they'd arrived at a suitable campsite. The feel of his strong fingers curled around hers had made her feel safe, warm and increasingly aware. Studying him now, she hadn't realized how starved she'd been for the sight of him, for the heart-stopping pleasure of his touch. She longed to reach over, to trace the faint scar that stood out on his bronzed cheek, to feel the thick silk of his hair. But she'd lost the right to touch him freely years ago.

Her first love. Did any woman ever really get over her first love? From the first day she'd seen him, riding into the children's camp and swinging down from a huge chestnut stallion, she'd wanted him. She'd wanted him with the fervor of the very young and the fearlessness of the very innocent.

He'd been standoffish at first, wary of trusting the "townies," as he called people from the area where she lived. Later she'd learned some hadn't treated him nicely. He'd been amused at the way she'd kept showing up shamelessly wherever he happened to be, helping Doc or brushing down a horse or taking a walk along the creek. Accidentally, of course. Nora smiled, remembering how blatant she'd been.

The afternoon she'd reached up and kissed him, he'd no longer been amused. He'd warned her—that he was four years older, that he had a reputation, that her family wouldn't approve of him, that he would soon be leaving. She'd listened solemnly, then kissed him again. This time he hadn't been amused—he'd kissed her back. Oh, how he'd kissed her back.

She'd been dating Ted Maddox for two years and had certainly been kissed before. But not like that. Rafe Sloan's kiss had started a fire inside her, one that had never dimmed. After that, he'd sought her out at every opportunity, finally convinced that her feelings for him were genuine.

They'd walked and talked and laughed, and they'd touched and kissed a great deal. Then one evening as they'd lain together in the sweet-smelling hay of the barn, touching and kissing hadn't been enough. With a soft sigh and a racing heart, she'd given him her innocence and discovered a shiny new world.

Looking at Rafe now, she wondered if he even remembered that time in their lives. He'd been so many places, seen so many things, and she was as she'd been—small-town and content to be so. Perhaps passion had been the only thing they'd shared. But what passion it had been, so strong that now, ten years later, the memory of those moments in his arms had her body yearning.

Resolutely Nora closed her eyes. If she didn't get to sleep soon, she'd be totally useless tomorrow. And tomorrow might be the day they found Bobby.

From a distance, Rafe heard the forlorn howl of a coyote, and then Nora turning restlessly in her sleeping bag. The smell of pine was thick in his nostrils, yet her special scent drifted to him. The coyote had made her uneasy, he knew, and he wished he could comfort her. But he also knew better than to touch her.

Always in the field, he'd had the ability to catch sleep when he could, to close his eyes and to awaken at the slightest shift in sound. Even unusual quiet would awaken him. But Nora hadn't been with him on those maneuvers, not physically, at least. She'd been with him, though, in his mind and in his soul. The mental picture of her had been there always, the way she'd looked the day he'd left, and the agonizing question that pounded in his brain then and now: why? Why hadn't she waited for him?

He hadn't planned to come back and confront her. But fate had moved him around the old chessboard and now here he was, and it was impossible not to ask. They'd be alone for some time, without Jack pretending not to watch their every move, and he would ask. No, demand. Maybe then, hearing some of the answers, he could forget her and get on with his life.

What was her son like? he wondered. As bright and quick and eager as she'd been? Filled with laughter and a love of life? But the Nora who lay beside him was quieter, calmer, her blue eyes shadowed instead of dancing with excitement. Of course she feared for her son's safety. Yet he had the feeling that even with Bobby back in her arms, there'd be a lingering sadness in her.

Rafe rolled to his side, cradling the rifle, and opened his eyes. She had her back to him, finally asleep. Tomorrow they would resume the search, the search for her son, the boy who should have been his. Life was filled with ironies, but perhaps this was the cruelest. He closed his eyes, willing sleep to come.

Nora awoke to the sound of birdcalls and the enticing aroma of coffee. She was a person who awoke slowly, her system sluggish until she'd been up a while and moving around. Stretching, she pulled herself upright and ran a hand through her hair as she opened her eyes.

He was sitting on a rock, watching her, his eyes hooded, his expression thoughtful. The sky, barely visible through the trees behind him, was just lightening with the first pink glow of dawn. She rolled her shoulders and rubbed at her calves, trying to relieve the unfamiliar soreness as she struggled to come alive.

"You still have trouble getting going in the morning," Rafe commented. "Some things don't change." Like the pleasure in simply watching her, as he had been doing for the past half an hour. Like his feelings for the woman in front of him. He clenched his teeth, fighting the knowledge. How could he care about someone who'd hurt him so deeply? No, he didn't care. But he still wanted her.

Nora rummaged around in her bag for clean clothes. "Everything changes, Rafe. Rule of nature: change and adjust, or become extinct." She got to her feet. "I think I'll visit the stream." Clutching her things, she turned and headed for the water.

A while later, she returned to find him bending over canned bacon sizzling in an iron skillet. "I'd have settled for just coffee," she told him as she walked over and poured herself a cup. Carrying it, she sat down cross-legged on her bedroll.

"It's the mistake most hikers make, not eating enough. Then they wonder why they haven't much energy." He handed her a tin plate of food, then filled his own.

Nora looked at her plate with little interest. She'd never cared to eat first thing in the morning, but she'd get some of this down somehow. She didn't want to give Rafe any reason to criticize her.

Rafe sat down, balancing his plate on his knees. "This mountain air is supposed to give you an appetite."

"You forget, I inhale this mountain air every day, though not quite so rarefied." Taking a bite, she gazed about at a string of western hemlocks bordering the small clearing of their campsite. "It is beautiful up here, isn't it?"

"I've always thought Oregon had a special beauty."

"But you left. Did you find what you were looking for?"

"Does anyone?" Rafe chewed on bacon and tasted regret. Swallowing, he turned to look at her. "Did you?"

"Some of it." She had Bobby, the home she'd wanted, work she enjoyed. That was more than many had. Life, she'd come to realize, consisted of trade-offs. She lifted her eyes to his dark profile. "Tell me about those faraway places you've been."

The steamy, bug-infested jungles of Nicaragua, the incredible bloodshed in El Salvador, the bitterly cold winters of Afghanistan—what could he tell her? "The names sound exotic and inviting. The places are not." He finished his food and set his plate aside as he gazed up at the sky. "Corruption, disease, illiteracy, terrorists. It's no picnic."

Nora sipped her coffee. "What do you do in those places?" She'd tried to imagine, but had fallen short.

How to explain the complex network. "Our government sends people into these countries to assist those fighting oppression. Sometimes our people disappear, get killed, captured or whatever. It's my department's job to find out, to get them out of there, if possible." It was a simplified version, but it would have to do.

She felt a chill race down her spine. She knew now why his eyes looked older. "Are you happy living that way, always on the edge of danger?"

Happy? It wasn't a word he thought about a great deal. Nor would he admit he hadn't necessarily had his fair share. As usual, he opted for a hint of arrogance. "Danger can be addictive, honey. It gets the adrenaline flowing." He shifted his gaze to hers. "Like making love." He watched the color move into her face as she turned to study the contents of her cup. "Tell me about Ted," he suggested, thinking that perhaps she needed to talk about the past as much as he needed to know.

Oh, she didn't want to do this, not now. "Shouldn't we get going?"

"In a minute. What's he look like?"

She'd forgotten that they'd never met. "His hair is blond and his eyes hazel. Recently he's grown a mustache."

"Is he fun? Is he interesting? Is he charming?" *Do you tremble in his arms like you did in mine?*

Nora raised her eyes to his, willing him to stop. The look held, and the silence stretched on.

"Why didn't you wait for me?" The words were out before he'd thought he was going to say them.

From the moment she'd heard he was on his way, she'd known they'd have this conversation. Why, then, wasn't she better prepared for it? "Why didn't you write me or call me? I waited..."

"Once I was in training and out of the country, I couldn't write or call anyone. It was part of the discipline of the program. I told you I'd be back for you as soon as the probationary period was over."

"I called Doc. He told me you'd be gone six months."

"Six months! You couldn't wait six lousy months?" Feeling the anger, he rose quickly, knocking their plates aside.

No, she couldn't have. How could she make him see? "I didn't know where you were, if you would return..."

Furious, he bent to grab her arms and pulled her up to face him. "I promised I would and you promised you'd wait. Don't promises mean anything to you?"

She closed her eyes to block out the intensity of his gaze. She'd known back then, as she did now, that she'd hurt him. But she couldn't tell him what pain he'd caused her.

Suddenly drained, Rafe let her go and stepped away, knowing it would be best if he put some distance between them. "I did call, when I came home for Doc's funeral. Jack told me that you were happily married to Ted and warned me to leave you alone."

Nora shoved her trembling hands into the pockets of her jeans as she blinked back the useless tears. "I didn't know about that."

He swung around, reaching for the control he seldom lost. "Why'd you marry Ted? Did you love him?"

Oh, God! The preacher's daughter, all alone and eighteen, hiding a desperate secret. Struggling to stay calm, she met his heated gaze. "It seemed like the right thing to do at the time."

"But he didn't make you happy, either. Did he, Nora?"

"No, he didn't."

He wanted to hurt her, the way she'd hurt him. "Maybe it's you, Nora. Maybe no man can make you happy. Have you thought about that?"

She felt the knife twist and fought desperately not to let him see the effect of his words. She gave a short, bitter laugh. "Yes, I have thought about that—a great deal."

Breathing hard, as if he'd just come off a run, Rafe bent to gather the plates. The cruel comment hadn't eased his own pain. "It's time to get moving."

Long past time, Nora thought as she stooped to roll up her sleeping bag.

Rotten. As he hiked up the hillside, Rafe felt rotten. He'd intended to mildly question her, not lash out with accusations. Evidently the pain in him wasn't buried as deep as he'd thought.

He'd always had trouble being indifferent to Nora. He could be kind and caring, or harsh and hurtful. What he couldn't seem to do was be casual about her. She was trudging along behind him like a trooper, worry over her son etched in the fine features of her lovely face, and he'd added to her unease. He felt rotten.

He had to make it up to her. Alongside a tree he stopped and turned so abruptly that Nora nearly plowed into him again.

"Oh!" She'd been walking with eyes downcast, silently mourning the loss of both their dreams. She looked up at him and hoped her eyes didn't look as bleak as she felt.

"I'm sorry. I had no right to say those things to you."

She understood more than she could explain to him. In a few days, when this was all over and Bobby was safe with her again, Rafe would be gone, chasing his dreams again.

She didn't want to be left with more bad memories. From somewhere she found a smile and gave it to him. "It's all right."

She'd always been forgiving, perhaps too much so. He had the odd feeling he didn't deserve it this time. He reached out his hand. She hesitated only a moment, then put her small one into his. Feeling better, he turned to resume the walk, his fingers curled around hers.

The climb was easier now, the heat less oppressive, with her hand back in his. Why was he so surprised? Hadn't she always been able to make him feel better?

He remembered a day, early in their friendship, when she'd hung over the stall door of the barn as he'd groomed a testy mare. She'd asked why she'd not seen him around town much before, for surely he'd come home summers between semesters. He'd explained that he wasn't exactly welcome in some places, because of his past wildness and because he was a half-breed. Her blue eyes had turned fiery in outrage. "How is it that they can't see the good in you?" she'd asked incredulously. One simple statement and he'd been lost.

Around noon Rafe dug out a couple of granola bars, and they ate as they walked, unwilling to lose time stopping. He kept the conversation light, hoping to lift her sagging spirits. They'd not seen any sign of Ted and Bobby, and he knew she was getting more anxious. Finally mid-afternoon they walked into a clearing, and Nora tugged on his hand as she stopped.

"Wait just a minute." Stooping, she examined the remains of a recent camp fire, filtering the charred wood slivers between her fingers.

Rafe hunkered down beside her. "What is it?"

"I've camped out with Ted several times. He always waits until the fire is out before moving on. For good measure he shreds each piece of wood remaining." She held up a handful of splintered wood fragments. "Like this. I know this sounds silly and I suppose other hikers do the same, but this looks exactly the way Ted leaves a camp fire."

Rafe didn't think it sounded silly. He stood and walked the area close by, bending to examine the ground closely. A few feet away he found what he'd been looking for. "Come over here."

Nora squatted beside him. "The same footprints, the larger tire-soled boot and the smaller one." She turned to him. "We must be on the right trail." Suddenly she rested her forehead on her bent knees. "If only we knew how far ahead of us they were."

He caught the anxiety in her voice. "However far, we'll find them."

Forcing herself under control, Nora stood. She couldn't afford the luxury of giving in to her emotions. "Let's go."

By late afternoon, Nora was having trouble putting one foot in front of the other. The buzzing gnats and mosquitoes were driving her crazy. She was hot, tired and cranky. And they hadn't run across any more signs that they might be closing in. How, she wondered, was her young son able to keep up this arduous pace when she was ready to drop? Still, Ted had an impressive head start. Perhaps she and Rafe could keep going longer, rise earlier. Anything to close the gap. The longing to hold Bobby was so strong she felt near tears. She could close her eyes and smell the small-boy fragrance of him after his bath, could feel his slim, tan arms slide around her as he endured one of her hugs. *Bobby!*

Sensing her fatigue and frustration, Rafe suggested they take a short break. He hated to spare the time, but he didn't want her cracking on him. He'd marched through wilderness trails and thick jungles with strong men and seen many crumble from the strain. Though Nora wanted to continue, he insisted, settling them both under a leafy tree at the top of a hill that overlooked a cool stream.

Hating to give in to the weakness of her body, Nora nonetheless ate a large orange, then gratefully flopped back onto the ground thick with pine needles. "Perhaps I should consider enrolling in an aerobics class," she said.

Leaning against the tree, Rafe found that his eyes wouldn't leave her. Hair windswept, face flushed, wearing jeans and a cotton T-shirt, she looked closer to eighteen than twenty-eight. "You're doing fine. This is one of the roughest trails I've hiked. You should see the equatorial forest east of the Andes in Ecuador. Hot and humid, with rats as big as a dog."

She shuddered at the thought. "I think I'll pass." With a groan, she sat up. "After this, I may never go hiking again. Maybe I'll even move away from here."

He didn't believe her. "Not you. You love it here."

"I guess you're right." She picked up a blade of scrub grass and stuck the end between her lips. "And there's my day-care center. I couldn't leave the children."

"I remember how much you loved children, how you said you wanted half a dozen." She'd once talked about having *his* baby. Rafe gazed off into a cloudy sky, pushing aside the thought.

"I guess that wasn't meant to be."

Rafe heard the sadness in her voice and touched her arm gently. "Jack told me about your miscarriages. I'm sorry. That must have been difficult for you."

Difficult? It had devastated her. "Yes. Ted took it very hard, too. Perhaps if I could have had another baby, he'd have been different."

Perhaps. But at least Ted had one son, which was more than Rafe had. Still... "Is that when he began to drink?"

Her eyes flew to his. "It seems that Jack told you everything." No, not everything. No one but she knew everything, though she'd told Dr. D'Angelo most of it.

"Don't blame Jack. I asked. I thought it might be easier to find Ted if I knew something about him, understood him a little."

"I'm not sure anyone understands Ted. Especially now."

"Drinking is usually the symptom of a deep-rooted problem. Did he want more children so badly that he began drinking? Or was there more?"

Nora sighed. "As you said, it's a symptom, but there were many things. The miscarriages, the fact that he couldn't seem to find a career that suited him, my going to work. I should have seen it sooner. Ted's not good at coping." She felt the old, familiar guilt wash over her.

"Is that why you wouldn't remarry him?"

She hated lies, hated the fact that her marriage had been built on one. If she hadn't agreed to the lie then, she wouldn't be in this mess now. Rafe's eyes were dark and waiting. "No," she said softly. Quickly she scrambled to her feet and picked up her backpack. "We've rested long enough."

Rising, Rafe touched her arm lightly. "Then why?"

Perhaps he deserved the truth. "Because I don't love him." Turning, she started down the trail.

She no longer let him hold her hand. Rafe noticed that she hung farther back on the trail from him, obviously needing some privacy. He let her have it, content to be alone with his thoughts, too.

She didn't love Ted. Had she ever? She must have, to have married him. Nora was not the kind of woman who would have had a child with a man if she didn't love the man, was she? Perhaps he should let it alone. Yet the need to know burned inside him.

What had happened after he'd left ten years ago? Had Ted returned at summer's end, found her mooning over another guy, and overwhelmed her with hearts and flowers, sweeping her off her feet? Nora hadn't seemed the type. Nor could Ted have pushed her into marriage, for even then she'd had a mind of her own. Had her family exerted pressure? Was it Jack who...

"Oh!"

He was turning around and retracing his steps before her exclamation had altogether registered with him. They'd been walking along a high ridge, and he hadn't glanced back at Nora in some time. Searching right and left, he couldn't see her. "Nora?"

"Oh, damn! Rafe, I'm down here."

He moved to the right, close to the edge and looked down. She was about a hundred feet down the embankment, her backpack caught in the treacherous stalks of a devil's club bush. He almost laughed out loud, a release of tension over the fear that had slammed into him for a moment there. It could have been so much worse.

Carefully scrambling down to her aid, he called out a warning. "Don't struggle and don't touch those stems. The spines of that plant are as sharp as porcupine quills." Reaching her side, he dug into his pack for the heavy gloves he always carried. "How'd this happen?"

"I was thinking about something and I wasn't watching where I was walking. I took a wrong step, and suddenly I was rolling down the hill." She glanced over her shoulder as he set to work freeing her with wire cutters. "Is there anything you don't have in that pack of yours?"

"Not much. Through the years I've learned to carry the essentials. These'll cut through barbed wire. Are you hurt anywhere?"

"Yes, my pride, I think. I feel pretty foolish and more than a little clumsy."

"Maybe you'll let me hold your hand again. I...ouch! Damn." Rafe flinched as one of the thorns found its way through the gloves and into his flesh.

"What is it?"

"Nothing much. Hold on another minute."

Finally he had her free enough to squirm out of the pack. Nora held it while he removed the rest of the barbs. At last she sat down on the scraggly glass as he removed his gloves. "Thank you. I'm sorry I...why, you're bleeding." She saw the short spiny thorn still in his flesh and jumped to her knees. "Here, let me take that out. Oh, that must hurt."

Handing her the cutters, he sat back and watched her grimace as she removed the ugly thing, then thrust it aside.

She groped for her bag. "I've got antiseptic in my case. Just a minute."

Florence Nightingale in blue jeans. With more amusement than pain, he watched her pour antiseptic onto a cotton ball and clean the ragged red cut on his right palm. The sting was worse than the thorn had been. When he told her so, she shook her head.

"Don't try to be macho man with me. Your skin is tough, but that's one nasty cut." She reached for bandages, then scooted closer on her knees, leaning over him to work on his hand.

"I used to be a Girl Scout," she confessed. "This is what our troop leader, Esmerelda Jones, called an open-hand bandage. You can move your hand, but the wound's protected."

"Esmerelda Jones? You made that up." He saw a quick flash of humor in her eyes.

"No, I didn't. Scout's honor."

Her hair fell forward, framing her face, as the approaching sunset turned the brown strands golden. He inhaled the warm, female scent of her and gave in to the need to touch her, lifting his free hand to her cheek.

Raising her head to look at him, Nora felt all the old longings spring to life. She'd put all her dreams to rest years ago, certain she'd never see Rafe again. And now here he was, making her want him again. Her heart began to pound as his eyes, nearly black, devoured her.

Rafe forgot all the warnings he'd been repeating to himself as he trailed his fingers along the silken line of her jaw, then cupped her chin. "You're so lovely. The loveliest woman I've ever known."

"That can't be so. You've been everywhere."

"And all along, you've been right here, in my backyard." But she'd been someone else's wife.

She seemed to read his thoughts; a hint of sadness moved into her eyes. Slowly she bent her head and placed a gentle kiss into the palm of his bandaged hand. Wordlessly she got to her feet and picked up her pack.

He wanted to stop her, to pull her to him, to kiss her beautiful mouth. He wanted to see if he could still make her throb with need, to make her tremble with desire.

He'd always wanted too much.

Rising, he glanced at the sky. "I think we can get in another hour if we're lucky." He reached out his hand. She gripped it carefully, mindful of his cut, and followed him back up the hill.

Rafe decided to set up camp at a small clearing a short walk from the river's edge. They ate their dinner around the camp fire, listening to the gurgling of the water as it flowed downhill. After the episode on the hillside, they'd both been subdued, trying to avoid emotional subjects. It wasn't easy, he decided, as he watched Nora shift restlessly while she finished her coffee.

"It's warmer tonight." Nora gazed up at the star-filled night sky barely visible through the trees.

"We're at a lower altitude here."

She glanced in the direction of the river. "Do you suppose the water's just as cold?"

"I imagine so. But the air's not even cool." He cocked his head at her. "Are you in the mood for a dip?"

She'd only splashed for moments in the stream this morning. Her hair needed washing, and she felt grungy. "More like a bath." She rose to get her soap and towel. "Do you mind? I won't be long."

"I'll come with you."

She stopped. "I...I don't have a suit." In his eyes she saw what he was thinking—that he'd seen her naked, the first man who had. She felt foolish, yet...

"It's not safe to be alone. I'll take the rifle. Wear your underthings, if it makes you feel more comfortable, but I don't want you out of my sight."

She could handle this, Nora told herself. Gathering her things, she marched to the water. It would feel good to be clean again. Behind her, she heard Rafe following. He would only be standing guard, she reminded herself. That was all.

Undressing under cover of a thick tree at the water's edge, Nora left her clothes on a rock alongside her clean ones. She grabbed her soap and shampoo and gingerly stepped into the water. Cold, very cold. But refreshing. She waded out and slipped under, wetting her hair, then rose to toss it from her face. Only then did she look back onto the river's bank.

Her mouth dropped open. He was undressing, his boots already off, as well as his shirt. "I thought you were going to stand guard?" Her words carried across the water, and he looked up.

"I'm leaving the rifle right here where I can reach it in a hurry if need be." Wearing only his briefs, he started in. "I just thought I'd rinse off. Get's pretty hot on the trail."

Nora eased more toward the middle, but found the bottom dropping quickly as the riverbed deepened. Frowning, she turned her back and began shampooing her hair. She dipped down to rinse off, then rose to blink the water from her eyes. The sky was already quite dark, but a nearly full moon lent a silver glow to the scene. Just what she needed. Glancing down, she saw that the lace of her wet bra was nearly transparent. Wonderful. She tossed her shampoo bottle to the shore and rubbed the soap along her arms.

"Nice here in the moonlight, isn't it?"

Nora swiveled about. How had he reached her so quickly, so silently? "Stay where you are," she warned.

"I only came over to borrow the soap. I forgot to bring mine in."

Sure he had. Cautiously she held it out at arm's length. He took it, his fingers barely grazing hers. But his eyes were dark and aware. Then he turned and moved back toward the bank.

Nora let out a slow breath as she rinsed off. She waited until he'd climbed out and walked upstream before she hurried to where she'd left her towel and clothes.

Dry and dressed, she strolled to join him, rubbing at her wet hair. He'd been standing with his back to her and now swung about and came closer. Almost lazily, he raised his hand and trailed his fingers along her cheek, down the smooth column of her throat, stopping just short of the fullness of her breasts. She felt the quick response and saw that he noticed the change, too.

"You want me. You still want me." His voice was husky.

Annoyed because he was right, Nora turned aside, stepped out of reach. She had a son, a business, obligations. And soon Rafe would be out of her life, rushing off to save the world. She'd have to remember that. "Perhaps, but I don't grab everything I want these days. Life's a little more complicated than that."

He let out a regretful sigh. "I've had my share of life's complications."

Even as she stepped farther back, she felt the familiar magnetic pull of his hold on her. Would she never get over this man? "Rafe, please don't complicate my life right now. I've got enough to deal with."

She couldn't have said anything that would have cooled him off faster. "All right. But answer just one thing for me. I asked you earlier and you didn't quite answer. Did you ever love him, Nora? In the beginning?"

Her shoulders sagged in weariness. She was fairly certain he'd never stop chewing on this particular bone. She raised her chin. It was time to see if he could deal with the truth, if they both could. "No, never."

"Then why did . . . ?"

"No more questions, Rafe. Not tonight." Turning from him, she headed for the camp fire.

Day Four

He'd forgotten how green this part of the Cascades was. Hiking along the riverbed, Rafe was fascinated by the shades of green offered by a variety of vegetation, from pale to a deep emerald hue. This area was lush and almost tropical in its atmosphere, at least during the middle of a sunny August afternoon. But it had gotten quite cold during the night.

So cold it had awakened him. Seeing the fire reduced to glowing embers, he'd gotten up and fed it more wood, then glanced over at Nora. Curled up in a ball, she lay on her side, shivering. Though she'd changed into clean shirt and jeans after stepping out of the water, and was covered to her neck by a thermal sleeping bag, she was obviously cold. He'd invited her into his larger bag, to share his body heat, but she'd refused. After their encounter on the riverbank, perhaps she was wiser than he, Rafe decided.

Behind him, he heard twigs snap under her boots as she followed, but he didn't look back. She was growing more tense with each hour, each day that passed, and he could do little to alleviate her tension. He'd never had a child, but could easily imagine the fears she struggled with, of Bobby hurt, or Bobby scared. He knew she was also concerned about Jack, if he'd had any problems getting back to town and how his foot was. And she had to be wondering about Ted's mental state.

Rafe walked around a moss-covered rock and heard the croaking of a spotted frog as it sat on a fallen log. Deep in thought, he hardly noticed. He'd forced Nora into admitting she didn't love Ted, had in fact never loved Ted. He'd also forced her to admit that she wanted him as much as she had as a girl. God knows he wanted her. But now what?

Nora was a woman meant for forevers. He wasn't sure he could ever give her that. When he'd learned she'd married another man, he'd set aside his own dreams of forever. Since then, he'd not allowed room in his life for thoughts of permanency. Yet Nora still tugged at him, still made him ache, made him yearn.

Ten years of working in intelligence and in field operations had taken its toll. Half as many years had depleted some men. He was a different man than the one she'd known back then. On those faraway battlefields, he'd lost his innocence, his youth, his trust in his fellow man. He couldn't afford to lose more. Yet she could do that to him, snare him, then turn from him again.

A golden-mantled ground squirrel scooted across his path, its cheeks bulging with some treat. Absently Rafe watched him as he slowed his pace. The tension between Nora and him was building, and they were both aware of it. Long before he'd claimed her body, he'd fallen in love with the person that was Nora. Though her body enticed him still, the woman she'd become drew him also, perhaps more. As then, he knew he couldn't touch the one without affecting the other. Not with Nora.

Sensing her close behind him, Rafe turned just as Nora placed her hand on his shoulder.

"Look over there, across the river," she whispered.

He spotted it right away, in the shadow of a huge Douglas fir. A black bear standing alongside a tree stump, busily scooping bugs from the decaying surface with her paw and stuffing them in her mouth, her brown eyes watching them.

"She saw us coming," Nora explained, "and chased her cub up the pine tree. See where he's hanging on? He can't be very old."

Automatically Rafe's arm drew her close as he kept a firm hold on the rifle. "Four or five months old, I'd guess, just a little guy. But that mother's pretty hefty, at least eight hundred pounds."

"She seems starved. Do you think she'd try to swim across the river and come at us? It's pretty deep in the center at this point." Nora was more fascinated than frightened. But she wondered how fast she could scramble up one of these thorny trees, and if that rather large bear would come after them.

"I doubt it. She probably picked up our scent some time ago and made sure her cub was safe. The black bears around here don't usually attack unless provoked. Once, when Doc and I ran into a large adult bear, it took its time looking us over, then turned and ambled off into the forest. Now, grizzlies, they're another story."

"I thought grizzlies were pretty much extinct in the Cascades."

"They are, fortunately for us. I think there might be a few left up by the Canadian border." He looked down at her. "You're not afraid?"

"Of the bear? No, not with the river between us. And I imagine, if worse came to worst, you know how to use that rifle. Have you ever had to shoot a wild animal?"

A wild animal and much more. Rafe started them walking again, keeping her within the protection of his arm. "Yes, but only when it was my life or his."

"Good. I'm appalled at men who kill for pleasure, even wild animals, unless they're about to attack a human. This Wilderness, and others like it, belong to the bears, the cougars, the wolves. And man has come along and senselessly killed most of them off. I don't understand it."

He gave her arm a squeeze. "A champion of wildlife, are you?"

"In a way. There was an article in the local paper recently about wolves. Most people automatically assume they're killers and actually there's been no authenticated case of a wolf attacking a human unless the person presented a threat to its young. With humans, protecting our young is considered a virtue. Wolves are good parents, always travel in packs, taking their young along. It's just that they're so scary looking."

"The howl of a wolf can sound pretty frightening."

"Man can be pretty frightening, too." She thought of Ted. Was he protecting his young this very minute, or was he the threat?

Sensing the sudden change in her, he tried to divert her thoughts. "So the wolf is a family man. I might have known you'd stick up for him."

With effort, Nora shook off her fear as she looked up at Rafe. "Yes, I always was for the family. And you were always the loner." She was hesitant now, treading on dan-

gerous ground. "Do you ever miss having a family,
children?"

He felt the flash of pain. It was because of her that he
didn't have a family, wasn't it? He wouldn't let her see how
much that still hurt. "My line of work is tough on a family. It's probably best that I go it alone."

So she'd been right, Nora thought. Rafe needed to be
free.

Her vision blurred. "Your work is enough for you,
then." That was the real reason he hadn't come back for
her. Deep down, she'd always known it.

Enough for him. Was it? He'd ignored that nagging
question for years, for he'd had no reason to face it. And
now there was Nora and her softly probing gaze. Stopping, he set down the gun and turned to her. "It has been."
He placed his hands on her cheeks, then slid them into the
rich chestnut of her hair. "Until I saw you again." Dipping his head, he touched his lips to hers.

He'd meant to taste, a quick kiss to see if his remembered dreams had had any substance. But the moment she
opened to him, he was lost, just as he'd been ten years before. Her fragrance wrapped around him, drugging his
senses, as his hands drew her closer. His tongue moved inside, and he felt her welcoming warmth. Rafe suddenly realized his memories had been only pale reminders of the
real thing. This was real and familiar and as incredibly exciting as he'd known it would be.

Her hands encountered his backpack, and she dug her
way beneath the canvas to touch the heat of his skin
through his shirt. His mouth was hard, yet tender on her
lips, his tongue fencing with hers and leaving her breathless. She'd tried to tell herself she could live without this,
that life consisted more of small everyday pleasures than of
intense moments. She'd thought she could make do, forget

the passion they'd shared, stop the incredible craving for that which could never be. But the moment she'd seen him walk onto her porch, her needs had shifted.

Moving her mouth over his, Nora inhaled the musky male scent of him, feeling the growth of beard graze her cheeks with sharp pleasure. She strained against him, closer, closer. *I remember you, love. I remember you well.*

How was it no woman had been able to fill this empty place inside him, except this one? Rafe asked himself. He'd tried to replace her, to forget her. But she'd always been there. Pride had kept him from returning again, and stubbornness. Stupid traits, and he berated himself for both. The here and the now and this woman were all that were important.

He held her tighter, and she responded, more alive than she'd been in a decade. She gave him her mouth as eagerly as then, her heart as willingly as yesterday. She'd never had a choice when it came to Rafe. Pulling back from him, she realized she was as in love with him now as she'd been the last time he'd kissed her. Loving him with all her heart hadn't kept him with her then, and it wouldn't now.

Rafe watched Nora step back and touch trembling fingers to her lips, still wet from his kiss. Did she regret giving in to her desire? He tipped her chin up and sought her eyes. "Are you sorry you kissed me?"

Sorry she kissed him, when she'd often awakened with the need to hold him so strong, so real in her that she'd had to get out of bed and pace the house to quiet her yearning body? She smiled then and reached to caress his stubbled chin. "Sorry? No. I've never regretted any of the kisses we've shared, only the ones we haven't."

He stepped closer. "Nora—"

"Shh, Rafe," she whispered, and moved on tiptoe to rest her cheek against his. "Just hold me a moment." She closed her eyes and clung to the solid strength of him. At last, with a regretful sigh, she released him. "It's getting late."

Rafe bent to pick up the rifle and reached for her hand. "Let's go." Mind and emotions churning, he set out along the narrowing path.

Night seemed darker in the wilderness, and evening came early. Rafe sat next to a dogwood tree and watched the moon play hide-and-seek among the giant treetops. The trail had steadily climbed, and they were at an elevation of at least five thousand feet at their campsite for the night. The cool air brushed against the pine branches, making them sway and sigh. Reaching into his bag, he pulled out a sweatshirt and slipped it on.

Glancing to the right, he saw the steady beam of the flashlight that Nora had taken with her to the pond just beyond the far row of trees. She'd wanted some privacy to clean up for the night and, because he could see her light through the trees, he'd given it to her.

She'd wanted to camp at this spot, even though he'd wanted to keep going a while, because she'd found more signs that indicated that Ted and Bobby had spent some time here. The remains of their camp fire, shredded as the one before had been, and more footprints, though vague. Nora was certain this was the spot where her son and ex-husband had slept, perhaps last night. And so he'd agreed.

While she was elated, Rafe was discouraged. The findings if real, meant that Ted and Bobby were still twenty-four hours ahead of them. To close the gap, he'd have to talk Nora into some heavy hiking tomorrow, starting earlier, moving faster. As he was wondering if she could handle a stepped-up pace, he heard a shriek from the direction of the trees.

Grabbing the rifle, Rafe leaped to his feet. He raced toward the pond, then slowed as he saw her standing alongside a tree, the flashlight trained on something she clutched in one hand. "What is it?"

She held up the item. "Bobby's hat," she said, her voice unsteady.

Taking it from her, Rafe examined the small Seattle Mariners baseball cap. "Are you sure? There are a lot of these around the Northwest."

"It's not even damp. It hasn't been lying here long. I was weaving the flashlight back and forth on my way back and spotted something on the ground. Bobby often tucks it into his back pocket when he's not wearing it." She looked up at him, her eyes bleak. "He'll miss it, I know. It's his favorite hat. He was wearing it when Ted picked him up."

Slipping his arm around her slender shoulders, he led her back toward their camp fire. "It seems as though we're on the right track."

Nora sat cross-legged on her sleeping bag and took the cap from him. She felt bone-weary, exhausted, defeated. Holding the cap closer to the fire, she turned it inside out. "Look at this, a couple of short, dark hairs that are wavy. Bobby's hair is black and quite wavy. I know that this is his." She ran her thumb along the bill. "Jack took him to a Mariners game last month and bought it for him."

Rafe thrust another piece of a log onto the fire, dusted off his hands and sat down beside her. Perhaps she needed to talk about the boy. "Is Bobby athletic?"

Her smile was filled with maternal pride. "Yes, he loves sports. He's on a Little League baseball team, the Blue Jays. He plays first base and he's saved the day more than once by getting a runner on first out with his long reach." She sighed, picturing Bobby's face as he concentrated on the game.

"Is that the only sport he plays?"

"No. Last winter they started a basketball team for the younger boys at his school. He was the first boy from the third grade to make the team. He's so tall, already up to my shoulders, and he's only nine."

In the shifting shadows of the firelight, Rafe watched her face grow lovelier as she spoke of her son. And he wished again that the boy was a child Nora and he had made together so he could join her in her love for him, in her fear for him. So much he'd missed out on, and he hadn't really known he was the poorer for it until now, until his return.

Anger and envy crackled through him, all aimed at Ted Maddox. Anger that Ted had stolen his girl, his future from him, and envy over the life Ted had shared with Nora, then somehow had tossed away. The man was a fool to let a woman like Nora get away from him. Rafe clenched his jaw, sure that if he'd had the chance back then to marry her, to make a life with her, he'd have made Nora happy. But in all fairness, Ted hadn't held a gun to her head. She'd turned away from him and reached out to Ted. Despite his desire for her now, how could he ever forgive her for those ten lost years?

He raised his eyes and saw her shiver as she sat staring at Bobby's cap, and his heart softened. That was the problem, Rafe thought as he shrugged out of his jacket and placed it around her shoulders. Nora always had his heart softening.

"Is he a good student?" he asked, hoping that more conversation would keep her from slipping into the lonely world of her fears.

Nora smiled and shook her head. "Not terrific. He's restless, a bit of a dreamer. And a scrapper, often getting into punching sessions with the other boys." She shot him a quick look, afraid she'd said too much.

Rafe gazed off into the starry sky, wishing he had a nickel for every fight he'd gotten into during his own school days. It seemed as though he'd constantly been defending himself against things said, real or imagined. But what did Bobby have to defend? he wondered. "Why's that?"

She shrugged. "Does a young boy need much of a reason? The male of the species, from the cradle on, has this need to prove himself." She looked into his eyes. He'd told her a great deal that long, hot summer, about how often his fists had gotten him into trouble. "Don't you remember?"

He nodded. "All too well." He watched her carefully tuck the baseball cap into her bag. "Have you got a picture of Bobby in there?"

She'd wanted this, yet feared it. With trembling fingers, she reached for her wallet and removed a small snapshot. "I took this on his last birthday." Heart in her throat, she watched him scrutinize the picture.

She wasn't much of a photographer, Rafe decided. The boy's face was oval, like Nora's, his wavy hair also very much like hers. His eyes looked dark and shone with that unmistakable spark of mischief. His smile was a little shy, reminding him of a youthful Nora, and there was something hauntingly familiar that he couldn't put his finger on.

"A good-looking boy. May I keep this—to study?"

The thing to do was to act nonchalant, Nora told herself. "Sure." She closed her bag, then pulled his jacket about her. His special scent surrounded her like a warm memory. "It's cold and I'm tired. I think I'll crawl into my sleeping bag."

"Good idea," Rafe said as he rose to arrange his own bag closer to hers. "I'd like us to get going at first light. We need to make better time. Will that bother you?"

"No. I'll keep up." She'd do anything to find Bobby, to get this nightmare behind them. Snuggling into her bag, she fought a slight shiver. Nights were the hardest, when her mind wouldn't let her rest as she imagined untold horrors. Days, at least, she was too busy concentrating on hiking to think too much. She closed her eyes, wishing the muscle cramps in her legs would ease up so she could get to sleep.

Rafe lay quietly on his side, very still as always. He'd trained himself to not move as he invited sleep and even as he slept. That trick had probably saved his life a time or two when the sounds of any restless movement might have been picked up by enemies tracking him. But Nora had had no such need and shifted now, rubbing her legs. Realizing the problem, he sat up.

"You've got muscle spasms. Let me help." He pulled back the edge of the sleeping bag.

"It's okay. They'll stop."

"They'll stop faster with a little help." Gently he rolled her onto her back. "Push down your jeans." In the firelight, he saw her eyes widen. "I can't rub your calves through denim."

"I think that might be a mistake."

He sat back on his haunches, exasperated. "Are you afraid of me, Nora?"

"No," she answered honestly. It was herself she feared.

"Do you think it's my style to force myself on a woman?"

Actually, even years ago, she'd been the one who'd initiated their first kiss, the one who'd later shamelessly strained against him, all but begging him to make love to her. Not only was it not his style to force, but he was so devastatingly attractive that few women could resist offering themselves to him, she was certain. "No," she answered in a quiet voice.

"Then let's have a little cooperation here."

Nervously she released the catch at her waist and raised her hips as she slid her jeans lower. Moonlight danced on his dark head as he pulled off her jeans and knelt alongside her. His hair, tousled and tossed in the night breezes, was endearingly unkempt. She looked away from his magnetic claim on her wilting good sense. His lean, hard fingers began to massage the soreness from her calves. "Oh," she moaned as he kneaded a particularly tense spot.

"You're not used to so much walking, especially up and down the hills. You've got knots of bunched-up muscles here." He ran his hand up her slender leg, then back down to the ankle, squeezing and stroking, and was rewarded with a soft sigh.

How many nights had he lain awake on the hard ground, on narrow canvas bunks, and once for nearly two months in an army hospital bed, dreaming of touching her like this? Like this and more. How many times had he relived the hours he'd spent in her arms when she'd made him feel as if he owned the world, the only woman who ever had? How many offers from other women had he rejected as unable to measure up to the yardstick of perfection that was Nora? He moved to minister to her other leg as he felt her breathing go shallow.

Silk and lace, the triangle she wore drew his eyes. He'd be less than human if he didn't respond, he reminded himself as he felt his body harden. He longed to trail his fingers farther, to lay his cheek on the smooth satin of her flat belly and feel her hands in his hair draw him closer. Then he would reach up under her sweatshirt and . . .

Abruptly, Rafe sat back. "There, that feel any better?"

Opening her eyes, Nora nodded. The knots were gone from her legs, but the tension from her awareness of Rafe had settled in a ball in her stomach. She sat up and reached for her jeans, but his hand stopped her.

"I have a suggestion. Sleeping in jeans can't be very comfortable for you. That's why I always take mine off. Let's move the sleeping bags together, and we can keep each other warm."

Gazing into his face, she saw that he meant it. "You can't be serious."

Rafe was up and rearranging his bag closer to the fire. "Sure I am." He patted the padded bed he'd made. "Come on, crawl over here and stretch out."

Anticipation laced with hesitation struggled inside her. "Rafe, I'm not sure I can do this."

The thing to do was to make light of it. Hands on his hips, he grinned down at her. "Think you can't handle the temptation and you'll jump my bones?"

Damn him for making fun of her very real reluctance. With a scowl, she scooted onto the spread bag. Turning on her side, she offered him her back.

Rafe shook his head as he lay down beside her. He had no intention of taking her, yet the need to hold her, just to hold her, had become a living, breathing desire. Now all he had to do was convince her that he posed no threat to her. Not, that is, unless she made the first move. Then it would be every man for himself. He arranged the other unzipped bag over them as a cover.

Slowly he inched closer, then trailed his arm along hers as she lay facing the fire. "There, isn't this warm and cozy?"

Nora shook his arm off and squirmed to the edge of the bag, her body no longer touching his. Why was this so difficult for her and so amusing to him?

"Are we pouting?" Rafe asked. After a long minute, when she didn't answer, he moved his face into her hair and nuzzled her neck. "I thought you said you weren't afraid of me?"

His breath was warming her, his body tempting her. She pulled away, then rolled onto her back, her raised hand keeping him at bay. His eyes were nearly black in the glow of the fire, reminding her of other dark eyes. Heart pounding, she knew she loved them both. "This isn't working."

Suddenly serious, he returned the look. "You're beautiful. What man wouldn't want to hold you? That's all it'll be. Will you let me hold you, Nora?"

All her life she'd detested force and those who resorted to it. She'd turned often from Ted when he'd been drinking and amorously insistent. But how could she resist a gentle question that left the decision to her, a decision she'd made years ago, anyhow? Without a word, she turned into him, her arms encircling.

Rafe let out a deep breath and held her lightly, without pressure. All those lonely years, this is what he'd wanted, Nora in his arms, willingly in his arms. To watch her smile in that soft way she had, to see her blue eyes light up for him, with the hot undercurrent of desire between them ever present... Oh, how he'd longed for just this. They had separate lives, separate dreams. But for a few hours, they could pretend that life hadn't cheated them.

Nora moved fractionally closer. He smelled so good, fresh like the stream he'd splashed in a short time ago, woodsy from the outdoors, his scent sharp and masculine. As always he could make her forget, make her want. But this time she wouldn't give in to her dreams of forever; only fools stuck their hands into the flame twice.

As she lay quietly in the shelter of his arms, she felt the unmistakable changes in his body and knew her own was not totally unaffected. "I should move back," she said quietly.

"Don't worry. Nothing's going to happen. Holding you like this, it's like a dream, one I've had many times when I've been on the other side of the world, lying awake thinking of you."

Nora's hand curled in the soft hair of his chest. Had they been the same nights she'd walked the floor thinking of him? "I thought about you, too. Many nights. But I'm not sure this is a good idea."

"Shh. It's a fine idea. A grown man doesn't lunge at a woman just because he wants her. You have nothing to fear with me."

Nothing except fighting her own need to lunge. She willed herself to relax. "All right, if you're sure I'm not making you uncomfortable."

He raised his hand to touch the silken strands of her hair, golden from the fire. "Uncomfortable was lying over there pretending not to want to be over here, with you."

"Truth of the matter is, I was having the same problem." Nora smiled and touched his stubbly face. Trailing her fingers upward, she reached the scar near his temple. "How did you get this?"

He shrugged. "An accident."

She raised a brow. "A masterpiece of understatement, I imagine. You don't want to tell me?"

Rafe sighed, settling her onto his chest more comfortably, the pressure in his veins easing. "It was a couple of years ago, in a particularly hot and miserable jungle. I'd gotten hurt, a knife wound in my side. The pain made me careless and I was captured."

She rose onto her elbow. "You were a prisoner?"

"Yeah, for about two months. Seemed more like two years. I was confined to a hut made of bamboo in an area about four-feet-by-eight. Food was some vile mixture of rice and fish, when they remembered to bring it, and my bathroom was a hole in the corner. By day, there was the heat and the flies. By night, bats would fly in the open windows and huge rats would race around the floor fighting over me. I had to get out or go insane."

She scarcely realized her hand had formed a fist. "So you got the scar escaping?"

He'd gotten that scar wrestling with the fat guard who'd miscalculated his cunning one evening when he'd brought his meal and turned his back for an instant. Rafe had been on him, enjoying the sound of air escaping from the man's lungs as his fist had connected, enjoying the satisfaction of hearing him hit the ground with a thud. Only fatso had had one last hurrah, swiping at him with his knife and nearly putting out his eye. Rafe had ripped the dagger from him and plunged the blade home. Bleeding and scared, but free, he'd run then, run like hell from the hell that had been his home for too long, vowing never to get caught again. And he hadn't been.

"Yeah, I got it escaping." It was time to change the subject. He rubbed a thumb along her chin, tracing a small, white scar. "And where did you get this?"

Even in the dim firelight, she'd seen the bleak look that had passed over him. She'd allow him a change of subject. "From Jimmy Hearns. Don't you remember when I told you the story, way back when?"

"Let's see," Rafe said, pretending to think hard. He remembered, all right. He remembered all their conversations. "Jimmy Hearns was the catcher at home plate who said you were out after your winning home run. And you didn't exactly agree. So, like a perfectly well brought up ten-year-old, you leaped on him and tried to rearrange his face. Is that about right?"

Nora laughed. "You do remember. I wound up with a cut chin, but Jimmy had a black eye that lasted two weeks."

"I think Bobby comes by his occasional aggressive behavior quite naturally. And you a minister's daughter." Shifting, Rafe rolled her onto her back. "A shy, quiet minister's daughter."

Still smiling, Nora looked up at him. "Was I shy and quiet?"

"Yeah, for about a day and a half. Then you all but ripped my clothes off."

"I did not! Rafe Sloan, what a terrible thing to say."

His face was close to hers now, very close, his body lined up along hers. He felt the ache return, more powerful than before. Supporting his weight on his elbows, he slid his hands into her hair and saw the smile on her face slip.

"You weren't shy with me, not even the first time, were you, Nora? You were as eager for me as I was for you. Do I remember the story about Jimmy Hearns? Yes, I remember everything you said to me, all summer long." Moving over her, he let her feel the hard thrust of his desire and heard her sharp intake of breath. "And I remember you in my arms like this, remember how it felt to be inside you while we made the whole damn world disappear. I remember kissing you until your lips were swollen, almost bruised, and yet you reached for more. Do you remember?"

The pulse pounding in her throat made it difficult to concentrate. "Why are you doing this, Rafe?"

He'd thought he could handle things, just hold her. He'd been wrong. "I want to make love to you."

"No."

Even though he'd known her answer, he felt the frustration. "Why? You're free and so am I."

A sigh trembled through her lips. "Because things are different now. We can't go backward. I'm not the same carefree girl I was that summer, and you're not the rebellious young man who wanted to prove himself to the world."

He sighed, a weary sound. "It wasn't the world I needed to prove myself to. It was to the town that never accepted me. And maybe prove myself to you."

"I never needed you to prove yourself. I wanted you to believe you didn't need the town's acceptance or anyone else's, that you were the finest there was, with or without their approval."

"You give me too much credit."

"Perhaps you give me too little." She touched his face gently, her fingers following the faint lines of his beard, trying to soothe him. "I always saw through you, through the arrogant rebel who wanted to take on the world with his fists. I believed in you then as I do now, or I wouldn't have trusted you to find Bobby."

His eyes bore into hers, as dark as ink. "Was that all it was, Nora, a strong belief in a young punk who attracted you?"

"You did far more than attract me."

"Are you afraid to say it?"

Hadn't she known he'd push her to this? "No. I loved you. Did you ever doubt it?"

"Yes, when I came home and found you married to another man." His hands tightened on her arms, his face becoming hard. "Why, Nora? Just answer me why."

She struggled to keep her eyes locked to his, to keep them unreadable. "Let it go, Rafe. All that happened ten years ago. It's over and done with."

Angrily Rafe released her and stood. "Is it, Nora? Will it ever be over between us?" He shook his head. "I don't think so." Grabbing his jeans, he strode off toward the woods.

Her body felt chilled without the warmth of his. Pulling the covers around her, Nora curled into a ball, her vision blurring from unshed tears. Sadness welled up inside her as she heard twigs snap under Rafe's angry footsteps. Would she ever be able to satisfy his questions? She wished she could, but knew it was impossible. She had too much to lose and Bobby to protect.

Nora closed her eyes, knowing it would be a very long night.

Day Five

*T*hey were no longer alone. He could sense it, smell it.

Rafe's eyes flew open as he lay perfectly still, scanning his surroundings. The bamboo walls of his prison were loosely tied together with a rough hemp roping. Through the cracks, the light that was never turned off in the hallway filtered in. He saw the fat guard who had the night shift press his ugly face into one of the larger openings and peer inside. Unhurriedly he began his frequent routine of loud warnings of what would happen to Rafe if he didn't cooperate with them. Striking the bamboo with the butt of his rifle, he went on in his broken English to list all that would befall Rafe's family back in the States if he didn't confess to being a spy. Little did they know that he had no family they could threaten him with.

The music began then, loud and thrumming, meant to keep him awake, to weaken him, to drive him into madness. A huge, hairy rat scurried past him, running from the *noise. The heavy, cloying heat of the jungle mingled with the scent of rotting garbage nearby. Rafe wound his arms about his head, trying to blot out the sounds, the smells, the horror. The guard poked the rifle through the bamboo slits, rattling the cage walls, his voice taunting, terrifying. Rafe smelled his own sweat and swallowed his fear. He would endure, until he could escape. And he would escape.*

He glanced over at the huddled figure curled up against the far wall. Skip was either blissfully sleeping through tonight, or he'd passed out again from the infected wound in his leg. If he didn't get medical help soon, he'd die. Rafe felt the anger, the frustration well up inside as he heard Skip moan.

Suddenly the small door swung open and another guard joined the first. Rafe sat up as they moved toward Skip's pallet. Each grabbed an end and hoisted the thin blanket roll that was wrapped around his friend. Silently they marched out carrying him. Rafe heard Skip's deep groan just before the door slammed shut behind them.

"Where are you taking him?" Rafe called out, fearful he would never see Skip again. "Please, no. He's sick." But only the shuffling of feet moving away mingled with the night sounds.

"No," Rafe yelled again. "No..."

"No, no," Rafe mumbled, his head thrashing. "Don't take Skip away."

In the bedroll alongside Rafe, Nora awakened and turned toward him. She listened a moment as he fought the demons in his dream.

"We have nothing to tell you.... Leave us alone." His face damp with sweat, Rafe held out his hands to ward off the unseen attacker. "Leave him alone." His eyes opened, but didn't focus. "No, no!"

She would have to waken him. "Rafe, it's all right. It's only a dream." She reached over and touched his arm.

Later she would recall the events in a blurry kaleidoscope of action. Faster than she'd seen anyone move, Rafe reached under his sleeping bag, grabbed a huge knife, rolled over and had her pinned to the ground with his heavier weight. Stunned, the air whooshed from her lungs and her eyes widened as he held the knife at her throat. His eyes were glazed, viewing a scene from his past, as she heard a low growl come from him. Terror all but clogged her throat.

"Please, Rafe. It's Nora." She tried keeping calm while her heart hammered in double-time. His arm pressed across her chest as the knife blade inched closer. Dear God, what had set him off like this? "Wake up, Rafe," she murmured, trying to penetrate the dream's hold on him. "It's all right."

Nora felt his body tremble as slowly his eyes cleared. He blinked as perspiration ran down his face. She saw recognition dawn as he continued to gaze at her, and felt a wave of relief that drained her.

"Nora?"

"Yes, Rafe. I'm right here." She dared to raise one hand and run it along his rib cage.

Still disoriented, Rafe glanced down and noticed the knife he held at her throat. With a small cry, he threw it aside and buried his face in her neck. "I'm sorry." He let out a shaky breath and clung to her a long moment.

She held him, just held him, trying to imagine the horrors he'd been reliving. Her hands under the loose shirt of his back found another scar, smaller but deeper. How many more had he gathered over the past ten years, since she'd last held him like this? And how many were invisible, the kind that scarred his mind and soul? She wanted to kiss them all, to make them disappear, to make him whole again. She knew she hadn't the right.

He was not a man who lost control easily or often. Rafe felt the humiliation of having lost it in front of Nora. It had been a very long time since he'd been vulnerable in front of anyone, and he wished he could have kept it that way. Not quite steady, he lifted his head and eased his weight from her. "I must have scared the hell out of you. I'm sorry."

She kept her hands on him, kept him from moving too far from her. "Don't apologize again. You couldn't help it. Does this happen often?"

He sighed as he settled himself alongside her, oddly pleased that she hadn't backed away from him. "No, not terribly often. Not anymore." Still more often than he liked. When he was anxious, when he was lonely, when he had too much time to think. Perhaps that was one reason he kept taking new assignments. A man who needed to stay alert to stay alive didn't have time to ponder his past.

Reaching behind her into her backpack, Nora grabbed a handful of tissues and gently patted his face dry, then dabbed at his neck and chest. "Have you seen a doctor? Maybe there's something they can do."

"You mean a psychiatrist? No, thanks." All the shrinks the government had sent to talk to Skip hadn't helped him in the long run. Maybe they'd helped push him over the edge. Rafe ran a hand through his hair, pleased to note he was much steadier now. "Time is the best medicine."

She curled his hand around hers, needing the contact. He'd frightened her far more than she'd let him see. But she'd been frightened as much for him as for herself. She didn't believe that Rafe would hurt her, but for some moments there, he hadn't been himself.

"Were you back in that jungle prison you mentioned?"

"Yeah." He stared up at a sky full of winking stars. The whole experience seemed as if it had happened light-years ago. How could it be so real in his dreams that he could forget the present and be back in his tormented past? "A lot of men have it much worse, men who've been prisoners of war for years." He slid his free hand along her waist, drawing her nearer. "Let's talk about something else."

Not so quickly, my friend, Nora thought. "Who's Skip?" She felt him withdraw fractionally as he shifted his gaze up to the treetops surrounding them.

"Did I mention him in my ramblings?"

"Yes. Did he escape with you?"

"Not exactly. We'd both been wounded, but his was much worse, a deep cut on his leg that had gotten badly infected. The bastards wouldn't give him the medication he needed, and he just kept getting worse." Why was he telling her all this? Rafe wondered. Maybe so she'd realize that while she was here playing house with Ted, his life hadn't exactly been a joy. Did he want her feeling guilty and repentant? He no longer knew what he wanted from Nora.

"Was he able to walk?"

"No. One day they hauled him out of there on a cot. He'd passed out. I was sure I'd never see him again. But I did, a year later, back stateside in a government hospital."

"Your captors must have softened then and treated his wound so that he escaped later?"

Rafe's laugh was bitter. "Fat chance. While I was busily plotting my own escape, somehow a couple of our guys rescued Skip and carried him to a helicopter. He was delirious and couldn't tell them I was still there."

"But he's all right now?" She knew she'd guessed wrong when she saw the flash of pain in his eyes.

"They had to amputate his leg past the knee. That was two years ago. There's an internal infection they can't clear up. The wound keeps draining and he can't be fitted for an artificial leg, at least not yet. He's in a wheelchair, his career over."

She squeezed his hand. "But he's alive. There are other things he can do with his life. Lots of men—"

"Yeah, I know. Lots of men live with handicaps. Skip's not real good at it. They've tried counseling, rehab, shrinks. He just sits and broods."

"Does he have a wife, someone who loves him?"

"He had a girl, but he sent her packing. He didn't want her pity."

"That's ridiculous. Chances are it was love she was showing him, not pity."

"Yeah, well, she didn't insist on staying with him, or fight real hard to change his mind. She just walked."

"Then she wasn't right for him. A woman who truly loved a man would be there for him no matter what happened."

Rafe swung weary eyes to her. "Is that a fact? Some women don't wait well. While the guy is getting himself together, another man shows up and she turns to him. To some women, it's out of sight, out of mind."

A bucket of cold water in the face couldn't have cooled her off more effectively. Quickly Nora moved away from him, averting her gaze so he couldn't see the pain in her eyes. "You're right. Women as a whole are a flagrantly disloyal group." Settling on her side with her back to him, she shut her eyes tightly. But the tears escaped anyhow as she struggled to lie still so he wouldn't notice.

Rafe shifted to his back and tasted the bitter aftermath of their conversation. So she didn't like hearing the truth. Tough. Nora Maddox was a beautiful woman, a loving mother, a kind person. She was also the woman—the *only* woman—who'd ever hurt him deeply. If he wanted to walk away from this second encounter unscarred, he'd have to keep that in mind.

Closing his eyes, Rafe fervently hoped they'd find Bobby and Ted tomorrow so they could both get the hell out of this Wilderness and on with their separate lives.

The only sounds to be heard were the noises of the Wilderness creatures and the shifting of the wind in the trees as they climbed a particularly steep hill in the heat of the midday sun. Nora adjusted the straps of her backpack more comfortably, then wiped her brow as she hurried to keep up the pace Rafe was setting. While she agreed they'd have to step it up in order to close in on Ted's head start, she had to admit the climb was taking its toll on her poor aching body.

And the silence, the tension between her and Rafe, was taking its toll on her spirits. Well, what had she expected? she asked herself as she ducked under a low-hanging branch. Emotions had always run high between Rafe and her. She simply couldn't be indifferent to him. When she'd learned he was returning to help her, she'd prayed they could at least be civil to one another. But even that was not to be.

Perhaps if Jack had remained with them, he'd have served as a buffer between two volatile people carrying varying degrees of hurt like extra socks tucked into their knapsacks. They were like two children scratching at scabs, unable to let them heal. They'd hurt each other before and they seemed intent on doing it again. Why, she wondered, did life have to be so damn complex?

"There's a swarm of bees ahead," Rafe said as he stopped to wait for her. He took her hand and guided her around them.

His tone was cool and definitely not friendly, but she did as he requested. She didn't want stubborn annoyance to result in a bee sting that would slow them down. She could tell the depth of his anger by the rough way he pulled her along in a wide circle about the buzzing bees.

When he calculated that they were free of the danger, Rafe let go of Nora's hand. She obviously didn't want or need his assistance. Which was fine with him.

He knew he'd hurt her last night. Not accidentally, but deliberately. While not particularly proud of it, he wasn't exactly remorseful, either. She deserved to know how he felt. Ten years was a long time to carry a load of resentment around. She'd never even said she was sorry, or that she'd possibly made a mistake, a huge one. She'd merely advised him to let it go. Rafe wished to hell he could.

It gnawed at him—the knowledge that she'd given herself to another man when she'd sworn she loved him. He couldn't have mistaken the depth of her feelings back then, when he'd been the first man to touch her, to show her the pleasures that could be between a man and a woman. And he'd been a boy then. He could show her so much more now. But she hadn't waited for him then and she didn't want him now. Correction: she didn't *want* to want him. But her body said otherwise.

Reaching the top of the rise, he paused a moment to catch his breath. It wasn't enough. He knew he could persuade her to make love with him, for the passion was there behind her smoldering blue eyes every time she looked at him. But he didn't want her that way. He wanted her to come to him, her eyes filled with anticipation, eager and willing and as wild for him as he was for her. And he wanted her to love him as he'd always loved her.

He started down the other side of the hill, kicking at a mound of dirt in his frustration. There were those who said that Rafe Sloan had come a long way in his life. He had respect, financial security, admiration. He'd risen above his impoverished childhood, his mixed-breed beginnings, his youthful mistakes. Yet he still longed for that which he'd merely tasted for the length of one short summer—Nora's love. And the need didn't please him.

He should have outgrown his desire for her by now. He'd thought to return and find he'd idealized his memories of her, that she'd be far less than he'd been remembering. In fact she was far more, the mature woman she'd become overshadowing the girl she'd been. Yet she still held that youthful appeal that had captured his heart. Stomping forward angrily, he wished he'd never laid eyes on her.

Shaking his introspective thoughts, Rafe raised his eyes and inhaled deeply. The unmistakable aroma of cooking meat drifted to him. Stopping quickly, he waved at Nora behind him, pressing a finger to his lips to prevent her from speaking out. Quietly she came alongside him, looking about as she did so.

Rafe moved soundlessly under cover of the largest tree near the path and peered through its branches. In a tiny clearing he saw the fire, above which dangled a small, skinned animal on a makeshift spit. Hearing Nora utter a soft sound behind him, he turned back toward her.

She'd moved off the path and was crouching with her back to him. He tried to see what she was doing when she spoke.

"Someone's laid a trap," she whispered. "This squirrel's foot is caught." She tried to pry open the jagged prongs of the animal trap, but couldn't quite manage it. The wiggling little creature wasn't making it any easier. "Rafe, help me free him."

He kept his voice low. "Let him be. He could be rabid, living up here in the wild."

"He is not." She tried to keep her temper in check. "Look at those eyes. He's in pain and—"

"Lady, step back from my dinner."

The voice was croaky from disuse but commanding in tone. Nora looked up into the double-barrel of a shotgun aimed at her head. It was held in the hands of a man barely five feet tall with stringy gray hair sticking out from under a disreputable green felt hat. His clothes were grimy and his blue eyes calm and unfriendly.

"Your dinner? How can you eat this poor defenseless squirrel?" The disgust in her voice was clear.

"Easy. I'd invite you to share, but you can see he's quite small. His brother's already on the spit. Now, step aside before I—"

In two long strides, Rafe stepped behind Nora and raised his rifle. "I wouldn't go making any threats, if I were you."

The man's eyes raised to Rafe's. They registered a flash of fear as he took in his opponent's size and the hard look of him. Quickly he reached a wise decision and lowered his gun. "Guess I'm not that hungry. You can free him, lady."

With a final tug, Nora pulled the metal jaws apart and the grateful squirrel hurriedly limped off. She rose to stand beside Rafe. "You can get sick eating wild animals."

"You can get sick not eating," the man said. He leaned his gun against the tree trunk and swiped at his brow with a dirty kerchief. "You folks from some sort of humane society?"

"No," Rafe answered. "Eating squirrels isn't the problem. Pointing your gun at us might be."

The older man jerked off his hat and shook his head. "Didn't mean no harm. Thought you were gonna steal my dinner."

Rafe lowered his rifle, but kept his hand on it. "We don't want your food, but maybe you could give us some help. Run into anybody along this trail lately?"

He narrowed his eyes shrewdly. "Maybe. Who you lookin' for?"

"Couple of hikers. The man's not too tall and has blond hair. And a boy of nine, tall for his age with dark hair."

Thoughtfully he scratched his thinning hair. "Saw a man and a boy fishing, yesterday or day before, I think it was."

Nora felt her heart lurch. "Where?" she asked.

He pointed to the path in the direction they were headed. "That way. The trail hits the river in another mile or so."

"Think hard," Rafe requested. "When exactly did you see them?"

The old man squinted up at Rafe. "You got any whisky? It always helps me think better."

Swearing under his breath, Rafe tugged off his backpack and opened a small zippered compartment.

"You've got liquor in there?" Nora whispered.

"I told you—all the essentials." He pulled out a silver flask. "Go get your cup."

Rafe watched the man eagerly scramble for his tin cup, return in moments and hold it out. He poured him a generous amount, then waited impatiently while he drank.

"Ah, that's good." He wiped his mouth on his filthy sleeve. "Let's see. Had to be yesterday, about sundown. Yeah, that's right. About a mile, mile and a half along that trail. They were sitting on a log on the edge of the river. The kid had a fish on his line and the guy was helping him reel it in."

Nora wasn't sure how reliable this mountain man's information was, but she had to ask. "Did they seem all right?"

"Looked okay to me." He finished off the whisky with a noisy smack of his lips.

Rafe put the top on the flask. "Do you remember what they were wearing?"

"Kid had on a blue jacket, some shiny material. That's all I remember noticin'."

"No hat?"

"No, neither of them had on a hat." Watching Rafe put away the flask, he realized he'd be getting no more whisky. He shoved the green hat back on his head. "Gotta get back to cookin' my dinner."

"Thanks for your help."

Muttering to himself, the old man wobbled past the tree and headed for the clearing. Rafe waited until he could see him bend over his fire, then hurried Nora along the path.

"You don't think he's a danger to us, do you?" Nora asked.

"I doubt it." His eyes scanned the trail before them as it wound downhill. The old guy had seen Ted and Bobby last night at sunset and it was scarcely midday now. They were gaining on them, albeit slowly. "We've got to keep going tonight as long as possible. The moon should be nearly full, so if you can manage we'll keep at it until we just can't see. All right?"

"Yes, fine. Bobby took along his Blue Jays baseball jacket. Do you believe that man really saw them?"

He could hear the heartbreaking hope in her voice. There'd be time enough later to tackle the unresolved problems between Nora and him. For now she needed his strength and some show of optimism about finding her son. "Yeah, I do," he said, grabbing hold of her hand. "We're going to find them, and soon."

The moon was high overhead when Rafe finally signaled that they should stop for the night. They'd been walking in the beam of the flashlight for some time now. He'd really pushed and he hoped it would pay off tomorrow. When they'd found the log the old man had mentioned, they'd spotted more of the footprints they now easily recognized. He'd seen the tears well up in Nora's eyes. At least she had to know Bobby had been all right as of last night. He'd had no trouble urging her on.

They spread out their things in a small clearing near the riverbank. Ahead a short distance a small waterfall splashed and sputtered, a pleasant backdrop of sound. Nora held the flashlight until he had a fire going, but neither of them was very hungry. They chewed on beef jerky and dried fruit while the water for coffee heated.

Noting the worried frown back on her face, Rafe searched for something to say to ease her mind. "You know, it's quite possible that Ted might have just meant to scare you and that he intends to return Bobby once they reach the other side."

Chewing, Nora thought that over. "Even so, Ted had no right using Bobby to get at me, whatever his motives. And when I get him back, I'm going to court. Ted's never going to get his hands on Bobby again."

Rafe leaned forward, dangling his arms on his bent knees. "May not be so easy. A judge could decide you jumped to conclusions, that Ted's always been good to the boy, that the note wasn't threatening in tone. Fathers have rights, too, you know, and most judges are men."

Nora's chin raised and her eyes narrowed. "Trust me on this. Ted will lose even his visitation rights. I've got an ace in the hole that I've never used, and he knows it. He's pushed me too far this time."

The mother bear protecting her cub. He should have known she'd feel that way. What ace in the hole? he wondered But on second thought, he didn't really want to know all of the nitty-gritty details of their marriage. Time to change the subject. "Do you still have Alfie?"

Her features relaxed as she turned to look at him. "My old stuffed dog? What made you think of him?"

He smiled. "You brought him with us that time we went camping? Do you remember?"

She remembered every moment of that camping trip. "Yes, of course. I still have him, tucked away in a trunk. Bobby slept with Alfie until he was about two. Then he shifted his attention to trucks and cars." She shook her head somewhat sadly. "I guess little boys don't need something to cuddle as long as little girls do."

"Maybe those lucky enough to have a loving mother like you outgrow the need sooner. Some little boys never do, only they switch from wanting to cuddle stuffed animals to wanting to snuggle with little girls."

Nora sent him a tolerant smile as she turned to pour their coffee. "Are we back to that again?"

"I'm not sure I ever left it." He accepted the cup of coffee as he studied her in the moonlight. A woman as lovely as Nora surely hadn't lived without male companionship for five long years. "Have there been men in your life since your divorce?"

He'd always been the most blunt man she'd ever known. Nora sat cross-legged and sipped her coffee as she wondered if he'd believe her. "No. And how has your love life been?"

Rafe grinned. "Touché. Am I being too nosy?"

"A little."

He shrugged. "I figured if I can't make love to you at least I can talk about it. Was your relationship with Ted at all satisfying?"

"Now that, my good man, is something we are *not* going to discuss." She gazed up at the night sky. "Look at those stars."

But Rafe wasn't ready to let it drop. "I figured you wouldn't have a baby with a man you didn't care about." Her eyes were a deep blue in the moonlight as she turned to him.

"You're certainly right about that."

Not exactly a satisfactory answer, but he could see she was growing wary of his questions. Time to switch to more neutral ground. "Why do you suppose Jack's never married?"

"Mmm, he's never said. I think it has to do with his work. Law enforcement, even in sleepy little towns, can be dangerous and demanding. Perhaps he didn't want to subject a woman to that life-style." She sent him a pointed look. "You should understand that. Didn't you say earlier that your work didn't mix well with domesticity?"

"I suppose I did, but it depends on the people involved." Rafe finished his coffee and stretched out his legs. "We have one agent, Ken Armstrong, who's married and has three kids. His home base is in Miami where his family lives. He's gone as much as the rest of us, but his wife understands and their marriage is strong."

"Maybe she's part of his strength," Nora offered.

"You could be right. Ken and I were lost together for three days in this stinking South American jungle a while back. You get pretty close when you're in that kind of situation, unsure if you're going to get out alive and in one piece. Ken told me that if he didn't have his family to go back to, he might not fight so hard to survive."

"What kept you alive, Rafe?"

His eyes, as he looked at her for a long moment, were soft and more vulnerable than she'd ever seen them. Then he blinked and put on his cocky grin. "Too damn mean to die, I guess."

Let it go, Nora told herself as she rose and glanced toward the waterfall. "I want to ask a favor of you."

"Ask away."

"I want you to stay here while I go into the river and bathe."

Rafe got to his feet and stood inches from her. "Are you afraid you won't be able to control yourself if I go in with you?"

He'd hit the nail on the head. She fought not to let him see. Bending to get her towel, she gave a quick laugh. "Your ego is monumental, did you know that? I'd just like you to keep your little rifle handy and your eyes on the lookout for intruders, four-footed or otherwise." Holding her things, she straightened and met his eyes. "Can you promise to do that?"

"I can probably manage that." Walking to the soft earth of the riverbank, he used his small shovel to dig a hole and bury their day's accumulation of trash.

"Good. And I'll return the favor after I've finished."

Once he was done with his chore, Rafe stuck the shovel into the ground and picked up his rifle. Easing onto a large rock, he turned to see that Nora was far downstream. By the time she stopped, she was only a shadowy outline in the moonlight. She placed her things on a fallen log and paused to look back at him.

"No peeking," she yelled.

Rafe waved at her as he cursed under his breath. He had half a notion to break his promise and run down there and jump in after her. He watched her undress and saw her silhouetted form move slowly into the water. Raising her arms, she strolled toward the deeper middle. His imagination filled in what his eyes couldn't make out, and he felt himself tighten.

What he was allowing her to do to him was unnatural, unnecessary and unfair. He could easily end it by going after her. But Rafe Sloan had never had to coax a woman into his arms and he wasn't about to begin tonight. Balancing the rifle on his knee, he scanned the area for any unusual movement.

The water was cold and invigorating. Nora rose from beneath, rinsing the shampoo from her hair, moving quickly, for she didn't want to spend too long in the chilly river. She glanced over her shoulder in Rafe's direction. He had his back to her. She smiled. So he'd decided to behave. She was half pleased, half disappointed. Annoyed with her ambivalence, she ducked under again.

Most likely Rafe's emotions were in as much a turmoil as her own had been since his return into her life. One minute he was cool and arrogant with her, the next he was warm, sexy, caring. And she found herself riding the same roller coaster, behaving erratically. She was used to a calm existence. This edgy excitement was wearing.

Tossing the shampoo bottle ashore, she began to lather her arms. They were getting closer, she could sense it. Maybe tomorrow night at this time she'd hold Bobby in her arms. She closed her eyes, raising her face to the heavens, praying that it would be so. At least she was comforted to learn that Ted seemed to be behaving rationally so far. Sitting alongside Bobby and helping him reel in a fish sounded good. She hoped she wasn't getting overly optimistic.

Nora rinsed, then rose to walk to the riverbank, feeling the night air cool on her wet skin. Quickly she dried off, then pulled on shorts and an oversize sweatshirt. Another night, two at the very most. One nightmare would be over when Bobby would be safely back with her. Then she'd have to face Ted and an undoubtedly messy court case canceling his visitation rights. But it had to be done. Bobby had to be protected. And she'd have to face Rafe's departure.

Wrapping the towel about her head, she began to walk back. That was one reason she hadn't given in to her desperate need to make love with him. The first time he'd left had devastated her. She might never recover from the second, if she entrusted her heart and her body to him again. Perhaps her heart would always be his. But if she didn't let herself taste again what could never be permanently hers, it might be just a little easier to watch him fly off this time. Maybe.

"The river's all yours," Nora said as she removed the towel from her hair and draped it on a branch.

Rafe smelled the clean female fragrance of her even before he heard her voice. Her wet hair framed her face in wavy ringlets. He held out the rifle. "Do you know how to shoot one of these?"

"Do you think I might have to?"

"No, and I don't think this is the time to teach you. Just hang on to it; the safety's on. If you see or hear anything suspicious, yell. I'm not going far." He pulled clean clothes from his pack.

"Right, chief." Nora sat down on the rock he'd vacated, turning her back to the river. She watched him walk past, then moments later heard him go into the water. Gingerly she propped the rifle against the side of the rock. What good would it do to hold the thing if she didn't know how to remove the safety, much less shoot it? Yelling would get her a lot further, for she had no doubt that Rafe would be at her side in moments.

She gazed up to find the night sky clear and cloudless, filled with hundreds of stars. The temperature was fairly warm in this lower valley area of the Wilderness, only a soft summer breeze restlessly shifted the evergreen fronds. The air was clean and sharp and heavy with the scent of pine. If only they weren't on such a dreadful mission, she might actually enjoy some aspects of this interminable trip.

Her curiosity itching, she turned to glance over her shoulder. He stood with his back to her, knee-deep in the river a mere thirty feet from her while the moonlight bathed him in its silvery glow. Without intending to, Nora swiveled all the way around, drawn by the attraction of his body as he stood unself-consciously bathing.

He was tall and beautifully formed, lean and muscular with broad shoulders and narrow hips. She couldn't help remembering how she'd once stood with him in naked splendor, her hands freely exploring every inch of his bronze skin. Deep inside she felt a powerful response to his maleness and knew she longed to run her hands over him again. As she continued to stare, he turned slowly to face her.

Nora swallowed as her blood began to race. He stood very still, his dark eyes watching her as water dripped from his coal-black hair, down the chiseled features of his face, and zigzagged through the thicket of hair on his chest. His strong arms hung at his sides and his thighs looked to be as mighty as tree trunks. Unable to stop herself, her eyes roamed over him as she saw him move toward arousal.

Was there a more powerful aphrodisiac for a woman than a beautiful specimen of a man who stood, obvious and unashamed in his desire for her, even from across the distance of thirty feet? Nora felt the breath tremble from her body as she slid from the rock and watched Rafe walk out of the water.

Taking his time, he dried off at the riverbank, then slipped on his briefs. Carrying the rest of his things, he came toward her, his heated gaze never leaving her eyes.

There was no escaping this, Nora thought. Her desire for this man was a living, breathing thing, her need for him something she no longer had the strength to fight. She wanted him, just as she'd always wanted him. To deny it would be sheer folly.

Hesitantly, she took one step forward and . . . the scream froze in her throat. Something strong, cold and slippery slithered about her ankles. Filled with fear, she couldn't make herself look down as her eyes clung to Rafe's.

"Stay still," he whispered, "very, very still." He'd seen her tense, then seen the snake coil around her legs. Though he knew that most snakes in the Wilderness area were non-poisonous, this was no time to take chances. Rafe's mind raced through the possibilities in seconds. He was without his boots and without his rifle. Retrieving either would take too much time.

In a swift movement, he grabbed the shovel he'd stuck into the dirt and batted at the snake's tail. As he'd hoped, the snake's head came around and up, just above Nora's left ankle. Taking careful aim, he lunged the sharp edge of the shovel into the base of its head. He heard a satisfying crunch, relieved that he'd hit his mark.

Nora screamed. She felt the snake's body uncoil and drop from her, then felt Rafe's strong arms reach out and pull her to him.

"Are you all right?" he asked, seeing her face turn impossibly pale. But before she could answer her eyes glazed over and she went limp, fainting in his arms.

Day Six

The shock of cold water roused her. Nora opened her eyes and found herself held securely in Rafe's arms. Her legs dangled in the river as he sprinkled cooling liquid on her cheeks. Realization rushed back with frightening clarity, and she shivered uncontrollably. Her arms tightened about his neck as she remembered the feel of the snake twining about her legs.

"It's all right, honey," he told her. "You're safe."

"I've never fainted before in my life," she confessed, upset with herself that she had. What must he think of her?

"You've probably never had a snake go for you before, either."

She shuddered. "Oh, God, it was horrible."

"It's over now." Rafe lifted her higher in his arms, holding her securely to him. When he'd realized she was about to faint, his first thought had been to pick her up before she fell on the snake. Then he'd waded knee-deep into the river, thinking the cold water would revive her quickly.

Angling his head, he studied her face and noted her color was improving. "Feeling better?"

"Yes. It's just that I'm not crazy about snakes."

"Not many people are." From what he'd heard of Ted, Nora had had to be the strong one in the marriage. Small wonder she hated feeling helpless.

"Is he . . . did you . . . ?"

"He's dead." He slid her down the length of his body until she was standing in the water. "I want you to stay here and not turn around for a few minutes. I'm going to bury him and I don't think you want to watch."

She trembled involuntarily at the picture in her mind. "You don't have to convince me. I won't look. It'll be awful for you, though. Why don't we just walk around him and go to our camp fire?"

"Because another animal might smell the blood and come investigate. We're going to be sleeping not too far from here, and I don't want to risk it. You sure you're all right?"

"I won't pass out on you again, if that's what you mean."

"All right. I'll let you know when I'm finished." Rafe walked to the riverbank and climbed out.

Nora heard the shovel scoop up the soil, then the dirt hitting the ground as he dug. "What kind of a snake was it?" she asked, raising her voice.

"Just a black water snake. Not poisonous, fortunately."

Nora felt a chill race up her spine, whether from the memory of the snake or the cold water she was uncertain.

With the shovel, Rafe lifted the limp body of the snake into the hole he'd dug. "You probably disturbed his sleep," he went on. "This kind often curls up on the banks of a river near a rock. They blend in so well that we may have walked past some others and never noticed."

"Comforting thought. I think I'll examine all future rocks carefully before I sit down again."

"Good plan." Rafe threw in the last shovelful of dirt and patted down the area. He squinted at the ground in the moonlight and decided he hadn't missed any remnants. Walking to the river's edge, he then bent to rinse off the shovel. "Okay, you can come out now."

Nora hurried out, her eyes avoiding the area of the rock. She grabbed her towel and began rubbing some warmth back into her chilled legs.

He waited until she was ready, then led her back to their camp fire. "Coffee's still hot. Want some?"

"No, thanks. I just want to crawl into my bag." While Rafe hung their towels on a tree limb near the fire, Nora scooted into her bedroll and curled up in a ball. Closing her eyes, she felt again the panic she'd felt as the snake had coiled around her. How many more mind pictures was she going to have to learn to live with? she wondered.

Rafe added more wood to the fire, then took a careful look around the area, finally satisfied that, for the moment at least, they were alone and relatively safe. He returned to Nora's side and stood looking down at her. "Would you feel better if I put up the tent tonight?"

She lifted her head. "You have a tent?"

He sat down on his sleeping bag. "I asked Jack to bring one along." He pointed to the tightly rolled yellow mound tied to the base of his backpack. "It's made of strong nylon, very compact and lightweight, but it offers some shelter. I prefer sleeping out in the open because I can hear better that way."

"Then why'd you bring it along?"

"In case of rain, or for a night like this, when it might give you a measure of comfort."

She remembered how thoughtful he'd been years ago, remembered the sensitive, tender side of Rafe that he'd let only a few glimpse. She wasn't feeling in the least sensual right now, but there was more to their relationship than sexual attraction, powerful though that was. There was an emotional bonding that had developed early and lasted. It wasn't the tent that would offer her a measure of comfort.

Nora turned back the edge of her bag. "I don't need the tent. I need you. Would you just hold me?"

"My pleasure." He'd been reluctant to suggest it, anticipating rejection again. As he adjusted their bedding, he wished he wasn't so damn pleased that she'd said she needed him. For tonight only, he reminded himself. Because she'd had a scare. Otherwise Nora wanted to go it alone. Though she'd chosen Ted over him, Ted had hurt her and she wanted to need no man in her life. As he lay down beside her, Rafe wasn't certain that he wanted to try to change her mind about that.

He also wasn't certain that he could lie with her, hold her, and not want to make love with her. Silently he waited for her to make the next move.

She'd invited him to hold her, yet he was inches away. Earlier, as she'd watched him walk out of the water, superb in his nakedness and obviously wanting her, she'd decided to take the chance. But that was before her encounter with the snake had cooled her ardor. Had she misjudged him, thinking they could just lie together? Didn't he want to be close to her except for sex? The thought had her turning to look into his dark eyes.

"Is something the matter?"

"I just wanted you to be sure."

"I'm sure. But if you'd rather not . . ."

He smiled and moved to encircle her. "Oh, I'd rather." He fit her small body against his own until she was snuggled tight up against him, then buried his face in the fragrance of her hair. "I very much would rather."

Nora sighed as she placed her arms over his as they rested on her stomach. His nearness would be less disturbing than warming. And right now she needed his warmth, his strength, his caring presence. Maybe he didn't care the way she wanted him to, but for a short while she could pretend.

"You sure smell good." His voice was low, almost a whisper.

"So do you." She paused as he shifted to lay his cheek close to hers. "Rafe, thank you for coming to my rescue."

"Anytime. Besides, I owed you one. Do you remember that time you rescued me from those girls in the barn?"

She smiled and nodded. Six of the older girls at camp, all in their mid-teens, had cornered him in the barn where he'd been grooming the horses. They'd been skimpily dressed, youthfully persistent and embarrassingly eager for his attention. She'd happened in and found him, red-faced and stammering, trying to fend off the most aggressive one who'd insisted on checking out his pectorals and had begun to unbutton his shirt. She'd sent the girls scooting, and he'd been enormously relieved. "Have you ever wondered what would have happened if I hadn't chanced by?"

He feigned a dramatic sigh. "I guess I'd have had to let them ravish me, one at a time."

"You lecherous man! They were all jailbait."

"So were you. Eighteen was underage in those days."

"I don't recall that stopping you from coming after me, after I made sure you noticed me."

"I always go after what I want." Except once. When he'd returned for Doc's funeral and learned that Nora had married, he'd left without seeing her. Perhaps he shouldn't have.

"You were always so sure of what you wanted. I thought you knew everything in the wide world." She'd been so young, so trusting.

"Yeah, I knew everything. Everything except who and what would make me happy."

"I guess we all have a little trouble with that. Are you saying you wish you hadn't gotten involved in government work, that you wish you'd have stayed here in Oregon?"

"Sometimes. If I had, you'd be my wife today instead of his." Rafe felt his jaw clench and made himself visibly relax.

"I haven't been his wife for five years."

He chose to ignore that. "You would have married me if I'd stayed, wouldn't you, Nora?"

They were strolling into the mine field again. "If you'd asked. You never did, not really. You always said, 'when I prove myself, when I return, after my probation.' You attached strings to all your promises."

"And you made only one promise, to wait for me. And you broke it."

Nora closed her eyes, wishing she could explain. "Yes, I broke it."

"I wish I could understand why you couldn't wait six short months for me to return."

She couldn't give him the answer he wanted, so she said nothing.

Rafe drew in a deep breath. This was making them both tense. "So what are your plans for the future, after Bobby's back, besides taking Ted to court?"

"The same as they've been for the past nine years, to do whatever's best for my son." And that wouldn't include a place in his life for an unstable man such as Ted, nor a man like Rafe whose first priority was chasing his own dreams. Ted needed professional help, and Rafe needed to be free. She'd see to it that they both got what they needed. And she'd go back to raising Bobby alone the best way she knew how.

"But you have needs, too. Bobby will leave you one day when he's grown, as he should. Don't you want more, someone of your own?"

She nestled closer to the long, lean body she'd yearned to lie next to again, and willed him to understand. "What I want can't come first anymore. It never can, once you have a child."

He wished he could make her see that she was wrong, even as he wondered if he had the right to try to convince her. "In nine years, Bobby'll probably go away to college. You'll only be thirty-eight, a young woman. Do you want to spend the balance of your life alone?"

"That's what you're doing, isn't it?"

He wouldn't let her shift the focus. "We're talking about you here. We can dissect me another night."

"All right. What would you have me do, run out to the highway and find a man to marry so I won't be alone?" She shook her head. "It's simply not that easy to fall in love, not for me, at least. If there's one thing I've learned over the past years, it's that living with someone you don't love, making love without loving your partner, leaves you emptier than before."

He'd guessed as much, that Ted hadn't fulfilled her. "Yet you married him anyway."

She could feel the slow anger building. "I am not going to beat this dead horse again, Rafe. I married him, I divorced him. I made a mistake. End of story."

"Well, at least you admit you made a mistake."

That did it. "Perhaps if you examined all the evidence in front of you, you might realize you made a few yourself." She threw his arm from her and moved away. "I'm warm enough now, thank you. It's well after midnight and we have to get up early. Good night."

He'd forgotten what a spitfire she could be when she got her dander up. He meant to get it up again, and again— until she told him all that she wasn't telling him. And he was certain there was more to tell.

Rafe lay on his back with his hands beneath his head, going over their conversation, hoping for a clue. It was clear to him that Nora was a born mother, who willingly put her child's needs above her own. He knew other women who did the same. But only a few fathers he could say that about, which didn't say much for the other men, but was nonetheless the truth. What kind of father would he have made? Rafe wondered.

Hearing Nora's breathing even out, he reached into his backpack and dug out the picture of Bobby that she'd given him. He held it up to the firelight. A handsome boy. A curious mixture of serious and silly. The mouth that was so like Nora's, and that wavy hair. For her sake, he prayed that the boy was safely sleeping not too far ahead of them, and that they'd find him soon.

Rafe put the picture away and lay back down. Since arriving, he'd spent five days and five nights with Nora. More hours in close quarters with a woman than he'd spent in years, perhaps ever. If the tension of the missing child were absent, their time together would, of course, be more pleasant. But even with that, even with their arguments, he enjoyed being with her. And if they could have progressed to sharing a physical relationship, it could be near-perfect.

From the first he'd enjoyed Nora, admiring her spunk, her sense of humor, her way of looking at the world. He liked the way she'd fought for the squirrel despite having a shotgun aimed at her head, the game way she'd scrambled down the sheer face of the cliff, the way she'd made him feel earlier tonight when he'd caught her looking at him standing naked in the river. Was this what marriage was like, this indefinable pleasure in the other person, this need to protect and comfort, this constant sensual awareness waiting in the wings?

What would it be like to commit to one woman, to build a lasting relationship? He'd thought he wanted that ten years ago, with this woman who lay sleeping beside him. But he hadn't fought very hard to get her back once he'd learned she'd not waited for him. Had he been secretly relieved that he'd be free to see the world and pursue his dreams unencumbered? Had he been blaming Nora all this time, when in fact she'd merely let him go? Hard questions and no simple answers.

In her sleep, Nora sighed softly and Rafe turned to pull her into the circle of his arms again. She didn't protest, but snuggled into him. He closed one hand over her breast and went still, waiting for her reaction. She didn't waken, but her hand came up and she placed it over his, pressing his fingers into her softly swelling flesh. She made a small sound of pleasure, then returned to her dream.

Rafe laid his cheek against the nape of her neck, inhaling deeply her womanly fragrance. They'd never shared a bed together, only the sweet-smelling hay of the barn and the hard ground under a sleeping bag. What must it be like to return at day's end to a smiling woman whose face lit up when she saw you? To share a meal with her every evening, and laughter and details of your separate days, then lie with her arms and legs wrapped around you each night, both of you sated from lovemaking, and her heart beating against your own?

* * *

The trail climbed steadily upward now, and the air turned cooler with each hour they traveled. Nora slipped on her sweatshirt at their lunch break, and changed from shorts to heavier sweatpants. Marching ahead of her, Rafe was still in short sleeves, seemingly oblivious to the chill. Already fully dressed, he'd awakened her at first light of dawn and they'd set out. He'd been curiously silent as they'd wound their way up the side of the steepest peak of the Mt. Jefferson Wilderness. Not angry or annoyed, more distracted and thoughtful. Wordlessly she'd followed, allowing him his privacy.

She had plenty to keep her mind occupied, searching the ground for more clues that Bobby had walked this way mere hours before. Nora was certain a nine-year-old boy, even one in good condition, couldn't have kept up their arduous pace, even if Ted had been able to. They had to be closing in on them. That thought kept her marching steadily forward.

The sun was already beginning its downward spiral in mid-afternoon when Nora heard the first shot. Freezing in place, she saw Rafe just ahead of her raise his rifle and look about. With a wave of his hand, he signaled her to duck behind a tree, then quickly joined her as another shot rang out.

Rafe spoke close to her ear. "You said that Ted sometimes carries a gun on these trips. Did he have one when he picked up Bobby?"

Her heart leaped to her throat. "If he did, I didn't see it."

The gunshots seemed to Rafe to be coming from the left, just past the thicket of trees. "I'm going over there to have a look."

"Not without me." Nora hooked her fingers into his belt.

He considered her for a moment. Maybe it was best that she stay close by, where he could watch out for her. "Walk slowly, quietly, and don't speak unless necessary. Sound can carry quite a distance at these heights."

He crept through the trees in an uneven pattern, Nora walking inches behind him until they came to a small rise. He motioned to Nora to follow him as he eased onto his belly and began to make his way up the incline. He heard her crawling after him and felt the fallen pine needles jab through his jeans as he inched upward.

Near the top he heard voices not terribly far away. Rafe waited until Nora reached his side, then signaled her to stop while he peered over the hill. Slowly he raised his head.

Three men in a grassy clearing were standing over the body of a slain mule deer. On the ground he made out the butchered sections of a large elk. The bearded man was attaching the kill to carrying poles while the taller man gave orders to the youngest one, who then moved to untie another deer from the tree where it had been hanging, its bloody throat a red gash in its dark hide. Rafe wasn't near enough to make out what they were saying. Three rifles were propped up against a stump of a tree. As silently as possible he crawled back down to Nora and whispered to her to follow him back to the safety of the trees.

"Poachers," he told her quietly when he figured they were out of hearing range. "They have elk and deer."

Thank goodness—not Ted and Bobby. She relaxed a bit. "How are they going to get a slain deer out of this Wilderness on these narrow trails?"

He hated to tell her and knew he had to keep her from crawling up for a look. "They quarter them, tie them on poles and carry them that way. Looks like they're almost finished.''

"Would it pay them to risk jail for a couple of animals?"

Rafe rolled to a sitting position and removed his backpack. "They must think so. Not too many people wander around this deep into the Wilderness. By the time someone would return to town and report them, they'd be long gone. Of course if that someone caught them in the act and posed as a threat to their operation, they could be in danger. Poachers are usually poor and real nervous about getting caught. They feed the meat to their families and sell the hides."

Nora gazed over her shoulder at the path they'd left. "If we move slowly along the trail, they probably won't spot us. We can't afford the time to just sit here and wait them out."

Rafe shook his head. "Poachers can get nasty if they feel they're about to be discovered, and these three all have guns. I hate to lose time, too, but our best bet is to wait until they leave and not let them realize they're not alone up here."

"But we'll lose all the headway we've made. I say we can make it if we're quiet."

Rafe sighed. She'd always been headstrong, stubborn and a few other unflattering adjectives that came to mind right now. However he swallowed his irritation, understanding her point of view.

"What if they decide to set up camp," Nora persisted, "and start back in the morning?"

"I doubt that. Look, I'm as anxious to get going as you, but I'm not going to endanger us." Seated behind her, he put his hands on her shoulders. "Relax. Time will pass faster." Slowly he began to massage the back of her neck. "A little tense, are we?"

More than a little. And his hands on her, as always, only added to her growing tension. Moving from him, she jumped to her feet. "I'm not waiting. We're close to finding Bobby. I can feel it. We can walk a wide circle on the far side of the trail, wind through the trees, and they won't see us."

Rafe could feel his irritation rising. "Keep your voice down. I'm telling you, it's too risky. I'm the one who's calling the shots on this little expedition, and I say we sit down and wait them out."

Angry, frustrated and annoyed at his bossy approach, Nora reached for her backpack. "*You* wait them out. I'm starting along the trail."

Rafe leaped to his feet. "The hell you are," he whispered harshly.

"The hell I'm not!" She struggled with the straps, trying to shove her arms into them.

Grabbing her backpack, he flung it to the ground and placed hard, restraining hands on her arms. "Will you lower your voice? You're going to get us noticed."

She narrowed her eyes at him. "All you have to do is let me go and get out of my way and no one will notice us."

In her anxiety to be free of him, Rafe was certain she didn't realize her voice was starting to carry. He could think of only one effective way to quiet her. Pulling her to him, he placed his mouth over hers.

He'd intended to silence her and no more. He hadn't expected the explosion that hit him every time his lips touched hers. He hadn't predicted that her arms, which had moments before been pushing him away, would shift and suddenly draw him nearer.

Her mouth softened, opened, invited. His tongue moved inside and found hers waiting for him. She moaned softly deep in her throat as she clutched at the material of his shirt. Rafe was breathing hard as he moved to kiss the pulse pounding at her throat.

"Are you out of your mind?" Nora asked in a husky whisper. "It's the middle of the day, we're only a few yards from men you just told me might turn their guns on us, and you want to play." She heard her own feeble protest and denounced the weakness Rafe always managed to find in her.

He touched his lips to her ear. "It's the only way I could think to quiet you. It sure beats tying you to a tree." Gently he lowered her to the ground and kissed her again.

This was crazy, this was madness, this was wonderful. His hands slid under her and pulled her hard against his broad chest. Nora felt five days' accumulation of beard graze her cheeks, and the sheer pleasure of his masculinity flowed through her. She inhaled the pine air and the essence of man and felt desire skitter along her spine.

His hard body was stretched out along hers now as his arms drew her closer. Her tongue danced with his, in remembrance, in celebration, in surrender. From the first stunning kiss they'd shared ten long years ago, she'd known what this man could do to her. Her arms gathered him to her, nearer, yet not near enough. Her breasts grew fuller, aching for his touch, as her body awakened to his sensual assault. Shamelessly she pressed herself to him.

All night long, as he'd lain awake hour after hour, he'd dreamed of this. Rafe moved his mouth along her cheeks, touching his lips to her closed eyelids, breathing softly into her ear and then absorbing her shiver of delight. His hands were in her hair, down her back, and moving lower to align her softness with his trembling body. He heard her frustrated groan at the barrier of clothes between them, and understood it perfectly.

She was his, he was certain. Always his. He'd known too many women to believe Nora could fake such a response. She'd never loved Ted, never wanted him like this. His head spun with needs, with doubts, with sudden new possibilities. She was a strong woman, capable of living without a man. If he wanted her back in his life, he'd have to prove to her that, though she could live without him, she would choose not to. As his lips returned to hers, he asked himself what he would choose.

Helpless. With no one but Rafe was she so helpless. His mouth captivated her while his hands moved beneath her sweatshirt. When they slipped to the front and closed around her breasts, Nora felt a moan begin deep inside. She, too, thrust her hands under his shirt, needing to be flesh-to-flesh with him. Her body shuddered as the whirlwind that was Rafe sent her senses soaring.

His fingers were fumbling with the drawstring of her sweatpants. Suddenly wary, Nora stopped his progress with her hands just as they heard the sound of hard boots tromping along a twig-laden path nearby.

Quickly Rafe rolled her beneath him, protecting her with his body as he burrowed them both into the dense overgrowth. Lying quietly, he let himself cool down, his gaze on Nora's face so near his own. Her eyes cleared slowly and met his finally.

"I'm not going to apologize," he whispered huskily, "not for something I've come to realize I want more than the air I breathe."

"There are no apologies necessary here." She'd always hated games. Perhaps it was time to stop playing this one. "In the unlikely event you haven't guessed, I want you, too. I've never stopped."

Jack, her parents, the people in town had often re-marked that Rafe's eyes were black and cold. They'd never seen them grow warm like she had, just now and many times before. He bent his head to touch his forehead to hers. Was it in relief, or gratitude, or merely in acknowl-edgment? She couldn't be certain. They heard the foot-steps slowly grow fainter. Nora cursed the timing as Rafe squeezed her shoulder and whispered her name.

Where they would go from here, she was unsure. She knew only that things between Rafe and her were far from over.

Nora's safety was still of primary concern to Rafe. He held her there under cover of the huge Douglas fir that blocked them from view. They lay close together until they heard only the familiar sounds of the forest.

At last Rafe got to his feet and pulled Nora up. She looked so soft, so inviting. With a swift movement he had her against him, his mouth covering hers. He encountered no resistance this time as she opened to him, her response instant and avid. Just as quickly she came down off her tiptoes and tenderly caressed his stubbly cheek.

"I'd love to continue this, but I think we have to get going," she said reluctantly.

"Would you really love to continue this?"

Nora picked up her backpack and adjusted it onto her shoulders. Did he imagine that it had been easy for her to stop when her body was screaming for release from the need he'd created in her? Five years of celibacy had not had her so strung out as five days and nights alongside Rafe.

She bit her lip, then looked up at him and smiled. "Everything comes to him who waits, haven't you heard?"

"Is that a promise?"

There was that word again. Nora sobered instantly. "Let's not make any more promises, Rafe. Let's just let happen what will happen, and hope for the best."

She'd phrased it better than he could have. Taking her arm, he nodded as he glanced at the late-afternoon sky. "Let's go, lady. We've got some miles to make up."

She was cold, hungry and bone-tired. Nora sat on the rocky riverbank, huddled in sweats and her heavy jacket, watching Rafe roll up his pant legs. "Your feet will go numb if you wade into that icy water," she warned him.

"It's not icy, just a little chilly." He turned his attention to assembling his fishing pole. "Besides, if I don't, we don't eat. All we've got left are dried fruit, beef jerky, some instant stuff and a couple of candy bars."

"I'll settle for a candy bar and a nice, soft bed. On second thought, you can skip the candy bar. I think I'm too tired to chew." She wrapped her arms around herself. "Are you sure you checked this area for snakes?"

"Positive. But you're going to have to turn on that flashlight and hold it for me. The trees are blocking the moonlight, and I can't see what I'm doing." Rafe stood and shook out his line. In daylight, he could whittle a branch and spear a fish faster than catching one with this makeshift pole, but it would have to do.

Reluctantly Nora stretched to turn on the flashlight and aimed it on him, feeling every muscle creak and groan. They'd walked until she thought she couldn't take another step, trying to make up for the time they'd lost waiting out the poachers. They'd followed the trail along the river, Rafe angling the flashlight's beam on the ground to light their way. It had been nearly midnight when he'd finally given in and set up camp. She'd insisted that he pitch the tent tonight, telling him he could sleep outside if he wanted to, but she needed the extra protection. And they hadn't spotted a single sign that Bobby and Ted had passed this way.

"There's no other trail they could have wandered off on, is there, Rafe?" She knew her voice sounded small and scared, and that's exactly how she felt.

How could a man steel his heart against this woman? he asked himself, not for the first time. "No, honey. We're on the right track, I promise you."

He'd begun calling her honey lately. Nora wasn't sure if it pleased or annoyed her. Right now she was too tired to argue the point.

Rafe knew that Ted and Bobby could have veered off the path and headed through the woods, especially if Ted was crazy enough to plan on taking up residence in the Wilderness. Even an experienced hiker could get confused in the forest and soon be lost. For long distances today they'd walked on lava rock, a hard substance almost impossible to track footprints on, even for experts.

Yesterday Rafe had gotten worried. He'd spotted the footprints that he now recognized as Ted's, but hard as he'd searched he hadn't seen the boy's prints. Distracting Nora, he'd bent to take a closer look and discovered that Ted's prints were deeper and wider, indicating additional weight. He'd likely been carrying Bobby, Rafe surmised. But why? Was the boy hurt, or just tired? Then, by afternoon, he'd spotted both sets of prints again, and he'd breathed a sigh of relief. But by evening he'd lost sight of both prints again.

If Ted had somehow gotten wind that he was being followed and if his mental state was deteriorating, he could be devious. The deranged often had a sixth sense about danger threatening them, along with an uncanny ability to cover their own tracks.

"Point that light down here, please," Rafe instructed as he knelt along the soft riverbank.

"What are you doing?"

"Got to dig around for some bait."

"Ugh! Now I know I'm not hungry."

"Just you wait until you taste my fried fish. Mouth-watering." Scooping up the tiny frog, Rafe turned his back to her. If she caught sight of what he was doing, she'd undoubtedly rush to the frog's rescue. When his bait was secured, he stood and waded into the water. He closed his mind to the chill and stepped over several rocks before throwing his line in. But he couldn't see where it landed in the skimpy moonlight.

"I hate to disturb your rest, but I need you to come closer with that light."

Sighing, Nora walked over to him and angled the beam. "This okay?"

"Not quite. Move back around me and shine it from that side."

Nora did as he asked, stepping carefully. Suddenly, her foot caught on something and she stopped. "Just a minute." Turning the light onto the ground by her feet, she looked down, then gasped out loud.

"What is it?" Rafe asked, glancing over his shoulder.

Nora knelt to examine her find. "It's Bobby's fishing pole, the one that Jack bought him for his birthday." Rising, she picked it up and frowned. "It's broken in three places. Splintered, actually." Fighting tears, she walked closer to Rafe. "Look. It's as if someone smashed it."

Day Seven

The itching was driving her crazy. Nora scratched at the hives on her neck as she sat on a mound of grass facing the campfire.

"Here, drink this." Rafe handed her a cup of instant soup, then poured hot water into the powder in his own cup. Sitting beside her, he stirred his soup and studied her. "I see you still get hives when you're upset."

Nora took a cautious sip. "I think I have a right to be upset, despite your very plausible explanations."

She hadn't bought his story, and he didn't blame her. The fishing rod he examined did look as if it had been snapped in a fit of anger. But Nora didn't need him to add to her worries. She was doing a fine job in that department all by herself.

He'd stopped all attempts at fishing when he'd seen how upset she was. Coming out of the river, he'd checked the pole with her and tried to keep her from jumping to conclusions, the same ones that had occurred to him. She'd gotten her emotions under control quickly, though he could see that her nerves were stretched to the breaking point.

"You're picturing the worst possible scenario. Try to think of a rational reason."

Her head shot up. "For a child's pole to be smashed apart? I can't think of a single rational reason for that to happen."

"Nora, I don't pretend to know much about fathering, but don't fathers get angry now and then? Harmlessly angry? Even mothers must occasionally. Maybe Bobby did something to irritate Ted, and to prove a point, he broke the boy's pole. Not a very adult thing to do, but things like that happen, don't they? And later, father and son reconciled their differences. Didn't Ted ever show anger toward Bobby when you were around?"

She'd listened to Rafe's words and knew there was some truth in them. But it didn't apply to their case. Ted never had shown anger at Bobby, at least not in front of her. Maybe because he knew she'd side with her son. Maybe because he never felt he had the right to reprimand him. Did he have a lot of anger stored up inside that he was now unleashing on Bobby? *Oh, God!*

"No, Ted was always gentle with Bobby." Closing her eyes, Nora laid her cheek on her bent knees. With all her heart she wished she could confide in Rafe. She'd carried her secret around so long, mostly alone. Though she'd confided some things to her doctor, Sam D'Angelo, even he didn't know the whole story. She needed to pour it all out, to feel Rafe's strong arms around her reassuring her that Bobby would be all right. Rafe was the only other person who should know all the facts, yet she couldn't tell him. Especially not now.

"That's not natural, Nora. Parents get annoyed at times with the best of kids."

"I'm telling you, I've never heard Ted even raise his voice to Bobby." Clutching the cup in an attempt to warm her cold fingers, she decided to shift the focus. He was getting too close. "Maybe Bobby broke the pole. He does have a bit of a temper now and then. Maybe he couldn't catch a fish and got angry." She didn't believe that for a minute. Bobby loved that silly pole.

Rafe saw her trying to replace the unthinkable with this new thought, and he let her. But personally he didn't believe a child of nine could have smashed that pole quite the way they'd found it. Was Ted turning violent? he wondered as he kept his features even for her sake. "That's a possibility."

"But Ted has always been so good about burying trash. He used to lecture us both if we so much as dropped a cherry pit." Without being consciously aware of what she was doing, Nora began to scratch her back.

"So he got a little careless. Perhaps it was getting dark and he was in a hurry to get moving." She seemed to be accepting the story he'd fabricated, the one he fervently hoped had some truth to it. If they did find Bobby hurt, he wasn't certain how Nora would react.

Seeing her discomfort with the hives, he reached into their supply chest and dug around until he found a plastic bottle. "Let me put some calamine lotion on those hives before you scratch yourself raw."

The will to resist seemed to have flowed right out of her. Nora finished her soup, set the cup down and turned to face him, offering her neck.

Gently Rafe dabbed lotion on the spots along her throat, blowing on the pinkish-white medication to hasten the drying. "Turn around and let me check your back." As she did, he raised her sweatshirt and found three angry-looking red dots. He covered them also and was bending forward to blow them dry when he saw her head drop down and her shoulders shake from her silent weeping. Setting the bottle aside, he turned her, then pulled her into the circle of his arms.

"It's okay, honey. Cry it out." He tucked her head into his shoulder, smoothing her hair as she clung to him. There were times when everyone needed to give in to tears, to frustration, to mounting fears.

She wailed, a primitive almost inhuman sound. He wept for her deep inside, for her fears for her child. He tried to imagine how he'd feel if Bobby were his. Enraged, victimized, vengeful. He tightened his hold on her.

"I'm so frightened, Rafe," she sobbed into his throat, gasping for gulps of air. "He's got my baby, and I feel so helpless. I hate him, Rafe. I hate him for doing this to me."

"I know, honey. We'll find Bobby, I promise you. Please believe me." He felt her pain as surely as he felt the moisture from her tears on his skin. He wanted to erase all the hurt from Nora's world, to deliver her son safely back into her arms, to smash Ted Maddox brainless. Nora had always made him feel protective, and now there was Bobby with his hauntingly familiar eyes and that mischievous grin. Yes, he would get the boy back for her if it was the last thing he did.

It seemed a very long time before she felt able to let go of him and wipe her damp cheeks. "I've soaked you, I'm afraid."

"It's all right. I'm glad I was here for you."

If only he'd been there for her ten years ago when she'd needed him so badly. Then they'd not be in this terrible mess. Nora blew her nose. There was no use starting on the if-onlys. "Thanks."

Leaning back, Rafe spotted something. He leaned behind her and plucked a lovely white flower from a dark green plant. Bringing it forward, he held it out to her. "Do you know what this flower's called?"

Nora brushed her hair back from her face. "I've seen lots of them, but I don't think I do. Why?"

"It's called a trillium. See how delicate it is? But its looks are deceptive. It's one of the hardiest plants in the Wilderness, surviving the harsh winters, caterpillars chewing on them, feet marching across them. Through it all, the gutsy little flower keeps poking up its pretty white head."

She took it from him and met his eyes.

"You're a lot like this trillium, Nora. A gutsy survivor. You've survived a bad marriage, and you'll survive Bobby's abduction." And she'd survived his departure by aligning herself with another man. Yes, she was hardier than she looked. He believed it and wished she would.

"Maybe." She'd survived the loss of the only man she'd ever loved. Would she survive his second leaving? Nora lowered her eyes. "I guess we all do what we have to do."

Leaning closer, he cupped her chin, forcing her to look up at him. "You're strong and you're very beautiful and..." *And I love you.* Even as the thought struck him, he knew it was true, had always been true. But he couldn't say the words. She'd made it clear she didn't want or need a man in her life. She'd rejected him once for another man. How much more would it hurt if she rejected him a second time?

Rafe cleared his throat. "... and you're doing fine. Just believe that and you'll be okay."

Believing Rafe again was something she had trouble doing. Of course he had come back when he hadn't had to. And he'd spoken of his friend Skip's weariness and disillusionment as if he shared those feelings. But looking into his eyes, she saw the same restlessness she'd spotted years ago, the curiosity to know everything and experience it all, to be on the move. This man would never be content again in a small town, if he ever had been.

Too bad because she loved him with all her heart and soul.

The first time she'd fallen in love with Rafe Sloan as a girl, it had happened quickly, like a fierce wind from nowhere, catching her unaware with the intensity of new passion. This time, as a woman, it had snuck up on her, calm and quiet, like a soft summer breeze, enveloping, warming. But no less devastating.

Nora looked over at the bright yellow tent, its open flap facing the fire. It looked small and cozy and intimate. Rubbing her tired eyes, she realized she'd never felt less like being intimate in her life.

Rafe got to his feet. "You look exhausted. I've fixed the bedrolls. Why don't you climb in while I beef up the fire?"

Stifling a yawn, Nora stood. "You don't have to ask me twice."

He took his time, gathering wood, securing the fire. Finally he lifted the tent flap and saw she was lying on her side, breathing evenly, sound asleep. Straightening, he strolled back to the fire and stood rubbing his chin. The new growth of beard was beginning to itch. As he was beginning to itch.

Itch to have this end, to get on with his life, or to change it. He hadn't faced a crossroads in years and wondered how it was that he was facing one now. Of course he knew the answer. Nora was back in his life.

Thrusting his hands into his pockets, Rafe walked the short distance to the trees bordering the river. Through the leafy branches the moon sprinkled silver shadows on the water as it splashed over the rocks. The tangy smell of damp earth and a thick pine forest mingled together not unpleasantly. From a long way off he heard the howl of a coyote and felt a shiver along his spine. Man was the interloper here in this Wilderness, and tonight he felt the part.

And he felt a bit of an interloper in Nora's life. Suppose they found Bobby tomorrow, unharmed and safe, to her great relief and joy. Suppose good old Ted would admit he'd been wrong and Nora, with her great capacity for caring, would forgive him, perhaps not even prosecute, just take away his visitation rights. Then all four of them would march down the mountain and ... and what?

Nora and Bobby would resume their lives and Ted would go back to doing whatever it was he did when he wasn't kidnapping children. And what about Rafe Sloan? Did he want to be on his way, to see where his next assignment would take him, to do the job he was trained to do? Or did he want to hang around and see if perhaps he and Nora could recapture what they'd once had? And what about Bobby?

Rafe threw a stone in the water and watched it sink. The two of them came as a package deal. He cared about Nora and thought she had some buried feelings for him, too. He didn't know how he'd stack up as husband material, and she'd had no shining example in Ted, either. Nora deserved a good man, a devoted husband, one who'd be at her side always. Could he commit to that? He knew zip about fatherhood. Suppose Bobby didn't like him, didn't want to deal with another man in his life?

And the ever-nagging question, the one that ate at him still—why hadn't she waited for him? Would he ever discover the answer to that, and if he did could he live with it?

Slowly Rafe turned and walked back to the camp. Putting the pot of water back on the fire, he decided to make himself some instant coffee. Nights like these, when questions and feelings churned inside him, he knew sleep wouldn't come easily. He'd be better off sitting out here than lying in there alongside a woman who caused more emotional reactions in him than anyone else ever had.

And still he wanted her. Rafe slid to the grass and waited for the water to boil.

It was going to storm. Rafe felt it long before the first drops fell on them in late afternoon. He checked the pale gray sky and decided that for now, at least, it was just a mild summer rain. But there was a restlessness in the air, a certain stirring of the wind he recognized, and the scampering of small woodsy creatures seeking shelter that told him that later the real storm would hit.

Stopping by a tree, he zipped open their supply case as Nora came alongside. "I've got a couple of plastic hooded rain capes wadded in here somewhere. Not real glamorous, but they should keep us relatively dry."

"I'm beginning to think that's a bottomless bag filled with unending surprises." She untied the sweatshirt she'd had hanging around her waist and shrugged out of her backpack long enough to pull the sweater on. The mountain air was definitely cooler as the trail climbed upward.

Unfolding the poncholike clear plastic raincoat, Rafe helped her slip it on, then let her assist him with his. He looked up to see a baby mountain goat stumble his way up the rocky hillside across the ravine to their left. "Looks like he's running for cover. This drizzle isn't bad, though. We can keep going until it becomes a downpour."

"Do you think it will?"

He could sense the rumble of thunder in the distance, though all he could hear were raindrops splashing on leaves and sliding to the already damp ground. "Not for a few hours yet. Let's go." Hunching down, he set out.

Behind him, Nora angled the loose hood over her head and followed. She hadn't packed rain protection in Bobby's backpack. It had been bright and sunny when he'd left, and she'd thought he'd be gone only a couple of days. Was it raining where he was? Was he getting wet, catching cold? Her lips a thin line, she walked with her eyes downcast, her thoughts as gloomy as the day.

They ran across the cabin just as the rain became heavier. Rafe, leading the way as usual, had just reached the top of a hill and glanced to his right. There it was, nestled among the trees alongside a shallow stream. He turned and waited for Nora to spot it.

"I can't believe my eyes," she said as she came to a stop. "Who would build that thing way up here?"

"It's a tracking station. The hunt-and-search team of the sheriff's department probably built it, and several others, years ago." He hefted his rifle and held it ready, just in case. "Let's go have a look."

It was hardly more than a lean-to. Weathered boards on four sides covered by a sloping tin roof. Near the front door stood a rain barrel next to a three-legged stool. Cautiously Rafe pushed open the door to reveal a room perhaps ten-by-twelve with a raised wooden floor. Two wide bunks were built into one wall, and a partitioned area suggested a bathroom of sorts. A rough wooden table and two ladder-back chairs sat in the center of the room, and a potbellied stove was in the far corner. Moving inside, he angled open the shutters on the two windows and let in more of the weak daylight remaining.

Nora shook the water from her poncho and walked in. "Look," she called to Rafe, who was inspecting the stove, "there's a kerosene lantern."

"I'll light it in a minute. I want to see if this thing works."

On the far wall Nora discovered a makeshift cupboard containing a small assortment of canned goods, a box of tea, several pots, paper plates and plastic utensils. A cardboard box served as a trash container for two empty cans. Gingerly she picked one up and examined it.

"Rafe, someone's been here—and not long ago. This corned-beef hash can has remnants in it that are still moist."

Rising, he walked to her and took a look. "In this damp atmosphere it takes a while for things to dry out. On the other hand maybe Ted and Bobby were here, maybe even last night. Or it could have been someone else. Take your pick."

He was right, of course. With a disappointed sigh she dropped the can and returned her attention to the cupboard. Beans, canned spaghetti, stew, more hash. "Who keeps this place supplied, do you suppose?"

Rafe was opening more doors, finding matches, a can opener, candles, more oil for the lamp. "The sheriff's department, I would imagine. Hasn't Jack ever mentioned these tracking cabins to you?"

"No. But he's not very involved in the hunt-and-search area." Removing her rainwear, she draped it over one of the chairs and put her backpack on the table. "If it's going to rain harder, this sure beats that tiny little tent." She watched Rafe take off his gear and return to the stove. He began to fill it with chunks of wood he'd found alongside. "Why didn't you join me in the tent last night?"

He shrugged. "I told you, I can't hear as well inside one of those. I don't mind sleeping on the ground."

"But both sleeping bags were inside with me."

"I managed." Stepping back, he lit a match and threw it inside.

He was being deliberately evasive, she knew. Was he finding it as difficult as she, lying alongside one another and not giving in to needs denied too long? She'd lain down thinking only of sleep, but if he'd come in, if he'd touched her...

The blaze roared to life. She walked over, holding out her chilled hands.

Rafe wiped his hands on his jeans as he turned to look at her. A damp curl clung to her cheek, and he gave in to the urge to brush it back. "Are you cold?"

"A little, but not for long with this fire. We couldn't have timed finding this cabin more perfectly."

He moved to light the lantern on the table. Stopping would slow down their progress, but they couldn't have made much headway in a downpour, anyway. Chances were that the two they were hunting also were holed up somewhere until the rain passed. He replaced the glass globe on the lamp and walked over to close the shutters so the moisture wouldn't blow in. Hands on his hips, he glanced around. "Not the Ritz, but not a bad port in a storm."

"Jack mentioned that Ted had purchased a tent before picking Bobby up. I sure hope it's a sturdy one."

"I'm sure it is. He's an experienced camper and he knew that they'd be up here for a while." Thinking to distract her, he went to the cupboard. "What would you like to eat?"

Nora walked over to join him. "I feel guilty taking someone else's food."

"We'll pay them to replace it, when we get back down." He gestured toward the cans. "What'll it be?"

Spotting the box of tea, she took it down. "I think I'd rather have a cup of hot tea for now." She picked up a pan and held it out. "I saw a rain barrel out front."

"I'll get some."

At the table, Nora spooned the dark leaves into two cups as Rafe returned to place the pan on the stove. Sitting down to wait, she rubbed her hands up and down her arms.

"You're still cold. Want me to dig out my jacket?"

"No, thanks. I think it's just the damp chill that's in the air more than anything."

That and the strain of worry, and the sleepless nights. He reached into his pack. "I have just the thing to warm us." He brought out the whisky flask and set it on the table.

Nora stared at the container and smiled. "You may recall that alcohol and I don't mix too well."

It had been toward the end of summer, when he'd learned he'd be leaving soon, that she'd agreed to go camping with him over a weekend. She'd lied to her parents, and they'd hiked into Willamette National Forest. He'd taken along some beer and placed it to chill in the freshwater stream while they'd played like two little kids in the water. She'd had only one bottle, but it had been enough to make her giggly and silly.

It had also made her sensuous and seeking. Rafe had needed no alcohol, for he'd already been drunk on Nora, on her beautiful mouth and her suddenly sure hands reaching for him. He'd made love to her there in the sweet-smelling grass of an August evening. And then later again, under the rushing waterfall. Oh, yes, he remembered all too well.

"We're a little older now, aren't we? And perhaps a little wiser?"

Nora went to get the water. "Older, yes. Wiser, I'm not sure." She fixed the tea and waited a few minutes while it steeped.

Rafe poured a generous dollop of whisky into each cup, then held his up. "Here's to luck being with us, and soon."

The perfect toast. She tapped her cup to his and took a warming sip. Lacing her fingers around the cup, Nora drank again, letting the hot drink work its magic.

The rain was coming down steadily now, a symphony on the tin roof above them. Rafe stretched out his legs. It was good to sit in a chair, to be warm and dry. He looked over at Nora and saw she was getting that faraway look in her eyes again. "Have you ever been drunk?" he asked, reaching for a subject that seemed harmless.

"You mean aside from that camping trip where you got me drunk on beer?"

"You weren't drunk that night, just feeling good."

She'd been feeling good because she'd been with Rafe, not because of the beer. "No, I'm not much of a drinker. We kept an occasional bottle of wine in the house. Ted drank, but he drank alone, never when I could see."

"That must have been hard on you and Bobby."

"Bobby was too young to be aware, but I wasn't. I'd come home from working at the nursery school and there he'd be, asleep in front of the television. He used to keep breath mints in his shirt pocket and he sucked on them constantly. I guess he thought I couldn't tell he used them to cover the smell of alcohol." She took a long swallow of tea, letting herself relax.

"Did he ever get mean or abusive when he drank?" Another question he'd been wondering about. He couldn't imagine Nora tolerating that sort of thing.

"No, on the contrary. He got depressed—sometimes he cried. Always he promised he'd never do it again." She shook her head sadly. She'd hated it, but she'd put up with it longer than she should have. Because she knew she was partly to blame for Ted's unhappiness.

"What did your folks think of Ted?" A minister might have trouble suggesting divorce to his own daughter, yet if her father had known of Ted's drinking...

"We'd grown up together, you know, and they'd known Ted since our school days. They were disappointed that we didn't both go on to college, but they seemed pleased that we married. And they adore Bobby."

He set down his cup. "That's not what I asked. What do they think of Ted?"

She finished her tea. "I never told them about his drinking. After the divorce, they heard about it from someone in town."

"Why'd you cover up for him?"

"I believe that what happens in a marriage is the business of the two people involved, and only them. I handled my problems the best way I could and I saw no reason to bring my parents into the situation. I didn't want them to somehow color Bobby's opinion of Ted."

He'd guessed her answer before she'd spoken. She'd been protecting Bobby, not Ted, as always. He stared down into the wet tea leaves in his cup. "Too bad we don't have a gypsy here. She could read the leaves for us and tell us what the future holds."

Anxious for a change of subject, Nora leaned forward. "I know a little about tea-leaf readings. Upend your cup slowly and let the leaves fall onto the table." She watched as he did as she suggested. "Ah, yes. See how the leaves drifted in different directions? Not a one is touching the other." She raised her eyes to his. "Your vagabond soul, searching, scattering every which way. Attached to no one, going it alone."

"Maybe we're more alike than you think. Upend your cup."

Nora let the leaves fall from her cup onto the tabletop. "Maybe not." Two of the larger leaves clung together while a third leaf, much smaller, had a corner touching them. Two other fragments hovered near the trio.

"Tell me what you think that means."

"It could mean almost anything," she answered evasively.

"All right, let me take a stab at it. This big leaf is you, and the larger one alongside is a man, the love of your life. This small one touching them both is Bobby. And these tiny particles are perhaps future children." He looked up at her bent head. "You're the kind of woman who's meant to have lots of babies."

Nora got up to get the pan from the stove. "It would seem the fates have decided otherwise." She spooned fresh tea into the cups and poured in the hot water.

"Those miscarriages were over five years ago. Did the doctor say you couldn't have more children?"

Nora reached for her cup, but he stopped her to add another shot of whisky. Even as she wondered if this was wise, she stirred the contents. "No, he didn't. He just told me my body needed a rest."

"You've had that. Perhaps it's worth another try."

She was getting impatient with his persistence. "In case you haven't noticed, I'm lacking a father for another child." It was time to lay it on the line. Her eyes caught and held his. "Are you volunteering for the job?"

A child with Nora. A little girl, with her delicate bones, her soft hair, those laughing blue eyes. "What if I were to say I am?"

She shook her head. "I'd say the alcohol's making your brain fuzzy."

But Rafe wasn't so easily diverted. "Do you remember how we talked about having babies together once?" Back when he'd believed she'd always be his.

He was making her recall the fragile dreams of their time together, when she'd still believed in white knights and forever-after. "We talked about a lot of things, Rafe, that summer when we were young and foolish."

"What happened?" he asked, sounding honestly puzzled.

"We grew up, I guess." She pushed aside her teacup and stood, feeling a little woozy. A clap of thunder sounded in the distance, punctuating her troubled thoughts. "Are you hungry?" she asked as she moved slowly toward the cupboard. "I'm starved." She didn't know if she could swallow a bite, but she had to stop this heartbreaking conversation. She stared unseeingly at the small array of cans. "What'll it be?"

When he didn't answer, she turned. He'd pulled Bobby's picture, the one she'd lent him, out of his backpack and was sitting hunched over the table studying it. Her heart lurched in her chest as she grabbed hold of the counter.

Not now, please, not now. I'll tell him later, I promise. Let me find Bobby first.

She would act normal, warm the food, distract him. "How's beef stew sound?"

"Fine," Rafe said vaguely. Would a baby he and Nora create look like this little guy? he wondered.

She struggled with the can opener. "Have we got anything in the bag to go with this?"

He and Nora both had dark hair, Rafe mused, though his was more black than brown. Hard to tell the color of Bobby's in this snapshot. The smile, as if hiding a devilish secret, was all Nora's. He'd never been a smiler. It was the eyes that didn't fit. He drained his tea and decided to try a whisky straight. He saw a flash of lightning through the ill-fitting boards. It was a night for drinking.

"Would you like more tea?" Nora asked as she passed by on her way to the stove.

"No, thanks." Probably the boy's eyes were more like Ted's. He grimaced as the whisky slid down his throat. No, Nora had said Ted's eyes were hazel. Bobby's were really dark. More like... Rafe sat up straighter. He looked over at Nora. She was busily stirring the contents of the pan. "When did you say Bobby would turn ten?" he asked quietly.

Oh, God! Nora felt her shoulders sag. It was worth one more shot. "In late spring." Slowly she set the pot down and turned.

"Late spring," Rafe repeated. He stared down at the picture a moment longer, then turned it to look at the back.

She fought a wave of nausea as she remembered what she'd written. Heart in her throat, she waited.

The handwriting was Nora's, neat and tidy. Robert Maddox, ninth birthday, May sixteenth. He'd left Nora the last week of August, after they'd said goodbye on that weekend camping trip. They'd made love time and again for three days and two nights. He'd returned for Doc's funeral in early March and learned that she'd married Ted. A Christmas wedding, Jack had said.

Stunned, Rafe turned the picture over and stared again at the boy. Bobby. Robert. Rafe's own middle name was Robert. And his eyes. That's why they'd looked so familiar. They were *his* eyes, because Bobby was *his* son. But how...?

Rafe got to his feet, filled with questions, and a burning anger. He walked closer to Nora, the picture still in his hand. She stood looking at him, pale and quiet. "It's true, isn't it?"

It was all over. There was no point in lying now, or in hiding behind evasions. "Yes."

He felt the rush of emotion and clenched his jaw tightly shut. Taking a deep breath, he made himself relax. "But how? We used protection. I made sure."

She colored slightly. "Not always, and sometimes not soon enough. And once, that camping weekend, under the waterfall, not at all. Do you remember?"

He closed his eyes a long moment. Yes, he remembered. But not having heard, he'd naturally thought... His eyes flew open and he stepped closer, grabbing her arms. "Why didn't you tell me?"

"I didn't know how to reach you. I called Doc, and he didn't know where you were, either." She felt his fury and his pain, but was helpless to ease either.

"You could have called someone at the government offices. They'd have found me."

Her throat was so dry she could scarcely answer. "I did call. They told me you couldn't be reached for six months, but they'd try to get a message through. I waited, but they never called me back." His fingers dug into her flesh, but she ignored the distress. "Please understand. I was eighteen, pregnant and scared, a minister's daughter. I had no one to turn to."

His voice was filled with all the anguish he felt. "But you found someone, didn't you? You found good old Ted. Did you lie to him, too? Lying by omission is still lying, Nora."

She felt the blood drain from her face, but her eyes never wavered from his. "No. I told him the truth. He... he insisted on marrying me, anyway."

Rafe was scarcely listening. "You could have told me later, when I came home for Doc's funeral."

Her eyes looked as bleak as she felt. "I didn't think you wanted me or our child. You hadn't written, hadn't called. I thought you wanted to travel, wanted your freedom."

"You robbed me. You took my son and gave him to another man. You took away my choices." He shook her once, hard. "You had no right!"

Her voice was empty, ragged. "You took away my choices first. You left me. I never meant to hurt you."

"Well, you managed anyhow, didn't you?" Abruptly he dropped his hands from her, as if touching her disgusted him. He felt white-hot rage building inside him. He had to get out of the cabin, away, far away. Scowling, he grabbed his jacket and headed for the door.

"Where are you going? It's pouring out there. Come sit down and let's talk. We've both made some mistakes . . ."

Rafe whirled on her, his face darker than the stormy night. He wanted to lash out, to hurt her as she'd hurt him. "No, *I* made the mistakes. In coming back here, in letting myself start to think there might be something between us still. You lied, you stole and you manipulated, not one man but two. Now I know why Ted drank." He yanked open the door, welcoming the rush of rain on his face.

She stepped closer, accepting his anger as she sought the right words to reach him. "That's not fair. Please, let me explain."

He let out a harsh laugh. "Fair! You don't know the meaning of the word. I don't want to hear your explanations. I want to get out of here. I need some fresh air." Stomping out, he slammed the door shut behind him.

Nora slumped onto a chair and laid her head on her folded arms. All along she'd somehow known this day would come. What she hadn't known was how much it would hurt.

Day Eight

By the time Rafe reached the bank of the stream, he was soaking wet. He scarcely noticed, his anger occupying his mind, his senses. Nora had deceived him in the worst possible way a woman could deceive a man.

He slumped down on a low tree stump and ran a hand through his dripping hair. He'd finally discovered her ace in the hole. Had she been so afraid of her parents, of what the town would say, that she'd given his child to another man, just for the use of his name? If, as she'd claimed, she'd loved only him, how could she have let Ted touch her? How could she have made love with him, Rafe, for three long months, from June through August, then married a man she didn't love in December?

The wind blew a gust of rain into his face, and he wearily wiped the moisture from his bearded chin with trembling fingers. She hadn't tried hard enough to find him, to let him know. If she had, he'd have come home, married her. He kicked at a stone as his conscience prodded him, making him remember how caught up he'd been in his training, his travels, his need to succeed. Well, he'd at least have told her he'd marry her as soon as his probation period ended.

Wouldn't he have? Of course he'd have done the right thing. But being painfully honest now, he'd have resented having to give up a career he'd yearned for. Was that why he'd not written, not called, neither Nora nor Doc? Subconsciously had he been protecting himself, believing that no one could interfere in his plans if they couldn't find him until he was ready to be found? No. He couldn't have been that self-centered, that callous. He'd loved Nora.

Needing to release energy, Rafe got to his feet and marched along the edge of the stream, stepping on sodden leaves underfoot. Yes, he'd loved her, but on his own terms. He'd wanted to have his work, to prove himself, then return to find her waiting to jump into his arms, go where he wanted to go, live as he wanted to live. And he'd left her to face a problem he hadn't even considered.

Ducking past a dripping fir, Rafe let himself remember the one time he'd run into Nora's father at the drugstore. The Reverend Curtis hadn't known who he was, but Rafe had recognized him. He'd had a man-of-principle look about him, a small-town narrow-mindedness, a man who saw things in black-and-white. Perhaps he wouldn't have sent Nora packing if she'd have told him she was pregnant at eighteen, pregnant by a half-breed loner who'd been in trouble most of his life. But the disappointment that would surely have registered on his face would have been terrible for his daughter to endure.

Circling back, Rafe made himself face some ugly truths. Nora had injured him, but how much greater had been his injury to her? He'd let her feel abandoned, though that had never been his intention. He'd narrowed her choices down to marrying a man she didn't love or being unable to hold her head up in the small town she loved. She'd had to raise his child almost without help, had had to go to work when Bobby had been just a baby, and had had to put up with Ted's drinking, as well. Rafe had put her through hell, and he'd not heard her once censure him for it.

He wanted to blame her because that would let him off the hook. But the truth was he had made himself unavailable at a time when she'd needed him. He'd been wrong not to keep in touch with her then, and not to understand just now. And still she cared for him. He could see it in her face, felt it in her touch. He didn't deserve her. His thoughts black, Rafe started back to the cabin.

Nora paced the small room, feeling alternately chilled, then too warm. Where was he? She'd stared through both windows, straining to see him in the darkness, but had seen no movement, no life. Rubbing her arms, she moved to stand by the stove.

Perhaps Rafe was right. Maybe after the divorce she should have tried to find him, written him of Bobby. Though the thought had occurred to her more than once, she'd stopped each time. He'd made no move to find her, or so she'd believed at the time. What if he'd thought all she wanted was financial help? She couldn't face Rafe thinking she was pleading for money. What if he'd been happily married and the news of an unexpected child had damaged that relationship? What if he simply hadn't answered, his silence letting her know he didn't want anything to do with her? She hadn't felt she could handle the rejection.

Reaching for a chunk of wood, she threw it into the pot-bellied stove and closed the door. Dusting off her hands, she then thrust them into the pockets of her jogging pants.

Perhaps she should have told Rafe about Bobby some days ago, after they'd left Jack. She'd had several opportunities. Yet none had seemed right. It wasn't exactly simple to say to a man you hadn't seen in ten years that, oh, by the way, you have a son. She'd had too many fears that he'd hate her. She let out a ragged sigh. Perhaps some of them were proving real.

He had to come back, she told herself as she walked to the door and opened it a crack. The rain was coming down in jagged sheets, making visibility almost nil, even in the slash of light. Thunder rumbled deeply, and a flash of lightning momentarily lit up the area. She thought she saw something moving by the stream. Grabbing her jacket and putting it on, Nora stepped outside, squinting through the trees.

Rafe had seen her come out and stand in a small pool of light from the doorway. He hurried to her.

In moments the pelting rain had plastered her hair to her head. As he stopped in front of her, Nora looked up at him. "I'm sorry," she whispered, no longer caring if she sounded as anguished as she felt. She wanted the hurting to end, for both of them.

His black eyes burned into hers as he slid his arms about her. "I'm sorry, too."

"Oh, God, Rafe." She clutched him, her tears mingling with the rain on her cheeks.

"Shh. Come inside." His arm holding her to him, he led her in, then pulled shut the door just as a clap of thunder echoed through the small cabin, followed by an even stronger one. He felt her shudder as she shoved the wet hair from her face.

She was drenched, shivering, crying—and she looked more lovely to him than ever before. Reaching up, he placed a hand on either side of her face and kissed her eyes, her forehead, down her cheeks, her dripping wet chin. Then he kissed her mouth, kissed her until there were no more yesterdays, only tonight stretching endlessly before them. When he pulled back he saw a tentative smile replace the fear on her face.

"I was wrong not keeping in touch with you," he said gently. "The thought that you might be pregnant never occurred to me, and it should have. Protection doesn't always work. If I had it to do over . . ."

"No," Nora said with a quick shake of her head. "Let's not do that to one another. I'd change a lot if I had it to do over, too. Guilt won't help us."

"If Bobby hadn't disappeared, would you have called me, ever?"

"I don't know." She was trying to be painfully honest. "At first I couldn't find you. Then after Ted left, I didn't know how to approach you. I hadn't seen or heard from you in years. I didn't know if you'd want to see Bobby or me." She sighed wearily. "I thought I was doing the right thing. But I made mistakes."

Rafe loosened his hold on her, dropping his hands to her shoulders. "Could you have let me go on forever, not knowing I had a son?"

"Probably not. If you'd have come back to Redfield for any reason and come around, I'd have told you. I would not want to keep you from your son."

He touched her gently, with wonder at the possibility of a second chance. "No more evasions between us, Nora. No more masking the truth or shielding one another. No more blaming each other for past mistakes. We've both made a few. In a way we both lost our innocence that summer. I've spent so many years wondering if what we had was really special, or if we were just two kids experiencing our first attraction. I need to know how you feel."

Eyes shining, she raised her hand to touch his cheek, then dipped her head to gently kiss the palm of his hand. "We didn't make love that summer because you were near and impatient and I was curious and ready. It wasn't budding manhood and proximity. It happened because I knew then exactly what I know now. I love you, Rafe. I've never loved another man. Never."

The words he'd wanted to hear for ten years roared in his ears as he crushed her to him and touched his mouth to hers. He was through with denials, with questions, with recriminations. This woman made his heart pound, his blood race, his soul come to rest. This woman, only this woman, was his.

The movement of his lips on hers had Nora opening to the welcome invasion of his tongue as her senses recognized his special taste. Her hands at his back clutched the sodden material of his jacket as she pressed her body closer, closer to the fire. He was back, he was here, he was hers.

When he lifted himself from her to kiss the smooth skin of her throat, he heard her sigh with frustration as she tried to push his jacket off. "We need to get out of these wet things," he said against her skin, hating to let her go even briefly.

"Yes." She pulled him toward the stove, then struggled out of her wet jacket.

Rafe stripped down to his jeans, then dug into the backpacks for their towels. Quickly drying his hair, he draped the towel about his neck before spreading their sleeping bags on the floor in front of the stove. Glancing up, he saw that she'd removed only her boots and socks and was towel-drying her hair. Smiling, he took the towel from her. "Let me do that."

He rubbed the short curls dry, then ran his fingers through the thick strands, watching the reflection from the fire turn her hair a golden-brown. "I've always loved your hair," he said as he dabbed the moisture from her face. He placed a soft kiss on her upturned mouth.

No one but Rafe had ever been able to make her feel beautiful with a single, simple sentence. Nora went up on tiptoe and shoved her fingers through his hair. "The feeling's mutual. Bobby's hair is just this color, and wavy like mine."

Rafe blinked away the quick stab of pain over the wasted years he'd not been around to watch his son grow. But there were more ahead. "It sounds like he's the best of both of us."

"He is."

His eyes held hers for a long moment. "I couldn't forget you. God knows, I tried."

"Stop trying." Nora studied him, still not sure she wasn't dreaming. She'd shared a marriage bed with a man she didn't love, and because Ted had been unable to reach her mind and heart, he hadn't been able to make her body respond. Rafe could make her respond in an instant. But this time she wanted more. She wanted it all. She wanted love. "Rafe, I need to know how you feel. I won't make love with a man again for the wrong reasons."

He smiled then, a smile filled with so much emotion that it made her knees weak. "How do I feel? I'm not sure I can describe it. You were always better with words."

"Try."

He pressed her head against his damp chest, finding it easier to speak of his feelings when she wasn't looking at him. "Like I've been wandering for a long time and I've finally come home. Like we've been given a second chance. Like maybe dreams really can come true."

Nora pulled back to look up at him, her eyes glowing with unshed tears. "Say it. I've waited so long to hear you say it again."

"I love you, Nora. Only you. I've never stopped loving you." He saw her eyes close, then watched a tear slide slowly down her cheek, and he was tremendously moved. His lips were a breath away from hers. "I love you," he whispered again.

The kiss started out sweetly as he tasted her salty tears, then escalated swiftly as he pulled her against him, taking her deeper. She responded instantly, her arms strong around him, her mouth open and seeking. This is what he'd remembered, the unashamed desire he'd never had to coax from her, the answering passion, the consuming hunger.

Grasping the hem of her damp sweatshirt, he pulled it over her head and dropped it to the floor as his eyes warmed. With a soft moan, he placed his hands on the fullness of her breasts and watched the pink glow move into her face. "We've waited so long," he said, his voice a husky whisper. "I'm going to make love to you until neither of us can move. Do you think you'll mind?"

"Mind?" Her hands moved to the snap at the waist of his jeans.

Rafe inhaled the rich scent of her, the one he'd never been able to push from his mind. "I didn't bring any protection. It's not something I usually carry on mountain hikes. But there are lots of ways to make love, so don't worry."

"I want you to show them all to me. But I should tell you that I'm on the pill."

He stopped, angling back to look at her. "Oh?"

"At first, it was to regulate me after the miscarriages. Then I stayed on because . . . because I didn't trust Ted."

His face darkened. "You thought he'd try to force himself on you?"

This wasn't what she wanted to discuss right now. "It was just a precaution. But he never tried, so let's forget it." His hands were doing wonderful things to her soft flesh. "Could we lie down? I'm not sure I can stand up much longer."

Rafe opened the door to the stove to afford them more heat and light. Slowly he eased her to the padded bedrolls, then followed her down. With deft fingers he slipped off her jogging pants and saw her shiver. "Are you cold?"

Her hands ran along his upper arms to his shoulders, touching the warm bronze skin as she'd been longing to do for days. "Cold with you? I don't think that's possible."

"You flatter me." He had her naked and paused to watch the flames reflecting on her satiny skin. Except for her breasts, she was as slender as the girl he remembered, small-boned yet long-limbed. Her blue eyes were dark with desire.

"I don't need to flatter you. From the first time you touched me, I've never been able to deny my response to you." Nora tried to lie still under his heated gaze, but lost the battle as her body began to arch toward him.

He reached for her hand and placed it on the zipper that strained over the throbbing evidence of his desire for her. "I've had a little trouble in that department myself." He felt her fingers tighten on him and couldn't stop the moan that came from low in his throat. "I want to take this slowly, but..."

She tugged at his zipper. "Don't go slowly. Ten years is a long time to wait." With a quick pull, she freed him. "I've run out of patience."

Shifting, Rafe removed the rest of his clothes, then lay back down to look at her. In her eyes he saw a hint of hesitation and uncertainty, and a desperate attempt at control. He wanted to shatter that control. "It's time, then."

"Yes, oh, yes." Greedily she brought his mouth back to hers. There was impatience in his kiss, one she shared. Memories of another time, another place, flooded her senses as he slipped his arms around her. The rough hair of his chest grazed her breasts, making them ache with need. Helplessly she gave in to the demands of her body as she lost herself in the power of his kiss.

His body was taut and straining alongside hers, and still he held off a bit longer, pushing himself to the limit. He sprinkled light kisses over her throat, then moved lower to put his mouth to her breast. He heard her whisper his name as her hands clutched his back.

He was a marvelously sensitive lover. Nora had often wondered if she'd only imagined his caring approach, or perhaps if time had enhanced the memory. But no, he touched her still as if she were fragile, precious, delicate—when she knew she was none of those. He kissed her as if he couldn't kiss her enough, as if he could go on all night, and she wanted him to. He held her as if she might break, and she loved him for it.

His fingers found her, and he felt her respond with a jolt she couldn't suppress. There was no need to prepare her, to wait any longer. Rafe captured her mouth as he slipped inside her. He swallowed her soft sigh of pleasure as her muscles tightened, welcoming him. He began to move, knowing the climb this time would be short.

The shabby little cabin with its hard floor and dusty walls disappeared for Nora. As if from a great distance, she heard the rain pound on the roof. Everything else centered on this man who was wrapped around her, who was deep inside her, who was again taking her to the heaven she'd only glimpsed as a girl. He lifted his head from her and she held on, eyes tightly closed, feeling the world about to shatter around her. Then suddenly she was soaring, flying out of control, fearful and delirious all at once.

Needing to feel even closer, she opened her eyes as the waves took her, and met Rafe's dark gaze. Then she saw his beautiful face change as he let go and joined her in this, their own special place.

Afterglow. Now as never before she knew what it meant. Nora opened her eyes slowly and saw that her skin had a rosy glow similar to the one she felt within. She was still wrapped around Rafe, her cheek on his chest, though she had no recollection of him rolling onto his back and taking her with him. Raising her head, she found his watchful gaze studying her, his eyes dark and unreadable. She tried a smile, but felt it slip a little, suddenly shy. Was Rafe experiencing regrets?

"If you're cold, I can shift one of the sleeping bags on top of us," he suggested, his voice sounding lazily content.

Her smile warmed. It was going to be all right. "I'm perfectly fine. Am I too heavy on you? I can move."

"Don't you dare." He placed his hands on her buttocks, pressing the soft flesh, reinforcing their joining. "I could stay just like this all night."

Nora crossed her arms over his chest and rested her chin on her hands. "What a good idea." She stretched to kiss his bearded chin. "I think you should keep the beard. I like it."

"Even after your face is red from brushing up against it?"

"Yes."

"Then I will."

She raised a brow. "I don't recall your being so amenable to my suggestions yesterday."

"I don't recall feeling this good yesterday." He moved his pelvis lightly and felt her immediate answer, returning the pressure. "It's good between us, isn't it, Nora?"

"Good? It's wonderful between us, mind-shattering, frightening."

"Just the lovemaking?"

"No. We got along pretty well back then, as I recall. Except when you dug your heels in and wouldn't take me anywhere in town, or let me take you home to meet my folks."

He nodded thoughtfully. "I was pretty pigheaded, all right. I wasn't used to being accepted, and I was afraid your parents would make you stop seeing me."

"Mmm, they couldn't have."

"If they'd known I took your innocence . . ."

She made a face. "Innocence has to leave all of us sooner or later. If you took mine, you left something far more precious in its place. Beauty. And it's never been beautiful for me since. Not until tonight."

He smiled, that slow smile she'd been waiting for. "You see what I mean about you being better with words than I?"

She closed her eyes dreamily. "You do all right, when you want to."

Rafe studied her face, noticing the faint smudges under her eyes. He should let her rest because they'd have to set out at first daybreak to make up for lost time. Already the rain was letting up. He hoped that by morning the sky would be clear. For a short time he'd made her forget about Bobby. But she'd soon remember and be anxious to get going. And now he was as anxious as she to get underway. To find his son.

He raised a hand to touch her hair. She was so soft, so warm, and he'd been denied her so long. He felt himself harden as he let his fingers trail along her cheek. "You're nodding off."

"Mmm, I know. I feel so comfortable, so satisfied."

His voice took on a teasing note. "Did you sleep while I made love to you years ago?"

"Only through the slow parts." She chuckled, then opened her eyes. "If you believe I could doze off whenever you're touching me, seriously touching me, then I've got a bridge I'd like to sell you."

He arched so she could feel his renewed need. "I'm seriously touching you." He skimmed his hands along her back, then buried them in her hair, bringing her face close to his. "Unless, of course, you'd rather sleep. Your choice."

Nora's face suddenly sobered as her blue eyes searched his. "No, I don't think so. Since I first met you, I've never had a choice about whether or not to love you. I simply did." Swiftly she touched her lips to his, hungry again for his kiss.

As Rafe began to move within her, Nora angled her head, rubbing her mouth over his, delighting in the scratchiness of his beard. She felt her blood heat, her pulse pound, her body awaken. When they'd been young together, their lovemaking had been unbearably exciting, coupled with the danger of the forbidden and their youthful lust. Now, after years of separation and the test of time, it was so much better, so much stronger. Taking over, she moved against him in the familiar dance of love.

He let her lead, let her do what she would, let her take him over the rainbow. She was all flash and fire, her small, searching hands racing over him while her mouth nipped at the fullness of his lip, then kissed away the small bite. In moments she had him tossing, straining, moaning—and he caught her small laugh as she returned to capture his mouth.

Then she had him striving, cresting, pouring into her. Struggling for breath, he felt her afterwaves as he cradled her close in his arms. When at last she lifted her head, she gave him a triumphant smile.

"Surprised you, did I?"

"You could say that. You've lost a few inhibitions since that day in the hayloft. I like it."

"Only with you, Rafe. Only you." Laying her head on his chest, she closed her eyes and sighed deeply.

In moments Rafe heard the deep, even breaths that told him she'd fallen asleep. Wrapped around her, he pulled the covers across them and closed his eyes.

Was it her imagination, Nora wondered, or was following the trail easier now that they were more in tune? The sun, after the rain, seemed brighter, the summer breezes more kind. Nothing had changed, yet everything had changed. Rafe loved her.

He was just as watchful of her as before, just as solicitous as he helped her around a particularly overgrown bend in the path, just as mindful of the pace she was able to keep. It was more an attitude difference. He smiled more, held her hand a bit tighter, touched her oftener. She was having a little trouble adjusting to the change. His thoughtful expressions told her he was, too.

As she squirmed around a sharp rock, Nora made up her mind that the next time they talked seriously she would reassure him that she expected nothing more from him because they'd made love. She'd wanted to experience the joy of their physical union again, and she'd needed to tell him that she'd never stopped loving him. But she had no illusions, as she had had years ago. She would enjoy him while she could, then set him free. Love wouldn't last if she caged him.

She wiped her damp forehead as she followed him up the steep incline. Being painfully honest, she saw her future basically unchanged. When she could take Bobby off this godforsaken mountain, she'd hustle him back to their little house and go on working and raising him the best way she knew how. She'd see to it that Ted got the professional help he obviously needed. And if she was lucky, Rafe would fly in occasionally to visit his son and to spend some time between assignments with both of them. It was more than she'd had before. It would have to do.

Loving a man from afar wasn't easy, but then she hadn't picked an easy man to love. One day when Bobby was older and could handle the truth, she'd tell him about his real father. Perhaps by then they'd be good friends.

Glancing up, she saw Rafe frowning as he shifted his gun from one hand to the other. He, too, was lost in new thoughts. If he had it in mind to play a larger part in their lives, the move would have to come from him. She wouldn't count on it, wouldn't plan or dream about it. She had once before and wound up with only regrets.

Walking several feet ahead of Nora, Rafe scanned the area as he climbed. He hadn't yet seen a sign of the two they were tracking this morning, not unusual after all that rain. Still it was beginning to worry him. No small pathways had wandered off the main trail. This was the only way they could have come. A small boy and an intense storm would have slowed them. Where were they?

At the crest of the hill, he stopped to stretch. He knew this Wilderness well, knew that at the most it was another three days' hike to emerge on the other side. It wasn't possible that Ted and Bobby had made such good time that they were already out of the wooded area. What was Ted's plan, once they did reach the Wilderness border, if in fact that was his goal? He'd left his car at the entrance point. Was he really mad enough to keep wandering the Wilderness with a small boy? Or was he too crazed to have a clear plan?

Rafe brushed back his hair thoughtfully, not wanting to consider that possibility. He'd just discovered he had a son. Would the fates be so cruel as to let a madman rob him of the child now, when they were so close? With a grim shake of his head he dismissed his thoughts, and put on a smile as Nora reached his side.

Grateful to stop moving in the hot afternoon sun, she nonetheless looked up at him curiously. "Why are we stopping?"

His smile warmed, turning devilish. "For this," he told her as he gathered her to him and bent to kiss her.

Her special tastes exploded on his tongue, chasing away his troubled thoughts. No other woman had ever tasted like this, darkly intriguing, yet warm and familiar. He felt her small hands try to burrow under his backpack in an effort to pull him closer to her. He did the same and gathered her body close against his.

Moving his mouth over hers, he heard her gentle sigh. She was opening to him, melting into him, responding with a fervor that matched his own. How could any other woman begin to match the magic of Nora in his arms?

Coming down off tiptoe, she smiled up at him. "Mmm, that beats a coffee break any day."

Rafe nuzzled her ear. "How is it I want you again, still, always?"

"Perhaps you're trying to make up for lost time." She touched her lips to the fascination of his bearded chin. "As I am."

He leaned back to look at her. "It's more than that. Do you think it would ease, this incredible wanting, if we were together day after day, night after night?" He'd been giving that a lot of thought this morning, more than he'd care to admit.

They were wandering into dangerous territory. "I don't know." She'd certainly be willing to try, but she could see the doubt in his eyes. "Let's not overthink it for now, Rafe. Let's enjoy what we've been able to recapture with each other and not sprint into the future just yet. It's all been a shade overwhelming, and I think we both need some time." Was that relief she saw in his expression?

He pulled her into a light embrace. She was right, of course. An admission of love between them didn't necessarily mean a necessity to change their lives just yet, if ever. Lots of couples shared a child and a love, yet went their separate ways.

Leaning his back against a tree that stood on the edge of the cliff, he took her with him, needing the contact for a few minutes more. He was glad she seemed to understand. They'd built lives that were vastly dissimilar. Though he loved her and would probably love their son and would want to be a part of their lives, Rafe had to admit he had his misgivings.

He'd never been a man who shifted into change easily. His chosen life-style had its drawbacks, especially during the past year or two, but it was one he was comfortable with, on the main. He'd long ago given up thoughts of domesticity, a nine-to-five job, the cottage with a picket fence. He'd never lived with any one person for very long, needing his space, his freedom. He'd never had anyone depend on him. A child was an enormous responsibility, marriage a huge commitment. Both possibilities had him uneasy as he stroked Nora's hair.

Nora stepped back, standing on the edge of the precipice. "Are you worrying already? Because you needn't, you know. I . . ." Her gaze had wandered down the hillside. "Look down there. I think I see something familiar."

Rafe turned to peer where she was pointing. He could make out a bag of some sort, bright blue, wedged into a thorny bush several yards below them. "It looks like a supply kit that's rolled down and gotten caught in that bush. Do you recognize it?"

Nora swallowed hard. "It looks like the one I packed for Bobby. I'd gotten it for his birthday. He picked out the color."

Rafe eased out of his backpack. "Stay here. I'll go down and get it."

There wasn't much growth to hang onto, to get a handhold. A few scruffy bushes sticking out of smooth lava rock. Sliding on his bottom, Rafe inched downward slowly, hoping he wouldn't suffer the same fate as the bag had and start tumbling.

The drop wasn't awfully sheer, Nora noted as she watched his progress from the top. Nonetheless, a fall would still be dangerous. Maybe she should have tried to stop him from going after the bag. What if it was someone else's and had been there a long while? She'd feel foolish, but she needed to know. Besides, most camping bags were olive-drab or a muted red. Not many were that neon-blue that Bobby had chosen.

Ted had been carrying it for him, the blue bag that she'd filled with Bobby's favorite snacks and freshly baked cookies, the morning he'd taken him away. She clenched her lips together, fighting a sob. That day now seemed an eternity ago.

At last Rafe had the bag strap looped around his arm and was starting the more difficult return trip. Jack had been right, she thought. Few men had Rafe's abilities in the wild, his sharp hearing, his patient persistence. And now, his added interest in finding Bobby.

Long minutes later, he grabbed hold of the overhanging tree limb at the cliff's edge and pulled himself up over the top. On his stomach he rested a moment to catch his breath before rising, as Nora took the bag from him. An involuntary sound escaped from her as she saw Bobby's tag on the strap where she herself had placed it. Rafe touched her arm, wordlessly conveying his understanding.

"They could have stopped here, you know, as we did," he told her, keeping his voice calm. "And the bag could have accidentally fallen. You mustn't think the worst."

With trembling fingers Nora unzipped the soaking wet bag. Inside she found two small packages of candy, some gum wrappers, an apple core wrapped in a napkin and Bobby's whistle. "Oh, no," she moaned, holding up the blue whistle hanging from a silver chain. "Bobby's been told to always wear this while camping, so he can signal in case he gets separated. Why did he take it off?"

Rafe examined the contents of the bag. Their supplies were undoubtedly running low, too, but Nora had said that Ted was an experienced camper who knew how to fish and find fresh water. They'd be all right, provided Ted was acting rationally. He closed the bag and turned to Nora. "It's hard to say why he took it off and forgot to put it back on. He's not the sort of kid who'd wander off, is he?"

"He never has. He always stayed right with us. But if Ted is acting strangely, if he's frightened Bobby, if..." She was unable to complete the thought, closing her eyes.

Pulling her to him, Rafe held her. "Nora, we've got to be strong and not jump to conclusions. And we've got to get going. We can't afford to waste any more time pondering possibilities."

He was right, she knew. Taking a deep breath, she stuffed Bobby's whistle into her jeans pocket. "I'm all right. Let's go."

The rest of the day's march was hot, humid and endless. Nora's thoughts alternated between impossible hope and frightening despair as she trudged along behind Rafe. Undoubtedly these past eight days had been the worst of her life. Would this nightmare ever end, and when it did, would the ending be a happy one? Silently she began to pray.

Daylight had gradually turned to darkness, and the moon, nearly full now, was high in the sky when Rafe finally allowed them to stop. He chose a campground near a stream with a high waterfall splashing furiously into it, the bank grassy and inviting. They were both too tired and too filled with concern to appreciate the beauty of the location.

As he set up the sleeping bags, he glanced at Nora removing her backpack. She'd been too quiet since finding Bobby's bag, her thoughts as dark as his own, he was certain. She needed to rest, if only she could turn off her mind.

They'd lunched late, munching on granola bars and dried fruit as they'd kept hiking. He still wasn't terribly hungry and didn't imagine she was, either. Quickly he gathered wood and had a fire going and water for coffee heating. "There's some beef jerky left, if you're hungry," he said as he rummaged through his bag.

Nora shrugged into a warm sweatshirt and shook out her hair. "Just coffee for me. You go ahead." But she saw that he zipped up the bag without eating. The tension of making little progress was getting to Rafe, too. She reached over to touch his hand, needing the reassurance of his strength.

Shifting, Rafe pulled her into the vee of his legs, leaning her back against his chest, and kissed her sweet-smelling hair. He felt her sigh as she placed her hands atop his where they circled her waist. This, too, was loving, he thought. This gentle offering of comfort, each to the other, as they worried about the child they'd made together.

Nora stretched her legs out and settled into him, closing her eyes. The darkness appeared more friendly now, simply because he held her, and she was able to relax.

Tomorrow, she told herself. Tomorrow they would find Bobby. Holding that thought, she drifted into an exhausted sleep.

Day Nine

Nora came awake slowly, then sat up with a start. She was in her sleeping bag, fully clothed, and realized she scarcely remembered falling asleep. Rising, she glanced at the sky and decided that the sun hadn't been up very long, either. However, the fire was going and the welcome fragrance of coffee drifted to her. Stretching, she wondered where Rafe had gone when she heard a grunt of satisfaction and looked toward the stream.

He was standing up to his knees in the rushing water, wearing only navy blue briefs, holding a speared fish on the end of a sharpened stick. Rafe removed the wiggling catch and tossed it into a pan on the grass to join two others already there. Unaware she was watching him, he leaned down to search the water for another, his spear held at the ready.

Nora removed her sweatshirt and pants, leaving on just her panties and a T-shirt for now. After breakfast, she'd bathe in the stream before dressing in shorts and a clean top, she decided. It promised to be another warm day, made hotter by the climb. Running her hand through her tousled hair, she returned her attention to Rafe.

What a prime example of manhood he was, tall and hard and solid. His legs spread, he spotted a fish and quickly plunged the spear. She heard his soft curse as he missed.

Two nights now, she'd lain wrapped in his arms. What a glorious feeling, to lie with the man she loved. Desire hadn't been part of their embrace last night, though she'd awakened several times to shift in her sleep and had reached out for him. Fatigue and worry had dulled her physical needs, if not her awareness of the very masculine man who'd held her. That, too, was part of loving, Nora acknowledged, though she'd not experienced much of it previously.

Rafe speared the fourth fish and returned triumphantly to the fire. "About time you woke up, sleepyhead," he said as he reached for the knife he would use to clean the fish.

Sitting cross-legged, she glanced at the watch tucked into her bag. "It's not even six yet." She stifled a yawn. "I really passed out on you last night."

Rafe placed a fish on the rock in front of him and sliced neatly with the sharp knife. "I was pretty tired myself. I thought we'd better have a good breakfast. The path may veer off from the stream and we might not have access to fish later on."

Nora poured their coffee, placing his cup where he could reach it. Sipping hers, she inhaled the fresh mountain air as her thoughts returned to her son. "Bobby's bound to have run out of clean clothes by now. I only packed enough for a couple of days. I wonder how he's managing, with not even fresh underwear."

Thinking of the many times he'd lived for days in the jungle, unable to bathe or change clothes, Rafe tossed her a smile. "Contrary to a mother's opinion, the male of the species can survive without a daily change of underwear. As I recall, when I was a boy I thought getting dirty was a wonderful experience. Some of the foster families I lived with were fanatics on cleanliness. Used to drive me crazy." He rinsed the fillets and tossed them into the frying pan, then reached for another fish.

"Mmm, I suppose his clothes are the least of my worries." She hugged her knees, watching him work.

Sensing her sinking into melancholia, he searched his mind for cheery thoughts. "Maybe when all this is over you and I can take Bobby camping. You said he likes to fish. I could get him a new pole or maybe teach him to spearfish."

It sounded good, Nora thought. Perhaps if she concentrated on the after-rescue rather than on the here and now, she would stay calmer. "Yes, that would be fun."

Finished with the cleaning, Rafe set the frying pan over the fire, angling it till it was just so. He sat down and took a swallow of his coffee as a new thought occurred to him. "And maybe before school starts, I can take him to D.C., show him where I live, my offices. He's probably never flown, right?" As he grabbed hold of the idea, he expanded on it. "I've got more time off coming. Maybe we could go to Disneyland." He raised his eyes to hers and saw she'd gone very still. "You could join us, you know." What had he said wrong? he wondered as he saw her shake her head.

"Bobby doesn't go anywhere without me. Not now, not ever." Nora heard the slight tremble in her voice. "Bobby's mine."

Rafe twined his fingers around the cup, trying to hold on to a sudden flash of temper. "Yours? Isn't he mine, too?"

"No, he's *mine*. Not Ted's and not yours." Her heart was pounding. Why didn't he understand? "I let Ted take him and look what happened. He's never going out of my sight again, not even with you."

She was upset because of the kidnapping and the long while it was taking to find Bobby, Rafe reminded himself. She didn't mean anything personal. He kept his voice level. "Surely you don't think I would take him away from you the way Ted has?"

"I'm the one who carried Bobby inside my body, the one who went to work so he'd have enough to eat when Ted was too drunk to care. I'm the one who watched him and worried over him and loved him when you didn't even know he existed." She jumped to her feet, having worked herself into a state. "He's mine, and no one has a right to him unless I say so." With agitated strides she marched to the stream and wandered in.

What, Rafe wondered, had brought on this outburst? He grabbed the frying pan only to burn his fingers on the handle. Swearing impatiently, he shoved the pan aside and took off after her. By the time he'd waded in, he saw that she'd made her way to the waterfall and was nearly under it. Maybe he should let her cool off alone. No, damn it, they needed to get this settled between them. He called out her name, but she didn't turn around. Annoyed, he followed her.

She was standing under the waterfall when he came up and grabbed her arm. "I want to talk to you." He pulled her toward him, but she resisted, then broke free of him. Turning, she walked into the heavily falling water.

Gingerly avoiding the rocks underfoot, Rafe went under. The water was falling so hard he couldn't see. Reaching blindly, he found her arm and jerked her toward him.

With a hard yank she pulled free of him and disappeared. Closing his eyes, he went after her.

Behind the waterfall, he discovered, was a small grotto-like area with a wide rock ledge and an air pocket. Mists from the water clouded the air as Rafe blinked to clear his vision until, at last, he could see. Nora was backed against the wall, watching him, her hair plastered to her head, her wet T-shirt sticking to her provocatively. He ignored the picture she presented and shook the moisture from his hair as he moved closer.

"What the hell was all that about?" he asked, nearly shouting to be heard over the roar of the waterfall.

She was calm now, perhaps because he wasn't. Her eyes as she met his were clear and determined. "I need you to understand. For nearly ten years now, even before he was born, Bobby's been my first thought each morning and my last thought each night. My disclosure to you of my feelings for you doesn't change that. I won't prevent you from coming to see him, but I won't let you take him away."

Rafe saw a red mist. He grabbed her forearms, yanking her so that her face was inches from his. "I have rights, too, or haven't you heard that fathers do?"

Nora held firm, matching his anger. "You gave up your rights the day you walked away from me and never came back till now. Legally Ted has rights since Bobby bears his name, but he gave them up with this . . . this crazy kidnapping stunt. Bobby's mine." She ended on a high note, her chest heaving from her effort at control.

Rafe's fingers on her arm tightened as he pulled her closer. "If you think, now that I know he's mine, that I'm just going to fade into the sunset, you can think again."

"And you can go to hell!" Squirming, Nora tried to extricate herself from his grasp. But he was too strong. And too fast as he suddenly lowered his head and captured her mouth.

He'd thought it the best way to stop her without force. Easing his hold, he increased the pressure of his lips on hers.

The kiss was hard, bruising, as each fought for control of the other. Nora struggled to keep from going under the sensual wave that threatened to distract her. But Rafe was relentless, his tongue gaining entry and mating with hers in a dance already so familiar, so enticing. His one hand went around back and inched down, aligning the lower half of her body with his own. His other hand slipped between them and cupped a breast already swollen and needing his touch. Anger and passion mingled and mixed as Rafe moved his mouth to the long column of her throat.

She was losing ground, Nora thought as her fingers clenched in his thick, wet hair. Then his hands went to her buttocks and he lifted her easily, bringing her breasts to his waiting mouth. Through the wet shirt he drew on her, and Nora was lost, drowning in sensation as she wrapped her legs around his waist and held on.

Rafe was driven by a kind of frenzied passion, the need to show her he couldn't so easily be discarded, the need to possess her completely, the need to make her admit her need. Backing her up against the slick wall of the grotto, he brought his mouth back to hers, kissing her long and fiercely until at last he felt her arms encircle him.

Then he was pulling her shirt off and tossing it aside before returning to caress her breasts with his hands, his hot breath, his seeking mouth. Her head fell forward to rest on his as a deep moan came from her. Setting her on her feet, he slid the swatch of silk she wore down and off. His hand found her and moved inside as her knees nearly buckled.

But it wasn't his fingers she wanted. Tossing about on a sea of sensation, Nora pushed at the waistband of his wet briefs until he stopped to help her free him. Lifting her again from the thigh-deep water, he leaned her against the wall and paused, waiting until she looked at him. Stretching his neck, he let his lips brush against hers, back and forth, until she lost all patience.

As he watched, she took hold of him and guided him inside her. His hands cradled her, shifting her weight until they were deeply joined. Placing her arms over his shoulders, she hugged him close as he began to move.

The rhythm was wild, both of them worked up to the height of passion. The thunderous waterfall drowned out her faint cry as Rafe plunged and withdrew, then plunged again, deeper, harder. She clung to him, her lips on his throat, her body straining. Then she cried out, and in another long moment he let himself join her, burying his face in her hair as he let sweet pleasure ripple through him.

Struggling to breathe and to keep them both upright, Rafe leaned into the rock wall with Nora in his arms, needing the support. She'd done it again, defused his anger and turned it into a passionate adventure. How could he stay angry with a woman who made love with him as he'd always dreamed it should be? In control at last, he eased back and brushed wet hair from her flushed face.

"You make me crazy, do you know that?" he asked, his voice still loud, but gentler.

In his arms, Nora sighed. "This isn't exactly an average morning for me, either."

"That's why men and women fight, so they can make up. They say anger fuels passion."

"They're right. You have me doing things I'd only fantasized about before."

He stroked her naked shoulder, his fingertips wandering down to caress the swell of her breasts. "Did you fantasize about me?"

"Yes." More than he would ever know, for she had no intention of telling him. His ego was already growing daily with the knowledge of what his touch could do to her. "Did you?"

"Constantly. Want to hear some of them?"

"Mmm, I think not, if we ever expect to get on our way." She eased from him and lowered herself into the water. "You've lost my clothes, I see."

"I'll find them." Ducking under, Rafe scrambled about until he came up with her clothes and his. Taking her hand, he led her through the waterfall and out into the weak early morning sunshine. As they stood near their camp fire, drying off, he decided to pursue their previous conversation. "Can you tell me why you flew off the handle like that? I was only trying to take your mind away from worrying about Bobby, and you compared me with Ted and his irrational behavior. I don't think I deserve that."

Rubbing the towel through her hair, Nora felt chagrined. She had been a bit hard on him. But she'd meant most of what she'd said. "No, you don't, and I apologize. It's going to take me a while to get used to your being back in our lives, Rafe. I don't know how active a part you plan to play." Nor even how large a part she wanted him to play.

He pulled on his jeans, watching her. "How active do you want me to be?"

No, he wasn't going to put the onus on her. "That's up to you, but it'll have to be on our turf. Visit Bobby here, get to know him. I don't want him traumatized by the introduction of another father when the one he's been used to is likely a sick man. He's probably going to have trouble dealing with Ted's illness."

Rafe stopped and reached to tip her chin toward him. "I haven't had experience fathering, but I promise you I want only what's best for Bobby, too. And for his mother. I didn't mean to imply I wanted to whisk him away. I only wanted to invite him—and you—to come see me, to spend time with me. All right?"

She nodded, automatically shelving the invitation. Who knew if he meant it and would even remember when he got back to his life in D.C. and wherever his work would take him next. Shrugging into her shirt, she glanced at the sky. "It's getting late. We've got to get going."

Bending, Rafe placed the pan back on the smoldering fire. "Not before we eat. Good sex always makes me hungry." He rose to his feet and took her into his arms. "How about you?"

Nora looked thoughtful. "I haven't had good sex in a long time. I think I could get used to it very easily." Too easily. She raised on tiptoe to kiss him, wishing the other things between them were as good as their lovemaking.

It was mid-afternoon when Rafe spotted the two sets of footprints he'd been seeking. The trail was inching downward at long last, and they'd been making better time since the walking was easier. For long stretches the damp earth of the fertile valley clung to the lava rock, making prints clearly visible. He bent to examine them and saw they were fairly fresh. Nora had seen them, too, and had hurried to catch up, pointing them out to him.

Glancing up at the rocky wall of the canyon, Rafe nodded, "I think we're getting close." He squeezed her hand reassuringly, yet he was reluctant to offer too much hope. So much could happen hiking in the Wilderness, even to experienced campers. Yet his own heart beat a little faster with anticipation. "Let's keep going."

Only another day and a half and they'd be out the west side, Rafe estimated. Though not without pitfalls, this area was not as dense and rugged as the parts they'd passed through. If Ted and Bobby were still walking as the footprints indicated, he was hopeful that they were all right.

The sun was low in the sky when Rafe thought he heard something resembling a human sound. He gripped his rifle and rested it on his arm, aiming forward. Stopping, he waited for Nora to reach him, then signaled her to listen with him. The moments stretched, then he heard it again. A sobbing sound. A glance at Nora told him she'd heard it, too.

"The canyon walls here are steep," he whispered, "and sounds from some distance can echo. We can take a chance and call Bobby's name out, hoping that if it's him he'll hear and shout back, revealing their location. But if Ted's upset, that could alert him and he might take the boy farther into the woods off the path. What do you think?"

Nora tried to reason out her choices. Her hands tightened on the straps of her backpack as she looked up at Rafe. "I trust your instincts more than mine right now. I'm too emotionally involved. You decide."

Grateful for her trust, he touched her cheek and nodded. "Let's get closer, see if the sound gets louder." Holding her hand, he followed the narrow path as it wound around. Walking carefully, trying not to make too much noise stepping on twigs underfoot, they passed a large jutting boulder. A keening sound, high-pitched as if that of a child, came again, loud and clear. He stopped and waited, but no man's voice followed. Rafe turned to Nora. "Call out his name. If it's Bobby, I want him to hear a voice he recognizes."

Trembling, Nora aimed her voice toward the path in front of them. "Bobby! Bobby, it's Mom. Are you there?"

She waited, clutching Rafe's hand while her heart lurched into her throat.

"Mom?" came a small voice from around the next bend, "Mom, is that you?" The sound echoed faintly through the canyon.

"Oh, God!" Nora murmured as she bit her lip, feeling her knees go weak. "Yes, Bobby. We're coming."

Quickly Rafe made his way down the sloping trail, an anxious Nora close behind him. They heard Bobby calling again, and again Nora assured him she was on her way. As they made the turn, Rafe spotted the boy huddled on a rock just off the dirt path. He fairly pulled Nora along as they neared, then stood back and let her rush to him.

"Bobby!" she cried out, and scooped him into her arms. Tears ran unchecked down her cheeks as she held him to her. "Thank God you're safe." Crooning, she rocked with him while he cried and let himself be comforted.

His eyes alert, Rafe scanned the area and saw no one else. He took a long moment to watch the scene in front of him, to look at the son he'd not seen before. Black wavy hair, a tan, wiry body and those familiar dark eyes. He wore a striped T-shirt ripped along one shoulder and dirty jeans with scuffed hiking boots. He seemed unhurt and to Rafe's suddenly misty eyes, he looked beautiful.

"Are you all right?" Nora asked Bobby, running her fingers along his arms and legs, looking for bruises. Her hands returned to push back his hair, to wipe the tears from his cheeks.

"I'm okay," Bobby managed, getting himself under control.

Fighting an unexpected rush of emotion, Rafe cleared his throat.

Hearing the sound, Nora remembered Rafe and swung about, her eyes shining. "He's all right," she told him, her voice quivering. She stood, but kept her hand on Bobby's shoulder. "Where's Dad?" she asked, looking around.

"He's hurt," Bobby said. "I couldn't help him." He moved to the other side of the path, nearer the edge of the cliff, and held on to a tree limb as he peered downward. "He's down there."

Instinctively Nora grabbed him and pulled him back. Carefully she leaned over herself. Ted lay motionless on a ledge of rock about fifty feet down. "What happened?" she asked as Rafe came over and knelt to look down.

"I was walking behind Dad and suddenly I slipped. I fell down that big hill and landed on this ledge. Dad was mad, but he came after me. He pushed me up ahead of him and just as I got to the top, Dad fell back down. I heard him yell real loud, then I heard this sort of thud. I was so scared, Mom." His thin voice shook as he choked back more tears.

"Of course you were." Unable to stop touching him, Nora sat down on the grass and pulled him to her. She glanced up as Rafe rose to examine the rope tied around the tree. "Ted's probably hurt, wouldn't you say?" she asked Rafe. The unspoken question, whether or not he appeared to be dead, passed between them in the look they shared.

"Yes, hurt, most likely." He held up the broken end of the rope as he turned to Bobby. For a moment, looking into those dark eyes so like his own in that small, frightened face, he had trouble speaking. "Did you try to rescue him, Bobby?"

"Who's he, Mom?" Bobby asked. His voice wasn't hostile, just curious.

"An old friend of mine. He's the one who led me to you."

"Yeah, I tried to rescue him," Bobby went on now that he knew his rescuer was a friend of his mother's. "Dad must have passed out, at first. Then he woke up and told me to get the rope from his bag. I tied it as tight as I could to that tree, then dropped the rest down to him. He tied the other end around his waist, then tried to pull himself up, but he couldn't manage. He tried again, and the rope broke. He said his one arm hurt real bad. I told him I'd crawl down and give him some water, but he wouldn't let me. He told me to keep calling out and maybe somebody would hear me and come help us.''

"How long ago did this happen?" Nora asked.

"Right after breakfast. Dad said we had to hurry and get out of here, that he wanted to take me to see his new house. He was hiking real fast and sort of talking to himself, you know. I couldn't keep up, and he kept getting mad."

Nora hugged him tight, seeing the unhappiness and confusion in his dark eyes. "It's all right." She needed to know a couple of things. "Did Dad drink any liquor while you've been up here?"

The boy nodded. "Every night. I told him you wouldn't like it, and he said you had no right to tell him what to do anymore."

Anger replaced relief inside her, but Nora banked it, not wanting to distress Bobby. "Dad's been upset lately, honey. I'll explain more later, when we're back home."

As he secured a second rope around the tree, Rafe listened intently, piecing together the story from what Bobby was telling Nora. He hoped Ted was all right, just passed out from the heat. He wanted him alive and well so he could tell him to his face just what he thought about what he'd put Bobby through. And Nora.

Rafe stood, testing the strength of the ropes, one anchored around his chest just under his arms and the other held loosely in his hand.

"Why didn't Ted use his rope when he went down to get Bobby?" Nora asked no one in particular. "It would seem logical to me."

Rafe sat down on the edge of the cliff. "I don't think Ted's been thinking logically lately. Stay near the edge in case I need you to toss down something, will you?"

"Of course." She shifted Bobby to the grass and reached for Rafe's hand. "Be careful."

His eyes warmed at the gesture. Flipping to his stomach, he eased carefully down the side of the cliff.

From the top, Nora watched Rafe descend. Ted hadn't moved.

Next to her, Bobby flopped to his stomach and peered over the edge. Then he turned, his face serious, to look at his mother. "Mom, why did you want me to move away with Dad? Don't you want me anymore?"

Nora thought her heart would break as she stared into his sad eyes. She grabbed his hand and squeezed it. "Is that what Dad told you?" When he nodded, she felt a renewed burst of anger. "Dad isn't well, Bobby. He's got some problems to work out and he needs a doctor to help him. The things he told you he made up. I never wanted you to live with him, and of course I want you with me. That's why I came looking for you. I've been miserable this past week, so afraid something had happened to you."

"How'd you know where to find us? Dad said we were on a secret trip and no one would figure out where we were. He said it served you right for not letting him come back to live with us."

Nora closed her eyes a long moment. "Uncle Jack's police officers discovered the path you'd taken. And he called Rafe, the man down there, to come help find you both because Rafe is experienced in rescuing people."

Bobby let that sink in. "Mom, you're not going to let Dad come back to live with us, are you? He's been acting funny. He scares me."

She slid her arm around his slim shoulders. "No, I'm not, Bobby. Not ever."

"Good. He gets mad a lot. He broke my fishing rod when I couldn't thread the line right. It was my favorite rod, the one Uncle Jack got me for my birthday. I cried, and he got even madder."

"We'll get a new rod, don't worry. Why aren't you wearing your whistle?"

"I took it off one night, and the next morning Dad shook me awake real early—it was barely light—and he said we had to get going. I forgot to put the whistle on. It was in my blue bag, and later on I asked Dad if we could stop to eat because I was hungry. He said no and made me keep walking. I was getting awful hungry and I asked if he'd give me my bag so I could check if I had any cookies left. He got mad and threw the bag down this hill and told me to keep quiet." He moved closer to her. "And I lost my favorite baseball cap. Mom, I want to go home." His voice ended on a near sob.

Nora's arm tightened. "We will, honey. Real soon. And I found your cap. It's in my pack." *Oh, Ted, what happened to you?*

Shifting, she looked down the cliff side in time to see Rafe land alongside Ted. She watched him bend to examine the prone figure.

Ted's pulse was steady and strong, Rafe discovered to his relief. He didn't care a whit about Ted, but he didn't want his death to be a bruising memory for Bobby. Stepping carefully on the ledge, he maneuvered the rope around the man's chest, tying it securely in place before trying to rouse him. It would be a great deal easier pulling him up awake than as deadweight. Easing Ted into a sitting position, Rafe reached for his canteen of water.

"Ted, can you hear me? Drink some water." He poured water on his face, then held the canteen to his parched lips.

Ted jerked his face away, then turned back and began to swallow. Coughing, he opened his eyes and stared unseeingly for a moment. He blinked several times and finally focused on Rafe. "Who're you?" he asked, his voice a croak.

"I'm here to help you," Rafe told him. "Let's see if you can stand."

"My arm," Ted said, grimacing in pain. "I think it's broken." With Rafe's help he got shakily to his feet and leaned against the rocky wall. Groggily he let Rafe examine his arm.

"Dad, are you okay?" Bobby's young voice echoed down the canyon.

Ted looked up, squinting. "Bobby, you got us help. Good boy." His eyes shifted, noticing someone beside him. "Nora? Is that you, Nora?" He sounded as if he were afraid he'd only imagined her.

"Yes, Ted. It's me. Let Rafe help you up."

With a puzzled frown, Ted turned to the man beside him who was tucking his injured arm into his shirt and buttoning it in place. "Rafe." He narrowed his eyes. "Not Rafe Sloan?" he asked, the hope in his voice that he was mistaken quite evident.

"Let's get you topside," Rafe said. "Then we'll do introductions. I'm going to climb up first. Keep that arm inside your shirt. When I signal you, grab hold of the rope with your other hand and brace your feet along the rock wall while I pull you up. Okay?"

Ted shook his head, obviously trying to clear his mind. "Just tell me, are you Rafe Sloan?"

"Yes."

A scowl appeared on Ted's face. "Of all people, you have to show up. How'd you find us?"

Rafe was getting annoyed. "Look, this is no place to chat. You want to get out of here before it gets dark?"

"Yeah, all right."

Quickly Rafe pulled himself up to the top, his hands inching up the rope, his feet scrambling for footholds along the way. Shoving onto the bank, he let Nora assist him, even though he didn't really need her help. As he sat up, she touched his face, a light quick touch, yet he felt it deep inside.

"Is my dad hurt?" Bobby asked.

Rafe removed his rope. "Broken arm, I think. Otherwise he seems okay." Bracing himself against the tree, he twined the rope around one wrist and grabbed it with his free hand. "All right, Ted," he yelled. "Here we go."

Nora lay on the grassy bank, her arm around Bobby, watching the rescue operation. Slowly, inch by painful inch, Ted was being pulled up by Rafe's powerful arms. She could see the sweat gathering on Rafe's forehead as he strained. Ted wasn't very heavy, fortunately, but he couldn't assist much using only his good hand. They'd found them just in time, she thought, as she glanced at the sky and saw that the sun was dipping low already. Thank goodness Bobby didn't have to endure a night alone up here, with Ted hurt below. She shivered and pulled the boy closer.

Finally Ted's good arm landed on the edge, and he grabbed hold of the extended tree branch. Still holding the rope, Rafe got to his feet and quickly gripped Ted's hand, pulling him up the rest of the way. His face twisted in pain, Ted sat down heavily and tried to catch his breath after the painful exertion.

Nora sat up and watched her ex-husband wipe his damp face with the sleeve of his shirt, as she struggled with conflicting emotions. She was glad Ted wasn't badly injured. He'd need his strength to heal his mind as well as his body. But she couldn't help feeling a deep surge of anger at the way he'd used Bobby because he was angry with her. And she felt no small amount of accompanying guilt, believing that had she never agreed to marry Ted and let him help her out of her own situation, he might not be here today.

Bobby walked over to Ted, but kept his distance. "You all right, Dad?"

Slowly Ted lifted his head and tried to give the boy a smile. "Yeah, son, I'll make it." He glanced over at Rafe, who was untying the ropes from the tree, and stared at him for a long moment, then turned his gaze on Nora. But he couldn't meet her eyes for long, finally letting his chin drop to his chest wearily. "I'm sorry, Nora."

She would feel sympathy for anyone wounded, and pity for someone helpless. But she couldn't find much forgiveness in her heart for Ted today. Maybe one day, but not just yet. Rising, she moved to where Rafe had left their backpacks. "Is the first-aid kit in yours or mine?" she asked.

"Mine," Rafe answered. He squatted alongside Ted and tried to use care in removing the rope from around his body. He could see that the injured arm was swollen, the material of the shirt tight along the forearm. Reaching into his pocket, he pulled out his Swiss Army knife.

"I've got one of those," Bobby said as he knelt alongside Rafe, then sat back on his haunches.

Rafe glanced at the boy, noting that his color was much improved. "I use mine all the time. Handy to have." How did a man talk to a nine-year-old son he'd just met? For that matter, how did a man talk to a boy, period? Rafe wished he'd had more experience with kids. Carefully he slit the shirtsleeve off Ted's swollen arm.

"Did you get yours in Switzerland?" Bobby asked.

"Yeah, I did. Did you?"

"My Uncle Jack gave it to me last Christmas." His eyes grew wide as he looked at Ted's arm. "Oh, that hurts, I'll bet."

Ted didn't answer, his hazel eyes studying Rafe.

Gently Rafe ran sensitive fingertips along the arm as Nora came over with the first-aid kit. "Luckily the bone didn't puncture the skin," he told her. "I'll go look around for something we can use for a splint, then you can bandage him."

Seeing Ted's pallor, Nora rummaged around inside the kit. Removing a bottle of aspirin, she indicated the canteen to Bobby. "Hand me the water, will you, Bobby?"

Rising, Rafe looked down. "I'm not sure aspirin's a good idea. He may have a concussion."

She hadn't thought of that. "Right. Some more water, then?" she asked Ted.

He looked at her hopefully. "I've got some whisky left in my case. Maybe I could—"

"No!" Nora said a bit more strongly than necessary. "No more, Ted. You're going to have to struggle through without alcohol from now on." Just then, she heard Rafe walk off.

Ted raised his head and finally kept his eyes on hers. "You hate me now, don't you?"

She glanced at Bobby, who was watching them intently. "I don't think this is the best time to discuss our feelings. When we get out of here—"

"I want to talk *now*. I want to explain. I never meant to hurt Bobby, Nora. Never." As if he were unable to control himself, the tears started.

She wished she could feel something besides pity for Ted. Thinking of Bobby, she handed him the water canteen. "Put this away for me, honey. And look in the pocket of my backpack and you'll find your whistle. I want you to put it back on."

"You found my blue bag?" he asked, scrambling to where the backpacks were piled.

"Yes." Turning back to Ted, she handed him a tissue from her pocket, keeping her voice low. "Ted, you need a doctor, professional help. What you did, taking Bobby like this, is a terrible thing."

He grabbed her wrist with his good hand. "I'm not a bad guy Nora. I just wanted all of us to be together again. I wanted to start a new life. I rented this nice house in Madras and I've got a job promised. I thought if I took Bobby there and you saw how happy he was, that you'd come, too." He looked suddenly dejected. "But the other tenant couldn't move out till next week, and I didn't know what to do until then. That's when I thought up this camping trip. But I was going to phone you when I got to Madras, honest."

Nora removed his fingers from her wrist. "What about the note? It didn't sound as if you were going to phone me, ever."

Ted made a dismissive gesture, waving his hand. "I just wanted to scare you a little, so you'd be anxious to come back to us when I did phone you." His face clouded as he shook his head sadly. "I made a mistake. I know that now. Bobby needs you. He missed you something awful after the first day. He cried, and I couldn't comfort him. I'm sorry, Nora. I won't do anything like this again. Please, give us another chance." His voice ended on a near sob as Rafe walked over.

His mouth a tight line, Rafe stooped down. He hated to see a man humiliate himself so. He couldn't even hate a man who was so pitiful. He watched Nora's eyes fill as she studied Ted, wondering what was going on in her mind.

She couldn't kick a man who was down, yet she had to be careful not to offer him false hope, either. The thing to do was to get off this mountain and get Ted to a doctor. "Let us stabilize your arm. We'll talk more later."

Squatting, Rafe wrapped gauze around the piece of bark he'd found and cut to size. Then he held it in place while Nora bandaged Ted's arm. After she finished, he rummaged in his bag and found a T-shirt. Ripping it, he fashioned a sling and tied it in place around Ted's neck, placing the arm inside.

Rafe rose and put away their supplies as he glanced at Nora. "We need to get going, to find a spot to set up camp before it gets much darker."

Nora helped Ted to his feet. "Can you walk?"

"I think so." But he was quite wobbly as he tried a few steps.

Rafe frowned. "Let me check your pupils. You might have a slight concussion." He bent closer, but Ted brushed him away. Rafe's temper flared. He grabbed Ted by his shirtfront and leaned down to him, his voice low and dangerous. "Look, chum, we've walked through hell to find you, but it's Bobby we were really after. Now you can come along and let us help you to the bottom and medical care, or you can be stubborn and stay up here alone. Your choice—and you'd better make it *now*."

"I'll go," Ted said quietly.

Rafe let go of his shirt and slipped a supportive arm around his back before turning to Nora. "We'll go first, and you two follow, okay?" He saw her nod as she helped Bobby into his backpack. Reaching to where he'd propped it against a tree, he picked up his rifle and balanced it along his free arm. "Everyone ready? Let's go."

The next two hours were slow going and difficult as the trail wound around huge trees and enormous jutting rocks. Rafe held on to Ted to keep him from slipping down the sloping path. He heard him draw in his breath sharply from time to time and knew he was in pain, but he was managing to handle it.

Behind them he heard Bobby chattering with his mother, noting on his glances backward that the boy didn't object to holding her hand. He talked about the fish he'd caught before his pole got broken, the wolf he'd seen high on a cliff and the frightening storm, as Nora gently drew him out. Rafe noticed she avoided references to Ted for now, and Bobby didn't mention him, either.

As he walked, Rafe deliberately didn't let his thoughts dwell on Bobby. He wanted to stop, to examine him, to question him, to get to know him. At the same time the whole idea scared the hell out of him. Three others were depending on him to get them down this mountain. He'd have to postpone facing his feelings about finding his son until they were all safe.

When they reunited with the stream that had taken a different path, Rafe decided they might as well set up camp since the thick trees seemed to block even the scant moonlight. Easing Ted to the ground, he rolled his cramped shoulders and removed his backpack. One more day should do it, he thought, wishing it would pass quickly.

Ted fell asleep while Rafe gathered wood for the fire and Bobby spread out their sleeping bags. Nora combined their supplies and threw together a makeshift dinner consisting of beef jerky, crackers, dried apples and a fruity drink made from a powdered mix combined with cold stream water. She didn't care what she ate, she realized as she watched Bobby tear off a piece of jerky. It was enough to feast on the sight of her son.

"Do you want me to set up the tent for you and Bobby?" Rafe asked.

"No," Nora answered. "It's a clear night. I'm beginning to like sleeping under the stars."

He smiled at her, noting how improved her disposition was since finding Bobby, the fear gone from her blue eyes. He wanted to touch her, to zip her into his sleeping bag and hold her all night long. But he couldn't, so he settled for just looking at her. Her change of expression told him she'd read his thoughts perfectly and wanted the same thing. He'd have to be satisfied with that knowledge.

Nora got Bobby settled in his bag while Rafe tended the fire. Exhausted, the boy fell asleep almost at once, his ordeal having taken its toll. Stooping, she brushed the hair from his face and bent to kiss his soft cheek.

"Nora?" Having just awoken, Ted's voice was hoarse as he called to her. He'd eaten very little and had been lying on his good side, cradling his injured arm since they'd stopped.

Taking a deep breath, she walked to his side. "Yes, Ted?"

"You didn't answer my question. Can we start over? Are you going to give us another chance?"

"You're tired and hurt. Let's not talk about this now."

He grabbed her wrist again as he lifted his head, his expression demanding. "I want to know!"

She saw Rafe rise and shook her head to hold him off. She had no intention of hiding the truth from her ex-husband. "No, Ted. You're sick. You need professional help. I promise you, I'll see that you get a good doctor."

"I don't need a doctor. I need you."

"If you don't agree to get help, you'll force me to press charges against you."

"Charges? For what?"

"Kidnapping. I have custody of Bobby. You took him without my permission for nine days. I have proof—your note, the police."

Ted's eyes turned bleak as the enormity of what he'd done began to sink in. He dropped his hand from her and made a gesture with his head, indicating the man stoking the fire. "It's because of him, isn't it? Because Rafe Sloan's back, you don't want me."

She sighed wearily. "No. We've been divorced five years. Rafe has nothing to do with this."

Ted shook his head knowingly. "It's always been Rafe and not me, hasn't it, Nora?"

She had no answer to that. Over his head, her eyes met Rafe's, acknowledging the truth of what Ted had said. Nora realized that the guilt she felt over Ted's condition was almost as severe as the pain she'd felt over Bobby's disappearance. Would it ever ease? she wondered.

Day Ten

The end of the trail. With a sigh of relief, Rafe, his arm around Ted, stepped off the path onto a small grassy bank that bordered a dirt road. Turning, he saw Bobby skip the last few feet, followed by his mother. It had been an interesting week and a half since they'd entered the Jefferson Wilderness, he thought as he eased Ted into a sitting position.

"Lean against this tree for a minute and rest," Rafe told him. Wordlessly the man did as he was told. Straightening, Rafe scanned the area. Not a soul in sight, not on the roughly graded road or in the small group of trees just ahead.

"I've never been on this side," Bobby informed them unnecessarily.

"Neither have I," Nora added, slipping off her backpack. She considered the possibility of burning the pack when she got home, thinking she'd never feel like camping again. "Have you, Rafe?"

"Not at this exact spot." He glanced at his watch and saw it was six in the evening. Not much traffic could be expected around the dinner hour. He cocked his head and listened. The sound he heard from a distance had to be saws. Most likely, they'd come out on a logging road. Now if only a truck would happen by—and soon. Rafe knew they always had CB's. Swinging around, he shifted his attention to his three companions.

Despite his minor ordeal, Bobby seemed none the worse for the hike, now that he was reunited with his mother. Yet he steered clear of the man he knew as his father, regarding him with wary looks. Rafe wondered what else had happened on their long hike that the boy wasn't revealing. As they'd ambled along the wider sections of the path, Bobby had avoided walking alongside Ted and had instead opted to walk beside him, directing questions and observations toward Rafe as his curiosity overcame his initial shyness.

Nora had told him that Rafe worked for the government and had been in tough spots before, spending weeks in forests and in jungles. Bobby's questions indicated he pictured Rafe as a modern-day caped crusader in army fatigues, which had made him smile as he'd described a few of his less dangerous adventures to the boy. Throughout the day Ted had shuffled along, grunting occasionally, rarely speaking, seemingly disinterested.

Bobby was quick, intelligent and friendly—like Nora, Rafe decided. He wasn't a complainer or a whiner, which on a day like they'd just been through, was a godsend. Now he busied himself pitching pebbles into the trees as he waited for the adults to make up their minds.

Setting down the supply case and his rifle, Rafe watched Nora offer Ted a drink of water from the canteen. She'd held up well, though she was tired and clearly ready for home. He noticed that she hovered over Bobby, more than she probably would under normal circumstances. Her relief at finding him mingled with the anger and pity she obviously felt toward Ted. The few attempts at conversation her ex-husband had tried with her after last night's uneasy talk, she'd rebuffed. Clearly she wasn't in the mood for more promises of reform or pitiful pleas for forgiveness. And Ted *was* pitiful.

Rafe rubbed his tense shoulder muscles as he watched Ted slump against the tree, cradling his arm. He'd walked as a man dazed all day, whether from Nora's censure or the realization of what he'd done, Rafe couldn't be certain. He needed medical attention first, and much more. Rafe took Nora aside.

"I think there's a logging camp not far from here. I can make out the saws and hear engines. I'm hoping a truck will come along and we can get the driver to radio for help." He kept his back to Ted, affording them some privacy.

"You'll call Jack?"

"Yes. We're a long way from where we entered. The nearest city, if I'm calculating our location correctly, is Corvallis, and that's some distance away. I believe Jack might be able to get us a police helicopter. It would probably be best to get Ted to the hospital in Bend instead of one way over here. He may be in a while. What do you think?"

"Yes, definitely."

Rafe glanced at Bobby and saw he was stooped down, studying something on the ground. He trailed his fingers along Nora's cheek, the need to touch her overwhelming him. Her blue eyes warmed, and she turned her face up to his. He took in a deep breath. "Almost over," he whispered.

"Yes. You've been wonderful."

"You mean because I didn't break Ted's other arm for what he's done to you and to Bobby?"

She reached to thread her fingers with his. "He's to be pitied, Rafe."

Rafe sighed heavily. "I know." He looked over where Bobby was, his dark eyes lingering. "He's quite a boy. You've done a fine job."

"Thanks. I think he's pretty terrific. Like his father."

He wanted to take her in his arms, to grab her and his son and get all three of them the hell away from here. Rafe cleared his throat. Shielding his eyes, he gazed down the road, wishing a vehicle would show. Soon it would be dark, and he didn't want to spend another night out here.

Nora caressed his bearded chin. "You're impatient, I know. Do you want to go on ahead, see if you can get to the highway and flag down a truck? We'd be all right waiting here for you."

"No. I won't leave you and Bobby alone with him. A logging truck should be by before long. They'll probably quit working as soon as it starts getting dark."

Nora turned to look at Ted asleep under the tree, his face lined with exhaustion. "He's harmless now. If you think you can make better time..."

Rafe had felt Ted's wiry strength as he'd assisted him throughout the long day. Even incapacitated, no man was harmless before a sympathetic woman who might drop her guard. Rafe slipped his arm about her. "Let's wait a while longer."

And they did, nearly an hour, as Rafe paced and checked his watch repeatedly and wondered if he were doing the right thing. Finally he heard the rumble of a truck engine coming closer. He set out a few yards to meet it head on.

In short order he'd flagged the trucker down. The man had gladly used his CB to contact the police and was assured that the chopper would be dispatched quickly. Thanking him, Rafe went back to where Bobby sat alongside Nora. Ted hadn't moved.

"I'll share my candy bar with you," Nora offered. "That's about all we have left." She gave one to Bobby and tucked the other one back in her bag for when Ted wakened, thinking he might need a spurt of energy for the last leg of their journey.

"No, thanks, you go ahead," Rafe said, flopping onto the grass beside her.

"Nope. We share or I don't eat." Her blue eyes sparkled through the challenge as she held the chocolate bar toward him.

"Think you're smart, don't you?" But he opened his mouth and took a bite, then lay back on the grass, chewing.

Their ordeal was nearly over, and Rafe felt conflicting emotions. He shifted his head so he could study Bobby from under lowered lashes.

A good kid, a son to be proud of, one to take fishing and camping when they'd recovered. What did he like to do, besides play minor-league sports? What did a father do with a son this age? Movies? Television? Rafe felt a momentary panic, thinking he didn't know how to relate to the child, to talk with him, even.

What if he stayed on a while and Bobby didn't like him? The boy's opinion would certainly color Nora's. And how did he feel about Nora now that they were nearly back in civilization? He wanted her, he even loved her, but could he get used to living with her? Rafe rubbed a weary hand over his eyes. So many unanswered questions. He closed his eyes.

Nora watched Rafe try to catch a moment's rest and longed to reach out and touch his face. Turning back to her son, she knew she couldn't. Bobby had some adjustments ahead, about Ted's illness and the whole experience he'd had with him. She didn't want to confuse him by displaying her feelings for Rafe, a man he knew only as someone from her distant past. Later, she hoped, she could explain the situation and her son could put it all in perspective.

"I know you're probably still hungry," she commented to Bobby as she disposed of the wrappers. "We should be on our way home soon."

"Are we really going to fly in a helicopter?" he asked, his young voice filled with excitement.

"Yes, we are. And maybe Uncle Jack will be on board to meet us. He's been real worried about you, too."

The boy frowned, remembering. "Dad shouldn't have hiked us so far. I told him I wanted to go back, but he just kept on going."

Taking a deep breath, Nora slipped her arm around him. "Bobby, sometimes grown-ups get confused, just like children do. They need help sorting out their problems, and there are doctors who can help them. Dad may have to stay in the hospital for a while. He's sick."

"I know."

She angled to look at him. "You do?"

"Yeah. He talks to himself a lot. He even has arguments with himself. I got kind of scared."

She squeezed his shoulder. "Don't worry. We'll get him all the help he needs." Sighing, Nora stood. These next few weeks were not going to be easy. She looked up at the sky.

"Why don't you watch for the helicopter while I go over and see if Dad wants his candy bar."

"Okay."

Walking over, Nora wished the copter would hurry. She was ready to drop, emotionally and physically.

The wide brown stripe painted down the middle of the tan hospital corridor was off center. Nora knew that because she'd been staring at it for the better part of an hour. Glancing over at Bobby, she saw that he'd fallen asleep on the two-seater couch under the window of the emergency-room waiting area. Fortunately it was fairly deserted tonight, with only one nurse at this end quietly doing paperwork behind a semicircular desk. Rafe had gone down the hall to the phone booths to make a couple of calls. Where was Sam? she wondered.

As soon as they'd brought Ted in and the resident on duty had taken him into a cubicle, she'd had Dr. Sam D'Angelo paged, but he wasn't in the hospital. So she'd phoned him at home, and his answering service said they'd locate him and give him her message. Sam was a family practitioner, a new breed of doctor who was as dedicated as the GPs of earlier years. Nearly every illness or injury found its way into Sam's office sooner or later. Nora had met him years ago and they'd developed a comfortable rapport and a trusting friendship.

Sam had assisted in Bobby's delivery and had helped her handle the devastation of the miscarriages. He'd also been the doctor and friend who'd helped her cope with Ted's drinking and her divorce. The doctors on duty could set Ted's arm and determine if he had a concussion or other injuries. But she wanted Sam's advice on what psychiatrist to call for Ted's deeper problems.

As a swinging door at the end of the hall opened, she glanced up hopefully, then stood to offer a relieved smile to the man rushing toward her. Sam's gentle brown eyes took in her fatigue immediately as he slipped a friendly arm about her in greeting. Tan and trim from years of skiing, he was rock-solid and she leaned into him for a moment.

"Thanks for coming, Sam," Nora said, wondering if this long day would ever end.

With a glance at her sleeping son, he led her back to the couch and sat alongside her. "I've just talked with Dr. Crane in ER. They've set Ted's arm—painful, but a clean break—and given him something so he'll sleep. He's got a mild concussion and he's dehydrated, but otherwise physically he'll recover."

Nora nodded. "Dehydrated probably because most of the liquids he's been consuming up till today involved alcohol, according to Bobby."

Sam took her hand in his. "Tell me what happened."

She did, sticking to the facts and trying to keep her emotions to herself. She wasn't sure she had, especially when she came to Rafe's involvement. Sam frowned thoughtfully at the mention of the name.

"I vaguely remember him from college. Hell of an athlete, wasn't he?"

"Yes. He graduated the same year as Jack."

Sam sat back, nodding. "I was a number of years ahead of them. He was Doc Sloan's son?"

"Adopted, yes. He's been a field operative for the government for a long while now."

"Sounds dangerous. You were lucky such an experienced man was available just when you needed him." Years of dealing with people had sharpened Sam's intuition. He waited quietly.

Nora wiped her damp hands on jeans that badly needed a wash. She'd never fenced with Sam. When Ted's drinking had first started, then escalated and she'd asked Sam for advice, he'd pinned her down, asked her to tell him everything about their lives if she wanted his help. She'd finally told him that Bobby wasn't Ted's, but she'd never revealed who the boy's father was. This was no time to finish that story. "Yes, we were. Jack called him."

"Where is Jack? I thought he'd be here."

"Out on a call. His office has let him know we're back, so I'm sure he'll be here as soon as he can." She touched Sam's arm. "What do you think made Ted do this, Sam?"

Sam shook his head. "It's hard to say, Nora." He looked up as a nurse walked by, giving him a nod in greeting. "Dr. Evans, the marriage counselor you'd both talked with before the divorce, told me that Ted has deep-rooted feelings of inadequacy and he's not good at coping. He also has delusions, such as if he gets his life in order, a steady job, and all, that you'll take him back."

"But Sam, Ted's taken things too far. He said he thought if he took Bobby to a new city and showed me they were happy, that I'd naturally follow. That's pretty twisted thinking."

"Of course it is. To us. Evidently not to him."

Bobby sighed in his sleep and turned over on the couch. Nora rose, too nervous to sit any longer. "What do you recommend for Ted at this point, Sam? I don't think Dr. Evans could get through to him. A psychiatrist, perhaps?"

Sam stood. "I've a friend who practises in Portland, Jim Davis. I've heard only good things about him. I could get in touch with Jim, if you like, and outline Ted's case, and see if he'd see him."

"Yes, please do." She ran a hand through her hair. "I must look a sight. And poor Bobby's tired and dirty, probably hungry."

Sam slid his arm about her, friend to friend. "You've been through a lot. Go home and get some rest and spend some time with your son."

Nora let out a long, ragged sigh. "I'm just so tired of all this, Sam. I want Ted well, but I want him *out of our lives.*"

"I understand. You have to know, though, that anything with the mind, the psyche, isn't cured overnight."

"Overnight? It's been years."

"It's not easy being patient, I know. Do you need a ride home?"

"No, she doesn't." Rafe watched as they both turned to look at him, evidently neither having heard his approach. He'd been watching the interplay for a while, first from the hall, then up closer, and he'd been wondering who the man with his arm around Nora was. He'd also been struggling with a surprising rush of jealousy, an emotion he hadn't felt in years.

Nora recovered quickly. "Rafe, this is Dr. Sam D'Angelo, our family doctor and an old friend. Sam, Rafe Sloan." She didn't quite know how to explain Rafe further, so she didn't try.

Sam swiveled, dropping his arm from Nora, and offered his hand to Rafe. "We've met, but it's been years ago. Good to see you again."

Rafe shook hands. "I remember, at Oregon State. You're a friend of Jack's."

"Yes." He stepped back and glanced down at Bobby, then back at Rafe. "I understand Nora and Bobby have a lot to thank you for. The Wilderness can be dangerous."

Moving closer to Nora, Rafe nodded. "I think we're all glad it's over." He turned to her. "I've rented a car and they're delivering it. Should be here any minute. The nurse tells me they're ready to move Ted to his room. He's still awake. Do you want to say a word to him before they wheel him up?"

Before Nora could answer, Bobby sat up, rubbing his eyes. "Mom, I'm hungry."

Nora reached to brush back his hair. "We'll be leaving in a few minutes. I'm just going to go check on Dad. Do you want to come with me?"

Bobby slumped back into the corner of the couch and shook his head. "I want to go home."

"I'll stay with him," Rafe offered.

Nora smiled her thanks and reached a hand out to Sam. "Thanks for coming. I'll wait to hear from you about your friend."

"Yes, I'll call you." Sam watched her walk back toward Admitting.

Rafe sat down alongside Bobby. "They have any golden arches on the way to your house?" he asked Bobby.

His eyes lighted up. "Yeah."

"Good. We'd better get some extra. I just talked to your Uncle Jack and he's going to meet us at the house."

"Uncle Jack's going to be mad that Dad broke my new fishing rod."

Leaning back, Rafe stretched his arm along the seat back. "We'll have to see about replacing that." He looked up to find Sam D'Angelo studying them. The doctor's eyes reflected his thoughts. In his school picture Bobby's resemblance to Rafe was subtle; in person it was unmistakable, especially the eyes. Nora had labeled Sam an old friend and their family doctor. Chances were she'd confided some parts of her life to him. Rafe wondered, as he waited for Sam to say something, how many others around Redfield would look at the two of them and wonder. Something else for Nora to deal with.

Sam shoved his hands in his pockets, his stance thoughtful. "You probably knew Nora back in those days, too, before she married?"

Rafe could see no point in lying. His instinct told him this man would do them no harm, but rather was trying to prove his own theory. He tried to keep his voice easy. "Yes, I knew her."

Sam's eyes lingered on him a long moment, then he nodded. "She's done a great job raising her son."

"I think so, too," Rafe answered.

"You going to come eat with us, Dr. D'Angelo?" Bobby invited.

Sam shook his head, but gave him a regretful smile. "Not tonight, Bobby. I've got a patient I have to check on." He turned to Rafe. "Tell Nora I'll call her tomorrow, will you?"

"I will." Rafe watched Sam D'Angelo walk away and wondered if the good doctor was married, and just how close his friendship with Nora was.

"Do you like chocolate shakes or strawberry?" Bobby asked, hunger obviously uppermost in his mind.

"Chocolate, no contest," Rafe answered.

"Yeah, me, too," Bobby said, grinning. "Strawberry's for girls."

Rafe had the urge to ruffle the kid's hair, but stifled it. Probably Bobby wouldn't welcome the gesture from a man he hardly knew. He'd have to take this slowly, let the boy get used to him. He wondered just how long that would take. Stretching his legs out, he wished Nora would hurry back.

"I can't remember ever being so glad to see someone," Jack Curtis said as he gave his nephew a big bear hug. "I sure missed you, sport."

"Me, too, Uncle Jack. Did you know we saw a wolf? He was way up high on a cliff and Dad was going to shoot him, but I asked him not to. He was kind of mean-looking, but he was far away. We rode on a helicopter. That was really neat." Bobby stuck his straw into his milkshake. "And my fishing rod got broken."

Taking a seat at Nora's kitchen table as she passed out sandwiches and french fries, Jack smiled at Bobby. "We'll get another one, and you can even pick it out." He turned to Nora. "You're sure a sight for sore eyes, too."

Nora stopped to squeeze her brother's hand. "I'm sorry you were worried, but we couldn't exactly phone you with updates. How's your ankle?"

He stuck out his foot. "I was on crutches for a couple of days, but I'm down to just an Ace bandage now." His gaze swung around the table, taking in all three of them, finally settling on Rafe. "I'm amazed no one else was hurt. That Jefferson Wilderness is one of the roughest areas around."

Rafe set down his sandwich and reached for his shake. "I'd have to agree. We were lucky."

Nora chewed on a fry. "More than lucky." She remembered the snake and shivered. "I wouldn't have made it without Rafe."

"The whole thing must have been a nightmare," Jack went on between generous bites of his burger.

The whole thing? Nora thought of the night in the tracking cabin, and the morning under the waterfall, and the simple pleasure of being with Rafe, free to look at him, to touch him. No, all of it hadn't been a nightmare. She bent to her food, hoping her face didn't reveal her feelings.

"And what about Ted?" Jack asked.

"His broken arm's been set and they've given him medication so he'll rest. The concussion's minor."

Jack's face became grim. "I'd like to have a word or two with him, as soon as he's rested."

"Let's keep in mind that Ted fell rescuing Bobby after a fall," Nora pointed out.

"Let's also keep in mind that Bobby wouldn't have been there at all if it hadn't been for Ted," Jack insisted.

She glanced pointedly at Bobby. "We can discuss this later."

"Right." Jack finished his sandwich and sat back. "Rafe, I don't know how to thank you for what you've done for my family."

My family, too, Rafe thought, but kept his expression carefully guarded. "No thanks necessary."

"Uncle Jack, Rafe knows how to spearfish with just a sharp stick. He said he'd show me how. Didn't you, Rafe?"

"Sure did." There was a shy eagerness about the boy that got to him, Rafe acknowledged, recognizing that he'd probably had the same look as a boy. Bobby hadn't had much male attention in his short life, with Ted so erratic and Jack kept busy with police work. At Bobby's age, Rafe had had only an overworked mother and a few school friends. He hadn't had a man take an interest in him and his needs until Doc. He was determined that wouldn't happen to his son. Of course Bobby had Nora, but a boy needed a father. "I remember some good fishing spots around here. Maybe we can go next week."

"So then, you're planning to stick around a while?" Jack asked.

"Depends." Rafe caught Nora's gaze and held it. What was she saying with those big blue eyes? he wondered. Stay or go? And which did he want to do?

"Isn't Washington wondering when you're returning?" Jack persisted.

"I called to get my messages earlier," he explained, more for Nora's benefit than to answer Jack. "I'll check in with my office tomorrow." He shoved back from the table. "I guess I'd better find a place to stay."

"You can bunk in with me," Jack offered.

"No," Nora said, not looking at either of them as she rose to clear the table. "We have a spare room. The least we can do, after all you've done for us, is to offer you a bed and a hot shower."

"I don't want to put you out," Rafe said. But there was more, and he needed to say it. "Or cause problems for you, especially with your family."

Nora tucked the paper bags, plates and cups into the trash container and turned to look at Rafe. "My family won't be a problem. I'd like you to stay here with Bobby and me for as long as you like. That is, if you want to."

Now Jack could stop speculating, she thought. Her parents would just have to adjust. She'd seen the unspoken question in Sam's eyes at the hospital the moment Rafe had joined them, the way he'd looked back and forth from father to son. Glancing at Rafe now, seated beside Bobby, she knew the truth would soon be out. Perhaps it was time.

Rafe had feared, once they returned to her hometown, that Nora would change, remembering that she was the minister's daughter. His pleasure at realizing she hadn't was mixed with relief. It would seem they'd both come a ways in their thinking. "In that case, thank you. I'd like to stay."

"Then it's settled." Nora turned her attention to Bobby. "Come on, sweetie. You need a quick shower and your own bed. There's fresh coffee if you two would like some. I won't be long."

Almost out on his feet, Bobby said his good nights and didn't protest as Nora hustled him along upstairs. Rafe poured them each a cup of coffee, bringing the mugs back to the table. Sitting down, he waited for Jack to speak, knowing he would after Nora had all but spelled it out for him.

"I owe you an apology," Jack began, his eyes on his mug.

That surprised Rafe. "How's that?"

"Years ago when you came back for Doc's funeral, I all but told you to stay the hell away from my sister." He shook his head regretfully. "That's the only time I've ever really interfered in Nora's life, and I've come to realize that I shouldn't have." He raised his eyes to Rafe's. "But at the time, I didn't know that she was carrying your child."

Crickets. He'd forgotten the sound of crickets outside the bedroom window on a summer night in Oregon. Rafe lay back on fresh-smelling sheets that undoubtedly had been dried on Nora's clothesline and sighed. Her guest room was comfortable, with a big brass bed and a cherry-wood dresser. But it seemed empty without Nora next to him.

He watched the moon dart behind a cloud as he raised his arms and laid his head on his crossed hands. The long shower he'd taken had relaxed him at the time, but the tension was returning. Just knowing she was in the next room was enough to make him restless.

Remembering his conversation with Jack, Rafe frowned into the darkness. He hadn't denied being Bobby's father, but had instead asked if Nora had told him or if he'd guessed. She'd not said a word. Jack hadn't been certain until he'd seen the two of them together, along with the way Rafe and Nora exchanged looks.

Jack had also talked of Ted, the problems in the marriage he'd observed, and his dislike of the weak man who'd married his sister. But typically he'd kept his feelings to himself during those years, just letting Nora know he was there if she needed him. Then stepping out of character, Jack had asked Rafe if he planned to stay on permanently, to claim the family he'd just discovered.

Rafe hadn't known how to answer that, and had been relieved when Nora had rejoined them. After Jack had left, Nora had seemed a little nervous, being left alone with him in her home. When he'd mentioned that he'd have to find a laundromat in the morning, she'd shown him where her washer and dryer were and then had gone up to shower, saying she'd see him in the morning. She had looked exhausted, and so, with a light kiss on the cheek, he'd let her go. He'd busied himself throwing in a load of his clothes. When he'd come out after his shower, her bedroom door had been closed.

On impulse he'd tiptoed in to check on Bobby. Sprawled in the maple bed, wearing only short pajama bottoms, he smelled little-boy fresh. Rafe had stood there several minutes, taking in Bobby's baseball and mitt on the dresser, a Batman shirt hanging over a chair back and a teddy bear that had seen better days slumped in a corner, a remnant of his early childhood. His son. He was having trouble getting used to the idea.

A night bird called out from the evergreen in the side yard, and Rafe shifted restlessly. The bed was a little too soft for his taste, and the springs squeaked under his weight. But it sure felt good after the nights on the hard ground. He was tired, yet not sleepy. He had just about decided to go look for something to read when the bedroom door opened.

She stood in a shaft of moonlight, wearing a pale nightgown that fell to the floor. Rafe drew in his breath and waited.

"I can't do it," Nora said quietly, closing the door after her.

"Do what?" Rafe asked, bending his elbow and propping his head up.

She walked over to him. "Go to sleep in there, knowing you're in here."

"You want me to leave?"

Nora sat down on the edge of the bed and laid a hand on his bare chest. "No. I want to join you. May I?"

Wordlessly Rafe opened his arms and she went into them. As she settled against his chest, she heard the noisy symphony of the springs. "I never realized how much noise this bed made. We'll wake Bobby."

"I seriously doubt that. However..." Rafe rolled to his feet and pulled her up with him. Then he eased them both down to the braided oval rug alongside the bed. "Better?"

"Oh! We don't have to do this. My bed is quiet."

He nuzzled her neck. "Mmm, I think this is nicer."

"I've never shared it with Ted, if that's what you're thinking."

"I'm thinking we might get spoiled by a soft bed. I'm more used to a hard floor." He stopped her protests with his mouth.

He hadn't kissed her, really kissed her, in two days, and he intended to make up for lost time. The sweetness he savored at first soon turned into the wildness he sought, as the kiss went on and on. His hands learned her anew, then wrapped around the straps of her gown. "This is lovely," he murmured. "Let's take it off."

She assisted him, then slid her hands down along his ribs and up into the thick hair of his chest. "I've been going crazy in the other room with the need to touch you."

"Touch me. I've been waiting."

She did and found him naked and arching toward her. "Mmm, I see you sleep in the buff."

"Do you object?"

"Object? I insist." She closed her fingers around him and heard him draw in his breath sharply. "Nothing this good should be covered up."

"That so? You don't think we might raise a few brows around town if we stroll about in the altogether?"

Nora pulled back to run a caressing hand along his bearded jaw and gazed into his dark eyes. "I have a feeling we're going to raise a few without trying."

"How do you feel about that?"

"How? That the past and the present is our business and no one else's. I don't owe anyone explanations."

"Not even your father?"

"Not even him, though I might give him one eventually. I've paid a high price for keeping my love for you a secret. I'm unwilling to do that any longer." She watched him carefully, but he didn't comment further as he trailed hot kisses along her throat and placed his hands on her hips. "How do *you* feel?" she asked.

"I feel that I can't wait another moment." Lifting, then lowering her, Rafe buried himself deep inside her. He sensed that Nora wanted him to say more, but he wasn't sure just what she was expecting to hear. He felt her heat surround him and decided talk could wait. This they both wanted, this they both understood.

Closing his eyes, he brought her mouth to meet his and began to move with her.

Day Eleven

Nora awakened alone in her own bed to the sounds of conversation coming through the door of her bedroom, which was slightly ajar. She sat up and listened. Bobby's young voice followed by Rafe's deep tones. The wish came from out of nowhere, the wish that she could waken each morning to the sound of her son and the man she loved quietly talking in the kitchen. Rising, she set aside the wish, knowing it could never be. She grabbed her robe and headed for the bath.

Splashing water on her face, she checked out the woman in the mirror. The strained look was gone, replaced by a hint of contentment. And she looked well loved, Nora thought as she pressed a towel to her pinkened cheeks. After making love to her on the guest-room rug, Rafe had carried her to her own bed. She'd fleetingly worried that Bobby would waken and come looking for her. But only for a moment. Then Rafe's strong hands and clever mouth had chased away all of her concerns as she'd shared a bed with him for the very first time. Yet aware of her apprehensions, sometime toward morning he'd returned to his own bed.

The woman in the mirror smiled back at her, looking as if all was right in her world. Well, almost all. Bobby was safe and Rafe was here with them. While there were more dreams she harbored, those two were paramount. Hanging up her towel, she recalled an old Bette Davis movie where the actress had summed up the situation well with a simple question. "We have the moon. Must we ask for the stars?"

By the time Nora got downstairs, Bobby was into his second stack of pancakes and Rafe was pouring himself another cup of coffee. They both greeted her warmly.

"Sit down," Rafe said, indicating her place at the table. "I'll get your coffee."

"Well, well," Nora commented, surprised. "It looks as if you two can manage quite nicely without me."

Rafe set down her coffee, brushing her hand lightly with his fingers. "We can, but we manage much better with you."

She was having trouble tearing her eyes from his. There was a different look about him, too, a look she couldn't quite read. She'd never seen Rafe in this domestic situation and it both delighted and worried her. The novelty for him might be there in the beginning, but she was certain boredom would quickly follow. He was too used to being on the move, on his own, to be contented for long in one place, with one woman. With effort, Nora turned to Bobby.

"Looks like you're starving this morning," Nora said, smiling at her son.

He looked at her sheepishly, then at Rafe. "Mom doesn't make pancakes very often. She says all that sugar in the syrup's bad for you." Bobby shoveled in another big forkful.

"Oh," Rafe said sitting down. "I guess I don't know much about what's good for young boys to eat."

Nora placed her hand on his. "It's all right once in a while, but we have to keep cavities in mind."

"Rafe makes these tiny little pancakes, Mom. They're called silver-dollars. You should try some. They're great."

"I had no idea you could cook outside of a campfire," she teased.

He shrugged. "Matter of survival. Want some silver-dollar pancakes, or are your teeth in jeopardy, too?"

"Not just now, thanks. I have trouble eating breakfast first thing."

"I remember."

Over Bobby's head, their eyes met in wordless communication. Nora felt the warmth flood her. Experiencing the pleasure of Rafe's special presence here in her home was a two-edged sword; facing his departure would hurt all the more, but there was much to enjoy in the meantime.

Turning her attention back to Bobby, Nora saw that he was wearing jeans and one of his faded rugby shirts. She was about to ask him where he'd dredged up that wrinkled thing when she glanced at Rafe. He was wearing jeans and a rugby shirt. The little monkey, she thought, suppressing a smile.

"Mom, can I be excused? I want to go see Alex."

Nora looked up at the clock, wondering if it was too early for Bobby to visit his closest friend, who lived six doors away. "It's only eight, Bobby. Won't Mrs. Masters mind?"

"Nah, they get up early. I want to tell Alex about seeing the wolf and about my ride in the helicopter. Bet he won't believe me."

"Carry your dishes to the sink and you may be excused. But Bobby, I'd rather you didn't go into details about Dad and his problems while you were camping, okay? Not to Alex or anyone. Just tell him about the fun things."

Bobby picked up his ball and mitt from the counter where he'd left them. "Sure, Mom. Thanks for the pancakes, Rafe. They were terrific."

"Remember, only to Alex's," Nora reminded him. "If you want to go somewhere else, you check in with me first."

"I will." He paused at the back door, turning to Rafe. "You're not leaving, are you?"

"No, Bobby, I'm not leaving." The boy smiled, and with a wave aimed at them both scooted out the door. Rafe felt a flush of pleasure he was unused to as he turned his gaze on Nora. "He's quite a boy."

"So you've said." She watched him struggle with his emotions and wondered what he was feeling and if he would tell her. But Rafe was very good at covering up. He put on his sexy smile, the one she loved so much, as he stood and took her hand, bringing her up with him.

"And his mother's quite something, too." Rafe slipped his arms about her. He couldn't help but marvel at the miracle of Nora standing before him in the sweet sunshine of morning, Nora smiling a welcome to his embrace, Nora his to touch and to love. He lowered his head to kiss her.

The kiss was long and lingering. Soon the memories of the passion they'd shared together the night before swamped Rafe's senses, and his hands molded her willing body to his. She was so soft and pliable in his arms, so responsive, and she smelled of soap and powder and woman. His tongue slipped into her mouth as her hands moved into his hair. The small house, the kitchen, the sunshine all floated away for Rafe and there was only Nora and the way she made him feel.

Rockets, Nora thought. Small explosions and a brilliant sky filled with a myriad of colors. Every time he kissed her the rainbow was filled with different hues, but no less thrilling. Would it always be so? she wondered as she pressed herself to his strong, lean frame. Her mouth moved over his, the gentle scrape of his beard on her face a sensual pleasure.

She went up on tiptoe as his hands slipped lower on her back. She could feel how hard he'd become, could feel her own body softening in welcome. So exciting to be able to arouse him with just a kiss. Her conscience warned that this was morning and they were standing in her sunny kitchen and not lying in the darkness of night locked away behind the privacy of her closed bedroom door. But her sensual spirit screamed that she had done without for too long.

How could this be wrong, wherever they were, Nora asked herself, when every part of her cried out for this man? This one man who, locked with her in passion or thousands of miles away from her, was never out of her mind or her heart. She would take what he offered while he would stay, then she would set him free at the first signs of restless discontent. After years of living unhappily, she would settle for half a loaf. It was more than many people had.

She heard Rafe's soft moan as he thrust his tongue into her mouth, then withdrew and thrust again. Her blood was racing, and she was quickly losing control. His hands were on her shoulders, then rubbing her back and...and she heard someone clear his throat. Someone very near.

Nora pulled back, blinking the mist from her eyes as she peered around Rafe's shoulder. Jack was standing inside the back door, wearing an embarrassed smile. Taking a deep, steadying breath, Rafe released her and coughed into his fist as Nora straightened her robe, feeling her face flame.

"I did knock," Jack explained. "Sorry."

"It's all right," Nora answered, turning to the coffee pot on the counter, buying a little time to compose herself. Never had she been caught in quite this position before. For the life of her, she couldn't understand why she felt guilty. She and Rafe were both free adults, not committed to another. Perhaps it was just the big-brother syndrome, she thought as she carried a fresh cup to the table for Jack and refilled their mugs. She noticed that Rafe was taking the interruption in stride.

"What brings you out so early, Jack?" Nora asked, seating herself. It was a dumb question, she immediately realized. Jack was always up and about early. And for the past five years he'd often dropped in on her just like this, giving a quick knock and then walking in. She gave him a shaky smile to take the punch from her words.

"I've been to the hospital. I thought you'd like to know Ted spent a comfortable night." He sipped his steaming coffee.

"Did you talk with him?" Rafe asked. He hadn't been as embarrassed by Jack's arrival as Nora, though the timing hadn't pleased him. After their conversation last night, he was fairly certain that Jack knew how he felt about his sister. He wasn't about to apologize for kissing her.

"Yes," Jack answered.

Nora frowned. "You didn't quarrel with him, did you, Jack? There seems no point."

"No, I didn't. He wants to see you, to apologize."

"He already has. But an apology isn't going to do it this time. Sam's contacting a psychiatrist in Portland."

"That's a long way. Ted would probably have to move there."

"That might be best for everyone," Rafe interjected. He finished his coffee and stood. "I've got a couple of calls to make."

"There's a phone in the living room, or you can use the one in my bedroom if you want more privacy."

"Thanks. The living room's fine."

Nora watched him turn and walk through the arch and down the hall. Would his office in Washington have another assignment ready for him? He'd said he had more time off coming, but would he take it now? How could she and Bobby and this quiet life compete with the lure of faraway places? Nora swung her gaze back to Jack and saw that he was studying her. After the passionate scene he'd witnessed this morning, she supposed she ought to say something. She kept her eyes steady on his. "Go ahead and say it."

"Say what?"

"That I'm lining myself up to be hurt again."

Jack shook his head. "It's your life. Do you love him?"

Nora's sigh was ragged. "I've loved Rafe Sloan so long I can scarcely remember *not* loving him." She gave a self-deprecating laugh. "But it's never been easy, and I don't imagine it ever will be."

"I thought so. And where do you go from here?"

"I don't honestly know. One day at a time, as they say."

Jack was thoughtful a long moment. "I talked with Mom and Dad. They're greatly relieved that you and Bobby are back, and that he's okay. Of course they don't know the whole story."

Nora laced her fingers around the cup and stared into it. "Maybe it's time they did. Think they can handle it?"

"I believe they're stronger than you think. And perhaps by now less judgmental. So are most of the people in town, if you'd give them half a chance."

She looked up, surprised. "What are you trying to say?"

Jack suddenly looked uncertain. "It's not my place to say, really."

"No, you started this. Tell me what you mean."

He took a deep breath and leaned forward. "That you should have trusted us. You didn't need to marry Ted, just because you were pregnant. Your family would have stood by you, been there for you, if you'd confided in us."

"Really?" Nora felt the anger flare and tried to keep it in check. "Did you think I'd never discussed unwed teen-age girls with Mom and Dad back then, and didn't know how they felt about them? Mom worked with the girls through the church and pitied them. Dad helped them, but privately was convinced they were of loose morals. Yes, they'd have stood by me, but could I have lived with the censure in their eyes? And the good people of this town would have understood, you say? The way they understood that Rafe was of mixed parentage, a boy orphaned at an early age, getting in trouble while he was looking for someone to love him?"

She got up to pour more coffee, needing to move around. "So Ted married me for his own reasons, but was he there for me, or did he hit the bottle, feeling sorry for himself when I couldn't give him a child of his own? I love Rafe, but he, too, was busy doing his own thing and not even calling to see how I was. And you, dear brother. When Rafe did come home and call, you took it upon yourself to warn him away and didn't even tell me he'd phoned. So you tell me, what shining examples have I had of people being there for me?'' Drained, she sat down.

Jack looked chagrined. ''I've regretted what I said to Rafe that day. I shouldn't have interfered. But I didn't know then that you were carrying his child.''

So he, too, had guessed. So be it. ''You still should have let me decide if I wanted to talk with him.''

Jack nodded. ''Yes, it was wrong of me, and I'm sorry.''

This was getting them nowhere. Jack wasn't really the problem, and she didn't want to quarrel with him. Reaching over, she touched his arm. ''It's water over the dam now. But I need you to understand that I did what I thought was right at the time. We've *all* made a few mistakes.''

He took her hand and squeezed it. ''Can we get past the mistakes? Do you believe that I didn't mean to hurt you?''

Nora's vision blurred. ''Yes, of course. These past five years, I wouldn't have been able to make it without you. I love you, Jack.''

Leaning over, he pulled her into a rough embrace. ''I love you, too. Please forgive me.''

She closed her eyes, her face in his shoulder. ''I do.''

Jack stroked her hair once, then pulled back, obviously uncomfortable with displays of emotion. ''I'm glad we got this out in the open. I want you to know whatever decision you make about Rafe, I'll support you.''

''Thank you.'' Nora wiped at her eyes as she sat back. ''It's been a trying time. I think it's best to put things on hold for now and see how we feel, not make any rash decisions we might have trouble living with later.''

Jack rose. "Are you going to the hospital?"

"I don't think so, but I will check with Sam. And I'll take Bobby over to Mom and Dad's so they can see he's all right."

"I've got to get to work. I'll call you later." He touched her shoulder lightly. "Tell me, if I'd have told you of Rafe's call back then, would you have seen him?"

Nora sighed heavily. "I don't honestly know."

Jack nodded, then left quietly, closing the door behind him.

Walking to the sink, Nora dumped the coffee she no longer wanted. The emotions of the past week were draining, she decided. Except for occasional visits from Ted, she was unused to the intensity and much preferred her quiet life. Yet she was glad she and Jack had cleared the air. Taking a tissue from the pocket of her robe, she dabbed at her eyes.

"Did you and Jack quarrel over me?" Rafe asked from the archway.

She shook her head. "No. We just talked about some things that needed to be said." She thought that he looked serious and somewhat worried. "Is anything the matter?"

He walked closer and touched her hair, so shiny in the morning sun. She was beginning to read his moods even when he tried to hide them. He didn't know if that pleased or disturbed him. "I don't think so."

"Everything all right at your office?" She held her breath, waiting to hear about the next assignment that would drag him away.

"Yes. But they told me Skip had been released from the hospital, into an apartment of his own. Yet when I called the number they gave me, there was no answer."

"Can he manage, living alone?"

"I don't know. I'll call again later." He moved his hands to frame her face. "Now then, where were we before we were so rudely interrupted?" Bending, he kissed her hard and long.

"Mmm, much as I'd like to take up where we left off, I do have a few things to do today."

Lacing his fingers behind her, Rafe leaned back. "Such as?"

"Talk to Sam about Ted, take Bobby to visit my parents so they can check him over. And I should call Wendy Brown, my assistant at the center, and find out what went on last week, if she had any problems."

"The center's not open on weekends?"

"No, and I hate to bother her on Saturday, but she'd probably like to know I'm back. Do you have something you need to do, or do you want to come with me?"

"As a matter of fact I have a couple of errands to run." He trailed his lips along the silk of her cheek. "In a little while. Do you know how good you taste, how wonderful you smell, how very much I want you? What is there about you that I can't seem to get enough of you?"

With a pleased sound, Nora snuggled up to him. "Do you know how much I'd rather stay right here with you than do all those other things?" She felt his hands slide to the front and inside the opening of her robe, then cover her breasts. Arching, she gasped at the contact. "Rafe, let's not start anything we can't finish. The door's unlocked and Bobby's liable to come running home any minute, with a couple of friends in tow."

The thought cooled him. He pulled back and smiled at her. "The joys of parenting." Suddenly he sobered, looking down into her blue eyes. "Bobby is a joy, Nora, one I'd given up on ever experiencing. Have I thanked you yet for giving me a son?"

"Oh, Rafe." Trembling, she reached for his kiss.

"My soup's too hot, Mom," Bobby complained.

Seated at the table across from him, Nora tasted hers and disagreed. However she didn't want to argue. "Then wait a few minutes and it'll cool. Drink some milk while you're waiting."

"Without cookies?"

Nora hid her smile. "I understand some people do."

"I'll bet Rafe wouldn't drink milk without a cookie, especially a homemade one from Grandma." Bobby swished his spoon through his soup. "Mom, why did Grandma cry when we went over there?"

Nora squeezed lemon into her iced tea, wondering how to answer him. So many reasons, she wanted to say, but Bobby wouldn't understand most of them. Her parents had both been happy to see their only grandson alive and well, and that alone had misted their eyes. Then while Bobby had gone outside to search for Muffin, his grandmother's calico cat, Nora had sat with her parents around the kitchen table for a long-overdue talk.

It hadn't been as difficult as she'd thought, telling them about Rafe and the love she'd hidden from them all these years. Perhaps her parents had grown more tolerant over the years and she'd failed to notice. Or perhaps they believed in the sustaining power of love more than she'd given them credit for. At any rate, the difficult part, and the part that had brought tears to both of them, was when she'd explained about Ted.

As Jack had suggested, they felt hurt that she hadn't trusted them enough to confide in them years ago and had instead opted for a loveless marriage. And they were angry, angry with Ted for his weakness and angry with her for not telling them the extent of his drinking problem. She, too, had cried then, cried for her share in Ted's problems and cried for the lost years.

In the end, they'd hugged her and told her they loved her and would support her future decisions, if only she wouldn't leave them out. And then they'd thrown the curveball, the one even Jack hadn't quite managed. Was she going to marry Rafe now? No, she'd had to tell them, keeping a smile firmly in place. Rafe needed to be free, but he'd likely be visiting their son frequently. Puzzled that she could accept that arrangement, they'd stared at her, looking as if they hoped she was kidding. If only she were, Nora thought as she returned her attention to Bobby.

"Grandma was crying because she was so glad you were back safely with us. She was worried about you."

Bobby tasted his soup, then made a face. "This isn't very good."

"Yes, it is. Grandma made it just this morning."

"Too many vegetables. I like chicken noodle soup better."

"Fine, I'll make some next week. Meanwhile, eat your vegetable soup." She watched as he halfheartedly ate a few spoonfuls. "I'm going to the hospital later to see Dr. D'Angelo. Do you want to come with me and stop in to see Dad?"

Bobby looked up, in his eyes a decided reluctance. "Do I have to?"

"Don't you think he'd like to see you?"

"Would you be with me?"

Nora leaned forward. Was that fear she heard in his voice? "Bobby, is there something you're not telling me, something that happened while you were camping with Dad?'' She saw him look down into his soup, averting his eyes. Alarmed, she touched his face so he would look at her. ''You know there's nothing you can't say to me.''

Finally he looked up. ''Dad said I shouldn't tell you, that he didn't mean it.''

Fear mingled with anger as she tried to keep her voice calm. ''Didn't mean what?''

''He hit me. I told you he was always getting mad. He said I wasn't walking fast enough so he yelled at me, then slapped me real hard. I started to cry. Then he did something real weird.''

She fought the quick rush of fury. ''What?''

Bobby's voice sounded young and unsure. ''He started to cry, too, and he picked me up and carried me for a while, telling me over and over that he was sorry. Mom, I don't want to be alone with him again. He scares me.''

She squeezed his shoulder. ''Don't worry. You never will be.'' *Ted, what's happened to you?* Nora shoved aside her soup, having lost her appetite. Even now, a week after the incident, she felt the anger. It was over, she reminded herself. Ted would never harm Bobby again.

''Why's he going to Portland?''

''There's a doctor there who hopefully will be able to help him.''

Bobby stopped to take a sip of milk. ''Is Rafe going to stay with us?''

Taking a deep breath, she decided to set aside her thoughts about Ted for now. ''I don't know. Would you like him to?''

He shrugged his slim shoulders. ''He hasn't taught me to spearfish yet. He makes good pancakes. You like him, don't you?''

The third time she'd been asked in one day. "Yes, I like him. How did you know?"

"You smile a lot when he's around. You never smile much at Dad. And you touch Rafe a lot, like you do with me." His dark eyes danced as he raised them to hers. "Right, Mom?"

She couldn't stop the faint blush. She'd been doing entirely too much of that lately, too. She ruffled his hair. "I guess you're right."

"Right about what?" Rafe asked, coming in the back door.

"Hi, Rafe," Bobby said, looking grateful for an excuse to stop eating his soup. "Where you been?"

Two hours, and she'd missed him. Nora fought the urge to reach over and touch his hand as he sat down, aware that Bobby was watching them. "Would you like some soup? It's homemade."

"No, thanks. I stopped in the diner on Summit Street. It hasn't changed in ten years. I couldn't believe it."

"You used to live here ten years ago?"

"Sure did. My dad was the town veterinarian. Do you like animals, Bobby?" Rafe saw the boy's eyes light up, and grinned.

"Yeah, but Mom's not crazy about them."

Rafe sent her a mock frown. "That's not how I remember it. I've got something outside that maybe will change her mind. Want to come see it?"

Bobby didn't need further coaxing. "Where?"

Rafe rose. "Come with me." He opened the door. "You can come, too," he said over his shoulder to Nora.

What was he up to? Nora wondered as she followed after them. Whatever it was had him excited. Rafe looked less hard today, less dangerous, almost boyish just now. Perhaps his son was a good influence on him. He was standing by his rented car, hands on his hips, watching Bobby peer into a brown box he'd set on the grass.

"Mom, look!" Bobby called out. "A puppy." He reached in and scooped up the small bundle of fur, hugging the sleeping dog to him. "Wow, a puppy. Is he yours, Rafe?"

"No, he's yours." Rafe stooped down to show him the dog's collar. From it dangled a silver heart. "See what it says here: *I belong to Bobby.* And your phone number. We can take it back and they'll put his name on, after you decide what it will be."

"Mom, he's mine!" Seeing his mother's face, Bobby's smile slipped a little. "Can I keep him, please?"

Rafe looked up to see Nora frowning. "Why wouldn't you let him keep the puppy?"

"He's allergic to most animals. That's why he had to give away the cat we had."

"Ah, but dogs are different," Rafe went on, rising.

"I don't know. His nose runs, his eyes get red. He may have to have shots—"

"Do you suppose you're overreacting?" He pointed to the look of sheer joy on Bobby's face as he held the puppy nestled in his arms, still fast asleep. "The only love money can buy, the man at the pet shop told me. Maybe he's worth a few sneezes."

It was easy for him to say, Nora thought. He'd fly off and she'd be stuck paper-training a puppy and driving Bobby to the allergist. Still maybe he wouldn't have such a strong reaction to a dog. Now, after the fact, how could she make him give the puppy back? Sighing, Nora nodded. "All right, you two. You win this time. Rafe, your intentions were good, I know. But next time, you might check with me first.''

"Okay, I will.''

He sounded uncharacteristically unsure of himself. She didn't want to ruin his tenuous confidence in fathering skills. As Bobby whispered to the puppy, she took the moment to slip her arm around Rafe's waist and hold him near. "It was wonderfully thoughtful of you." He looked down at her, a little sadly she thought.

"I guess I don't know much about what's best for kids.''

"I'll bet you're a quick study." She slipped her hand under the hem of his shirt and caressed the warm, smooth skin. "Have I told you yet today that I love you?" she asked in a husky whisper.

It occurred to Nora how infrequently Rafe had heard those three little words from someone who meant them from the heart. Her own heart turned over at the quick way his eyes warmed as he brought her into the circle of his arms.

He lowered his head so that his mouth was a breath away from hers. "I love you, too. So much so that it frightens me.''

She knew how difficult that had been for him to admit. "Don't be frightened, not with me. I won't make demands on you, ever.''

"You already have. Unspoken demands are the hardest to ignore." He touched his mouth to hers, keeping the kiss light.

Remembering Bobby, Nora pulled back and found him watching them. The puppy, finally awake, was licking his face.

"I guess Rafe likes you, too, Mom. Can I keep the puppy?"

She smiled at her son as she walked over to pet the dog. "Yes, at least for a while. We have to make sure he doesn't make your allergies flare up."

"Let's hope they don't," Rafe said as he opened the trunk of the car. "Because I can't take this stuff back."

Nora peeked in as Bobby excitedly exclaimed over each item. There was a wicker dog bed with a red cushion, a Snoopy food-and-water dish, rawhide bones to chew on, assorted toys and enough food to take him out of puppyhood.

Checking her expression, Rafe grinned. "Think I overdid it a little?"

She smiled back, keeping her voice low. "Just a little." She turned to where Bobby was trying to interest the puppy in a rawhide bone. "I think he's a little too young for that yet, son. His teeth are too small. Why don't you take him in the kitchen and see if he's hungry?"

"Okay. Will you bring his stuff? I have to carry him."

"Yes. By the way, what are you naming your new puppy?"

"Rambo," Bobby answered immediately.

Nora laughed at the thought of the small brown beagle with that big name. "Rambo it is." Still smiling, she watched him walk to the house, then grabbed the dog's bed from the trunk.

"Rambo, eh?" Rafe lifted the dog-food bag and toys. "I guess Bobby won't be interested in this, then." He thrust a package toward her. "I saw you had a VCR so I rented a movie I thought he'd like."

Nora opened the bag. When she read the title, she grinned up at him. "*Bambi*?"

"A little too young for nine, going on ten, right?"

"I'm afraid so."

With a sigh, he slammed shut the trunk. "I told you I was lousy father material."

"You're trying too hard, Rafe. Remember what the man at the pet store said, that a dog's love is the only love money can buy."

He frowned. "You think I'm trying to buy Bobby's love?"

"Aren't you?"

He shrugged. "Maybe I am."

"You don't have to. It may take a while, but it'll happen."

"I feel like I have so much time to make up for." He sounded frustrated, annoyed, impatient.

"But not with gifts. You have the ability to make people love you without giving them gifts. You never lavished me with gifts, and I've loved you forever."

His eyes lit up. "I want to give you gifts, too. I saw this great necklace downtown and I almost—"

"No." A simple gold ring she'd have accepted. "I don't want necklaces."

"Then what do you want?" he asked seriously.

You. Only you and our son. Why can't you see? "To enjoy our time together," she answered carefully.

With a puzzled frown, Rafe walked ahead of her into the house.

Nora knew her answer hadn't satisfied him. He would simply have to read between the lines and figure out the rest himself.

Day Twelve, etc.

Rafe couldn't remember the last time he'd slept in so late. A glance at the clock told him it was nearly nine in the morning. Stretching, he lay back again, luxuriating in the quiet. He'd had another of his dreams last night, waking in a cold sweat. Nora had calmed him, then held him. It had been past three when he'd finally fallen back to sleep. Yawning, he decided to enjoy the lazy morning. He wouldn't be staying much longer.

They'd come out of the Wilderness a week ago, and the days since had been full as he'd spent time getting acquainted with his son and tried to fit into a domestic routine. He was learning, though it wasn't easy for him. There were moments of intense pleasure as well as moments of utter frustration. In all honesty, Rafe thought he'd be hard put to say if he was making progress in his adjustment or not.

A child's voice from the day-care center in the backyard rang out in the clear morning air through the open window. Nora was back working there daily, leaving him with a soft kiss and a promise to return often, which she did. Late afternoon, when the children would leave, she'd come in for good and tell him about her day. Her eyes would be bright as she fixed dinner and made him laugh with her stories of the kids and their adventures.

And then there were the nights when he held her close to his heart, and made love to her until they were both spent and exhausted and happy. It had been her idea that they not hide their feelings for each other from Bobby and after that first night, she'd moved him into her bedroom. Oddly enough, Bobby had never commented on the switch, nor appeared to notice. Reaching over, he touched the pillow where hours ago her head had lain. Already he'd begun imagining her beside him at his meals, beside him in a big bed this winter, beside him as they guided Bobby into adulthood. Always beside him. The images warmed him and unsettled him.

Rafe rolled out of bed and marched down the hall to the bath. Bobby had spent the night at his friend Alex's house, so Rafe was alone. Turning on the jets, he stepped under the shower spray. He worked up a lather, feeling mostly at peace with himself. Being here had relaxed him. Maybe too much. He hadn't had so much time off at one stretch in years. He hoped the idle hours hadn't made him soft, or careless. Either could cost him his life.

That's one of the reasons he'd decided that he'd leave soon, to get back in shape, to let distance lend some perspective, to give them all a little breathing room. Bobby had been great, but Rafe wasn't sure if, on a scale of one to ten, he wouldn't stack up as a poor three or four as father material.

Rinsing off, he stuck his head under the spray and reached for the shampoo, going over the past week in his mind. He'd bought Bobby the wrong kind of fishing pole, one much too long and advanced for him. So he'd taken him spearfishing and somehow, Bobby had poked the sharpened stick into his middle finger, requiring two stitches. And while Nora had been at work, he'd taken him to a matinee only to discover the swearing, the blood and gore in the adventure film he'd chosen had been so constant that he'd hustled Bobby out after less than half an hour. Sighing, Rafe rinsed his hair and turned off the water.

Nora had been very patient with him, even when she'd had to leave the center to meet him at the hospital because they wouldn't sew up Bobby's cut without a parent present. He'd wanted to grab the doctor by his white jacket and tell him that he *was* the boy's parent, but he hadn't. Then there'd been the evening that Nora's parents had come over for dinner.

Rubbing himself dry with a big towel, Rafe smiled at the memory, though he hadn't been smiling then. Even Nora had been nervous, completely forgetting to serve a vegetable dish she'd prepared earlier and left to keep warm in the oven. The Reverend and Mrs. Curtis had been polite, seemingly interested in his work, but cool. Decidedly cool. Or perhaps that was just their normal manner. Bobby had been his usual self, the only relaxed one at the table. Rafe had offered them wine, and they'd declined, informing him that they didn't drink, looking a little taken aback when he'd obstinately filled his glass and Nora's to the brim. They probably decided then and there that Nora was involved with another drinker. And Rambo had topped off the evening by wetting on the Reverend's shoe. Yes, it had been a night to remember.

Walking back to the room he shared with Nora, Rafe admitted ruefully that her parents might never accept him, even if he would move back permanently. That didn't particularly bother him, except for Nora's sake. Though they tried, Nora's parents had been conditioned from childhood to be wary of men like him. He was more interested in Bobby's acceptance and Bobby's love. The boy liked to go places with him, talked to him at great length, but he'd yet to make the first move, to kiss him good night, to hug him or spontaneously run into his arms. Maybe he was expecting too much too soon.

Rafe buttoned his shirt and reached for his slacks. Nora had told him of Bobby's revelation that Ted had slapped him. Rafe had suspected as much, but had thought it best to let the story come out naturally. Of course she no longer asked Bobby to go to see Ted. Yesterday Ted had been released from the hospital and transferred to Portland.

After learning what he'd done to Bobby, Nora had been too furious to visit Ted again. Rafe didn't blame her. He only hoped Ted, when he recovered, would plan to stay out of their lives. If not, he would find a way to persuade him. There was no way Ted was ever going to get near Bobby again.

The phone rang, and Rafe moved to pick it up as he felt a smile form. Probably Nora calling to check in with him, as she often did. But the words he heard wiped the smile from his face quickly. A few minutes later he hung up, his expression grim. It would seem fate had stepped in and hurried along his plans. Checking his watch, he left the room in search of Nora.

But she wasn't in the day-care center, Wendy informed him. She'd had to drive home a sick child, first locating the mother. Of all days, Rafe mumbled to himself as he returned to the house. He simply couldn't wait.

Picking up the phone, he called the airline and booked himself on the next flight out. He'd have to hurry, but he'd make it, turning in his rental car on the way. Quickly he threw his clothes into his leather bag and made for the door. He'd call Nora tonight and explain.

Something made him stop and reconsider. Once before, he'd left and she'd had to wonder. He wouldn't put her through that again. Finding paper and pen, he scribbled a note, telling her an emergency had come up in D.C. and he'd had to leave, but he'd be in touch later with a complete explanation. Propping it next to the coffeepot, Rafe took a last look around.

Rambo, in his box by the back door, whimpered in his sleep. Bobby's mitt lay on the kitchen counter next to his ball. Rafe ran his fingers along the worn leather. A small bouquet of roses Nora had picked from the side yard earlier that morning sat in the center of the table. He could almost pick out her special scent in the room, as if she'd only recently dashed through, her fragrance mingling with that of the flowers. He would miss this, Rafe acknowledged. But perhaps it was time to go.

Quickly he left the kitchen and headed for his car.

Nora opened her back door wide so Wendy could walk in. "My guess is that Kathy's rash is roseola, but it could be measles." She stepped in after Wendy. "Her mother's supposed to let me know tonight, after she's had the doctor look at her."

Wendy ran a hand through her short hair. "With measles cases on the rise again, I feel we ought to consider making immunization a requirement. What do you think, Nora?"

"I agree. Would you like a cup of coffee?"

"That sounds good. This has been some day." She plopped into a kitchen chair and eased off her shoes. "I don't think we stopped for five minutes."

"Isn't that the truth?" Nora peeked into Rambo's box and saw that it was empty. From the living room came the sound of a television show. "Bobby, have you got Rambo in there?" she called from the arch.

"Yeah, Mom. He's on my lap."

"Watch that he doesn't wet, will you?"

"Okay."

She moved to the sink to wash her hands. Fresh coffee would taste good. The coffee pot was still plugged in from the morning, she noticed as she reached for the soap. A note was propped next to it. Must be from Rafe, she thought. She'd been wondering where he was since noticing that his car was gone. She'd been too busy today to check in with him. Behind her, Wendy was going on about one of the four-year-old boys who'd bitten a toddler, wondering what they were going to do with him if he didn't stop biting his classmates. Drying her hands, Nora reached for the note.

Her heart skipped a beat as she read. An emergency in D.C. He'd call later with a full explanation. She tried to panic as she read his words again. Why hadn't back to tell her in person?

"Say, honey, where's your fella?" Wendy asked stretched her legs out and wiggled her toes. "I've gotten used to him joining us for coffee at the end of a hard day.

He sure is the handsomest son-of-a-gun I've met in a month of Sundays. I . . . Nora? Is anything wrong?''

"Rafe's been called back to Washington," Nora said, amazed that her voice sounded so calm. "Some kind of emergency." She set aside the note and picked up the coffeepot.

"Oh, yes. I meant to tell you that he came looking for you this morning, right after you'd left to take Kathy home. I told him you'd be back in about an hour."

"Did he say what he wanted?"

"No. I saw him walk back to the house. I'm sure he'll be in touch soon."

Nora wished she were as confident. Shutting off the water, she measured coffee, fighting all the insecurities that came rushing back with full force. Rafe had seemed happy and relaxed this past week. They hadn't quarreled. Bobby was obviously a joy to him. Of course she'd noticed some restlessness. Never having lived with him before, she didn't know if that was part of his nature or if he'd been getting ready to move on.

Last night he'd made love to her and there'd been no special intensity, no poignancy that might have made her suspicious. He'd had another bad dream, but he'd handled it better this time. She knew he was impatient with his fathering skills and frustrated that they weren't inbred. But that was such a minor thing, one that only time could improve.

Nora plugged in the coffeepot with a sigh. She'd have to think of this fatalistically, as she'd been gearing herself up to do. If he came back, she'd be happy. If he didn't, she'd adjust. Trying to concentrate on that philosophy, she turned back to Wendy.

"You're upset, aren't you, honey?" Wendy said as she rose. Slipping an arm about Nora, she hugged her. "Don't you fret. Your fella's crazy about you. I can tell. He looks at you same as George used to look at me, God rest his soul. Thirty years I lived with that man and he never stopped looking at me like I was a tasty treat on his plate. Mark my words. You don't have to worry about your fella. He'll be back."

Her fella. Since meeting Rafe, Wendy had never used his name when speaking of him, referring to him instead as her fella. Was he? Nora wondered. Had he ever truly been hers in any sense of the word?

"I'm fine, Wendy. I'm sure I'll be hearing from Rafe soon." She moved from her and sat down. "Did you bring that new schedule we've been working on? With school starting next week, I know we're going to have to adjust some drop-off and pick-up times."

"Got it right here in my purse." Wendy hoisted her large leather bag into her lap and started rummaging about.

She'd put Rafe's sudden departure out of her mind for now, Nora decided. Keeping busy was the answer. She glanced at the clock. Nearly six. Three hours later in Washington. Was he in his apartment, or conferring with someone at his office this late? She didn't even have a number where she could reach him, though Jack did. Not that she intended to call. She would wait. She was good at waiting. She'd certainly done her share of it through the years.

Wendy spread the new schedule on the table, and Nora shifted her attention to revising it.

* * *

Fresh from his bath, Bobby came bouncing down the stairs and into the living room. "Mom, why are you sitting in the dark?"

Nora tore her gaze from the window where she'd been staring out and glanced up at her son. "Oh, I just didn't get around to turning on the light." Lost in thought, she hadn't even noticed the lateness of the hour. Reaching over, she snapped on the lamp. "Ready for bed?"

Bobby sat next to her and snuggled up, something he rarely did anymore. "I guess so. Mom, why did Rafe leave?"

She hugged the small, warm body to her, needing the contact more than he did tonight. "I told you, he had some kind of an emergency come up at his office. They needed him so he had to return, probably to help straighten things out."

"But he said he'd call and he hasn't."

"He probably went straight from the airport to his office and he's working, trying to solve the problem." She hoped she sounded more certain than she felt. Bobby was asking the same questions she'd been asking herself, and she'd come up with only vague answers.

"You always tell me that it only takes a minute to make a call and let someone know you're okay. He should have called."

The honesty of children. "You're right. He should have. But let's not judge him too harshly. He probably has a very good explanation."

"Okay." Sounding unconvinced, Bobby fussed with the seam of his pajama bottoms. "I thought he liked me."

Surprised, Nora leaned back to look at his face. "He does, very much. Why would you think otherwise?"

"He left without saying goodbye, even. You don't do that to people you care about, do you?"

Emotion clogged Nora's throat. One of the difficulties of raising a child was having to explain the actions of adults in terms the child could understand and accept. She swallowed hard as she took his small hand in hers. "Bobby, I believe Rafe cares about you and me a great deal. But he's an important man with a large, responsible government job. He can't just walk away from that and stay here with us indefinitely. Do you see?"

"Yeah, I guess so. Dad used to leave us a lot, too. Remember?"

She remembered, all right. Putting on her best attempt at a smile, she brushed the hair from his forehead. "Looks like it's just you and me again. Do you mind very much?"

"No, it's okay."

With all her heart, she wished she could offer him a better explanation. She tried to think of a distraction. "Tomorrow we should go shopping. Get some new clothes and your school supplies. You've got to look spiffy to start the fourth grade, right?"

"I guess so." He heard Rambo whine from his box. "Can Rambo sleep with me tonight, Mom? I'll watch him real good."

She kissed his soft cheek and nodded. "All right, but let him out before you take him up." She watched Bobby dash off to the kitchen, and sighed. Shifting her gaze back to the front window, she saw the big fir tree sway slightly in the night breeze. Moonlight lit the yard, turning everything silvery.

It would be one in the morning in Washington by now. The emergency must have been a whopper. She'd tried all evening to give Rafe the benefit of the doubt, but with each passing hour she'd lost heart. He was gone. She could feel it. Hadn't she known he'd leave them one day? Absently she scratched at a bothersome hive on her shoulder.

"Mom?"

She turned to see Bobby standing at the bottom of the stairs, his puppy in his arms. "Yes?"

"Do you think Rafe will miss us?"

Blinking through the mist, Nora nodded, then turned back to the window so her son wouldn't see her tears.

A chilly September wind whipped around Nora's legs as she locked the door of the center and walked to her own back door. An early frost was headed their way, or so the weatherman had predicted. Already, the sky wasn't as bright a blue as last week, she thought as she gazed up, and the clouds were thicker. The leaves would soon be changing colors and dropping to the ground.

Many people loved the fall best, but she'd never been very fond of it. It was a time when you watched living things slowly die and soon they were buried under a blanket of white. It reminded her too much of endings instead of beginnings. No, she much preferred spring when everything came to life. Opening the door, she hurried inside.

Removing her sweater, Nora rubbed her arms. A cup of fresh coffee would hit the spot. Wendy had left early for a dental appointment. Mrs. Masters had taken Alex and Bobby to the library and wouldn't have them back for another hour. Nora welcomed the peace and quiet of a little alone time after the busy, noisy day she'd had. She could use a little time to think.

Or could she? Inevitably, her thoughts moved to Rafe. It was only a week since he'd left so abruptly, yet it seemed much longer. He'd called her the next day, sounding distant and distracted, telling her that Skip was in the hospital. He didn't volunteer much more, except to say he was busy catching up with paperwork. She hadn't pushed. If he came back, it would have to be because he wanted to, not because she'd coaxed him to return or made him feel guilty. Hadn't she sworn to herself that she'd free him when he became restless? They'd hung up and Nora had felt empty, as she still did. She hadn't heard a word since.

She plugged in the coffee pot, then opened the refrigerator door, wondering what to make for dinner. She'd taken a pound of hamburger from the freezer yesterday to thaw, then hadn't had the energy to prepare it last night. So they'd ordered a pizza, despite her reservations about serving junk food. Tonight she'd have to give Bobby a decent meal. If only she felt more hungry. Dispiritedly she closed the refrigerator door. Perhaps after her coffee, she'd be better able to come up with an idea.

Slipping off her shoes, she heard Rambo scratching the sides of his box, wanting out. Leaning down, she rubbed the soft head. "We're going to have to get you a pen of some sort, fella," she told him. "You're outgrowing this box and we just can't trust you alone in the house, yet."

Picking him up, she walked with him to the back door. "Need to go out and run around a little? Sure you do." She stepped out and set him on the grass. He made her smile as he sniffed around at the shrubs, his little tail wagging. Sliding her hands into the pockets of her slacks, she stood waiting for him to run off some of his pent-up energy.

"Excuse me, miss," said a deep voice behind her. "Are you the lady of the house?"

Whirling about, Nora caught her breath as she recognized the voice. Rafe? "Yes, I—"

"Good. I'm looking for Nora Maddox. Nora Curtis Maddox. Is that your name?"

What was he doing? she wondered, taken aback. He stood before her, clean-shaven and wearing an expensive-looking suit and that same heart-stopping smile, his dark eyes capturing hers. He held something in one hand behind his back. Taking a deep breath to calm her pounding heart, she decided to play along. "Yes, I"m Nora Maddox."

He held out his right hand. "Pleased to meet you. I'm Rafe Sloan and I haven't lived here for a long time. They told me at the flower store in town that I could find you here. You see, I'm a sucker for blue eyes, and the florist told me yours are the prettiest for miles around. I'm inclined to agree."

She touched her hand to his. "Thank you."

"You're welcome." Now that he had her hand, Rafe held on. All the way here in the plane, he'd struggled with several scenarios on how to approach her and had decided on silly. Just now, when she'd turned, he'd seen surprise, then a quick flash of anger when she recognized him, and finally a wariness in her eyes as she tried to decide how to react. If he could keep her wondering, get in his explanation before she rebuffed him, then maybe he'd have a chance.

"They didn't know what your favorite flower was, so I took a chance." He held out the small bouquet. "I used to know a girl once—she had blue eyes so much like yours—and I gave her these trilliums. The florist had a hard time locating them, but I insisted. You see, they remind me of her. She's very strong, a true survivor."

Nora took the flowers from him, burying her nose in the delicate blossoms. "Perhaps she's not as strong as you might have thought."

"Oh, I think she is. Like those little flowers, people haven't always treated her fairly, abandoning her to struggle alone. Yet she survived beautifully. She's to be admired."

"Maybe admiration wasn't what she was after."

"Sometimes admiration is the first step toward love, don't you think?"

Nora met his eyes again. "I don't know. I've tried loving, and I find I'm not very good at it." Finished with his business, Rambo scampered to her. She picked him up. "I have to go inside."

"A cup of coffee would sure taste good. That is, if you don't mind offering one to a stranger."

How long was he going to keep this up? Nora turned toward the house. "Certainly. Come on in."

She settled Rambo in his box and poured each of them a cup of coffee, carrying the mugs to the table where he'd seated himself and was quietly watching her. She sat opposite him, keeping her features even, wondering where all this "let's pretend we're strangers" was leading.

"This is a nice home you've made here," Rafe went on, noticing her face had turned cool. He'd have to get to the point soon or she'd run out of patience. "And it's a nice town you live in. I lived in this town once, and I couldn't wait to leave. You see, I had this dream. I wanted to see the world, to make a difference, to become someone."

"And did you?"

"Oh, yes. I'm respected, admired, even feared in some circles. But just recently I discovered something."

"What was that?"

He leaned forward, his fingers circling the cup, speaking from the heart. "That girl I spoke of earlier, she was part of the dream. But I wanted her on *my* terms, when *I* was ready, when *I'd* made my mark in the world. When I learned she'd married someone else while I was busy elsewhere, I turned away, blaming her, never once questioning that she might have had a very good reason. Recently, when I returned and realized I still loved her, I still wasn't ready. I wanted her to make all the compromises, to fit herself and our child into my life, my schedules. I was afraid to admit that I might actually like coming back, settling down, being a husband and father. Because then I would have to change, to adjust, to adapt. And to admit I might have been wrong."

He stopped to take a swallow of his coffee, trying to find the right words. Silently Nora waited for him to continue. "So I grabbed the first opportunity to leave, telling myself I needed to return to work, to do what I did best, to pursue my dream."

"So why did you come back again?" she asked softly.

"Because I discovered I was chasing the wrong dream." He looked up, realizing it was now or never. Nora would either understand, or she wouldn't. "It's not enough to be respected and admired for your work. If pride in your work is all you have, you come up empty-handed in the end. If you're not *someone* to someone you love, you're no one."

Her hands were trembling as she set aside her cup. "When did you come to realize that?"

"Last week, at Skip's funeral."

She saw it then, the pain in his eyes. "Oh, Rafe."

"He killed himself, Nora. Took an overdose and never recovered. He'd lost the will to fight. He turned away the people who loved him. His perception of himself was all wrapped up in his work. He saw himself as a strong field commander, a leader. When that was taken from him, in his mind he had nothing left."

"I'm so sorry." She reached to touch his hand.

He grabbed her fingers hard. "I don't want to wind up like Skip, Nora, thinking my work is all I have to live for. *You're* my dream, the better part, the important part. You and Bobby. Marry me, please. Let me be a part of your lives."

Eyes shining, Nora hurried to him as he made room on his lap. His lips were cool, but she warmed them quickly, her hands framing his face. His arms tightened around her, and she gloried in being held again. He was back. Rafe was back, and suddenly her heart felt lighter.

Reluctantly Rafe pulled back, needing to say it all. "I stayed long enough to clear up the paperwork on a few cases that were incomplete. I have a lot of accumulated time and I think a vacation is in order. Then maybe I'll take their offer to get involved in training new men. Or maybe I'll find something around here. Then again, I've always wanted to try writing a book."

She had one more burning question. "You're sure you're not doing this for me?"

"Very sure. I'm doing this for *me*. Another thing I had to come to grips with was that all my life I've wanted to have a home, to be a part of a real family. I wanted it so badly, yet I never thought I'd have it, so I denied wanting any such thing. I'd been a loner so long. Yet inside, I've never stopped yearning." His hand moved into the silkiness of her hair. "And always, when I thought of a home or a family, you were at the center of my dream. And now, there's Bobby. I know I've given you both a hard time. I hope you believe that this time it's for keeps, if you'll have me."

She drew in a long breath, afraid to believe that her dream was finally becoming a reality. "Yes, I'll have you. I've waited for this day so long that I'd almost given up hope of it ever happening. Almost. All I've ever wanted was to belong to you."

Rafe smiled into the blue eyes he loved. "You've belonged to me from the first moment I saw you. It's just taken me a damn long time to realize it." He kissed her then, lingering a while, letting the slow pleasure grow.

Trailing her fingers along his jawline, she frowned. "You shaved off your beard."

"I'll grow it back, if you want. I wanted to look the part of the upwardly mobile businessman, complete with fancy suit, so you'd be impressed. Are you?"

Nora smiled. "Absolutely. I've always wanted to be kissed by one of those yuppie types."

"Glad to oblige." He touched his mouth to hers in a gentle, loving kiss. "Say, where's Bobby?"

"At the library with Alex. He should be home any time. He's going to be glad to see you. He's been moping about since you left."

"Really? I wasn't sure if he liked me or..."

"Oh, he does. But he's a little afraid to let himself care. Ted was always leaving, and I think Bobby is holding back, waiting to see if you're going to stick around before he invests his love in you."

"Smart kid." He kissed her slender neck. "Like his mother." Hungry for her, his mouth captured hers again. He was just getting into it, when he heard the back door open. Releasing his hold on Nora, Rafe turned to find his son standing in the doorway. "Hi, Bobby."

Bobby's surprised look was replaced by a wary one. "Hi."

Nora rose and moved to the counter. "Want some hot chocolate?" But Bobby didn't answer, his eyes on Rafe.

Rafe stood and walked closer to the boy. "I see you've been taking good care of Rambo."

"Yeah." Bobby glanced at his mother. "What's for dinner?"

Nora knew what he was feeling. She also knew the two of them would have to settle it between them. But perhaps she could nudge a little. "Rafe's come back, and he tells me he missed us a lot."

"I sure did. Maybe we could all go out to dinner tonight, sort of a celebration. What do you say?"

"Sure." He tossed a scruffy football into the corner and watched it bounce. "How long you staying this time?"

"I'd like to stay for good. I asked your mother to marry me."

His eyes shifted back to Nora. "You want to marry him?"

"Yes, Bobby, very much."

Bobby kicked the toe of one shoe with the other. He kept his eyes cast to the ground.

Rafe walked over to him. "It was wrong of me to leave in such a hurry, but I had some problems to work through. I'm sorry. I won't do it again. Do you believe me?"

He shrugged. "I don't know. You said we'd go to Disneyland before school started and we didn't."

"I know. A very good friend of mine died, Bobby, and I had to go back for his funeral. But I'm here to stay now, I promise you. How would it be if we go to Disneyland during your Christmas vacation?"

His face brightened a little. "Okay." He walked over to Rambo's box and leaned down to talk to his puppy.

Nora sighed as she slipped her arm around Rafe. "Give him time," she whispered. "He'll come around."

Rafe let out a deep breath. "I hope so."

Picking up his dog, Bobby turned around. "When you marry Mom, then you'll be my dad, right?"

"Yes."

"I made the basketball team. Mom's not real crazy about basketball, but she always comes to my games alone. Most of the guys have their dads come. Maybe you could show up once in a while?"

Rafe swallowed past a lump. "I'll be there. You can count on it. I used to play basketball when I was in school." He glanced at Nora. "Maybe we could set up a net and backboard in the yard somewhere, practise a little."

"I don't see why not," Nora answered.

At last Bobby smiled. "Great." Nuzzling his dog, he left the kitchen.

Nora hugged Rafe close. "See what I mean?"

He let out a relieved breath and pulled her into the circle of his arms. "How'd you get to be so wise?"

"I'm not particularly wise. I am patient, though." And it's finally paid off, she thought as she held him close to her heart. "I love you, Rafe Sloan."

"And I love you, Nora. Now and always." Lowering his head, he kissed her.

Home. This time, he was home to stay.

* * * * *

Back by popular demand, some of Diana Palmer's earliest published books are available again!

Several years ago, Diana Palmer began her writing career. Sweet, compelling and totally unforgettable, these are the love stories that enchanted readers everywhere.

Next month, six more of these wonderful stories will be available in DIANA PALMER DUETS—Books 4, 5 and 6. Each DUET contains two powerful stories plus an introduction by Diana Palmer. Don't miss:

Book Four	**AFTER THE MUSIC** **DREAM'S END**
Book Five	**BOUND BY A PROMISE** **PASSION FLOWER**
Book Six	**TO HAVE AND TO HOLD** **THE COWBOY AND THE LADY**

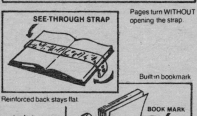

Diana Palmer's fortieth story for Silhouette . . . chosen as an Award of Excellence title!

CONNAL
Diana Palmer

Next month, Diana Palmer's bestselling LONG, TALL TEXANS series continues with CONNAL. The skies get cloudy on C. C. Tremayne's home on the range when Penelope Mathews decides to protect him—by marrying him!

One specially selected title receives the Award of Excellence every month. Look for CONNAL in August at your favorite retail outlet . . . only from Silhouette Romance.

CON-1

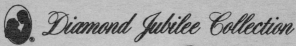 *Diamond Jubilee Collection*

It's our 10th Anniversary...
and *you* get a present!

This collection of early Silhouette
Romances features novels written
by three of your favorite authors:

ANN MAJOR—*Wild Lady*
ANNETTE BROADRICK—*Circumstantial Evidence*
DIXIE BROWNING—*Island on the Hill*

* These Silhouette Romance titles were first published in the early 1980s
  and have not been available since!

* Beautiful Collector's Edition bound in antique green simulated leather to
  last a lifetime!

* Embossed in gold on the cover and spine!

This special collection will not be sold in retail stores and is only available
through this exclusive offer.
Look for details in all Silhouette series published in June, July and August.